# Silent Legacy

## *Discovering Family Secrets*

Diana Church

Grateful acknowledgement is made to the following for permission to excerpt their work:

*Emigration to America.* Christophorus der Stelzfuß, (Pegleg), 1883 edition of the *Lutheran Almanac,* edited by Pastor Martin Christian Daniel Hafermann. (Translation by Rudy Wiemann, Reprint by Ostfriesen Genealogical Society of America, Volume 13, January-March 2010).

The *Lutherisch Emigranten-Mission* from Stephanus Keyl Collection 1838-1906, Collection No. M-0011. Courtesy of Concordia Historical Institute, St. Louis, Missouri.

*New York City Tenements.* Excerpts courtesy of the Lower East Side Tenement Museum, http://www.tenement.org.

*Cover Photo*: The home where Katie lived with her grandparents. This photograph is reprinted with permission from Hilde Stein.

Library of Congress Control Number: 2014912698

CreateSpace Independent Publishing Platform,
North Charleston, SC

ISBN-13: 978-1500538910

ISBN-10: 1500538914

For Monica, Larissa

and

Christian, Katherine, Elizabeth,

Robert, William, Betsy

# Table of Contents

# SAN FRANCISCO

# The Bequest

The mystery began with a stack of letters, an omen, foretelling of many records that would reveal long-buried family secrets.

On a cloudy, drizzling, fifty degree day in San Francisco, the postman climbed the steps of an older apartment building. He unlocked a metal cover which displayed the contents of twelve mailboxes and filled all the slots—all except one. The mailbox of Miss Helen A. Cooper was filled to the brim.

Exasperated by the delay, he turned around and knocked on the manager's door. "I'm sorry to bother you, Ma'am, but I can't deliver anything to Miss Cooper. Please ask her to pick up the mail and make space for more deliveries. I'll return tomorrow with the other letters."

"*Ja, ja*. I'll go talk to her now." Agnes Mueller returned to her apartment and picked up the master key. She climbed the creaky stairs to the third floor, recalling that she hadn't seen Miss Cooper lately. Walking down the long hallway, Agnes reminded herself to talk with the Coronado Advisory Board about updating the common areas; the carpet was threadbare, the wallpaper was faded and torn, all should be replaced. Then she remembered; Miss Cooper was a member of the advisory board and she didn't like to spend money.

On arriving at Helen Cooper's apartment, she knocked on the door; no answer. She knocked again and called her name loudly. No one came to the door. Agnes Mueller unlocked it with her master key.

Cautiously, she opened the door and saw an older woman slumped in her chair, her eyes open and a trickle of blood dried on her face.

"*Mein Gott!*"

Agnes crossed herself, slammed the door shut, ran down the hall and hurried downstairs to her apartment. Shaking uncontrollably, she unlocked the door, picked up the phone, and dialed the police.

"Nine-One-One. What is your emergency?"

"I'm Mrs. Mueller, at the Coronado Apartments on Twenty-Ninth Avenue near Golden Gate Park. Tell police to come immediately! Miss Cooper *ist* dead!"

∞∞∞∞

Ten minutes later, San Francisco Police Officer David Ryan knocked on the door of the manager's apartment.

"*Hallo, danke Gott,* you're here. Come *mit* me." They climbed the worn stairs to the third floor and walked down the shabby hallway. She unlocked the door and gingerly pushed it open.

In the living room, Helen Cooper was sitting in an old recliner chair, dead. The smell lingered pervasively.

Officer Ryan quickly walked across the room and turned off the *Blue Danube Waltz* recording. "We don't need to stay here." He led Mrs. Mueller into the hallway.

Leaving the apartment door slightly ajar and unlocked, Officer Ryan said, "I'll call for an ambulance. We'll have to tell the coroner because she died at home. She looked pretty old—did she have any relatives?"

"*Nein,* they're all dead." She said, crying quietly.

4

"Perhaps you should return to your apartment," he said. "I'll handle this and return the key to you."

"*Ja, ja*, a good idea."

After Agnes left, Officer Ryan placed a handkerchief over his face and went inside the apartment to look for anything that would help decide the next step. It didn't take long. On the oak mission-style desk in a corner of the living room he found Helen A. Cooper had left instructions to be cremated at Cypress Lawn Memorial Park in Colma, California.

Beneath these documents, the officer found her Last Will and Testament. He also discovered a large, manila folder of documents: stock certificates, certificate of deposit receipts, oil leases, and Addendum A.

When the ambulance arrived, the driver called Cypress Lawn. The cemetery official instructed him to deliver Miss Cooper's body to the county morgue. Officer Ryan then locked the apartment, took the creaky stairway to the first floor and knocked on the manager's door.

Agnes Mueller opened the door. "I found some documents on the desk. Here is an address," he said, while handing her a slip of paper. "Her attorney is George Smoot; please ask the mailman to send all the Cooper letters to Mr. Smoot."

"*Danke,* I hope *die* attorney will decide what to do soon—I must lease her apartment again," said Agnes.

Officer Ryan handed her the apartment key and continued, "I'm taking the cemetery contract, the Last Will and Testament and a manila folder of documents to Laura Dodd, who is the police department investigator. She'll give these documents to the attorney and stop by to look at the Cooper apartment tomorrow morning."

"Okay, I *vill* be ready for her," replied Agnes, still a bit rattled by the death of one of her oldest residents. When Officer Ryan left, she had a cup of tea—it had been such an unsettling afternoon.

∞∞∞∞

On Friday morning Laura Dodd briefly reviewed the terms of the will, noted Helen Cooper's attorney was George Smoot from Lardner, Alexander and Smoot, and filed the papers in her briefcase. Leaving the office, she drove to the Coronado Apartments, knocked on the door and introduced herself to Mrs. Mueller.

"Hello, I'm Laura Dodd, from the San Francisco Police Department. May I have a key to look at the Cooper apartment?"

"*Ja, ja,* here it is. Take the stairs to the third floor. Her apartment is on the right. Just lock up and bring me the key when you are done."

Laura climbed the ancient stairs to the third floor, unlocked the door, then walked through the musty apartment, checking to see if anything looked unusual or if there was any evidence of a break-in. The kitchen was clean and there was a normal supply of food in the cupboard and refrigerator. The living room window and corner bedroom window were draped with old-fashioned handmade lace valances and each had a view of the Golden Gate Bridge. She jotted a note on her clipboard—even though this was a small and very expensive apartment—the view must have been important to the elderly woman.

After completing her initial survey, Laura began taking Polaroid photos and listing details to match the pictures. She photographed all the furniture, the faded paintings, old documents, family photos, a Tiffany lamp, mission-style furniture, and many books about collecting lace and Native American crafts plus several novels and history books written in German. The elderly woman seemed to have a variety of interests but was mostly a pack rat. The living room floor was strewn with stacks of old *American Indian Art* magazines, newspapers from Oklahoma in the 1920s, a few genealogy books and some charts with family names.

Walking into the bedroom, Laura found framed pictures carefully placed on top of the chest of drawers: a 1902 death certificate signed by a Lutheran pastor, the wedding photo of a young couple with a handwritten label, *Katie and Chris 1908*, a photo of several men and an oil derrick in the background, and a faded photo of a man and two teenage children, identified as *Anna, Vater, Fred*. She also took photos of the hand-made doilies, lace-edged pillowcases and a 1935 Oklahoma signature quilt, all kept in the bottom drawer of the bureau.

Hidden underneath the linens, she discovered a tattered leather journal titled *Marie—1888—New York City*. A ticket from Antwerp to New York City was pasted on one page, while addresses for the *Lutherisch Emigrantenhaus Association* and *YWHA* were listed on the following page. Throughout the journal, German handwriting mentioned a location called *Altenkirchen* and the names of Fritz, Katherina, Friedrich, Johann, Georg, Lena, Katie. The last page, dated May 23, 1892, had two scrawled lines:

*Katie is four years old today.*

*Leaving for Josephine, Nebraska tomorrow.*

Finishing the photos and her notes, Laura did a final walk-through inspection of the apartment. She locked the door and returned the key to Mrs. Mueller, then drove to her office and called Mr. Smoot to schedule an appointment.

∞∞∞∞∞

Although a steady rain created traffic delays, on Monday afternoon Laura arrived at the office of Lardner, Alexander and Smoot for her two o'clock appointment. The secretary escorted Laura to an elegantly furnished corner office and introduced her to George Smoot.

"Hello," said George. "Please have a seat. Officer Ryan called last week to let me know about the death of Helen Cooper. He said you'd be contacting me."

"Yes, I've brought the Last Will and Testament document and other financial papers that were found on her desk," Laura replied. "There's a very interesting 1888 journal, some family photos, a stack of genealogy charts, and a framed 1902 death certificate. I've also included my inventory photos."

"Thanks for bringing these items to my attention. Is your investigation complete?"

"Yes. I didn't find any evidence of foul play. The case will be closed when we receive a medical report from the coroner's office."

"Okay, I'll be in touch with you if I need anything else," said George. They shook hands, and he escorted Laura to the elevator.

∞∞∞∞

By Tuesday of the following week, George Smoot had received a copy of the medical report and scheduled a late afternoon meeting with his partners. They met at his favorite place for discussions—a small, exclusive conference space with its own fully-stocked bar in a nearby cabinet. The room had a stunning view of San Francisco Bay. It included a finely crafted burled walnut conference table, deep-cushion leather chairs and small Impressionist paintings by Degas, Monet and Sisley.

George greeted Michael Lardner and Peter Alexander; each of them poured a glass of Scotch and sat at the conference table. After a general progress report on a few other cases, George began a discussion of the Helen A. Cooper Estate.

Referring to her death certificate, he said, "Helen Cooper, age eighty-five, died instantly of cardio-respiratory collapse on January 18, 1986; a contributing condition was chronic brain syndrome (dementia). The police have completed their investigation, her death certificate was filed by the coroner and cremation occurred yesterday."

"I'd like your opinion about publishing an obituary. Miss Cooper noted in her will that she didn't have any children and we don't know of any extended family relationships or organizational affiliations. Do you agree an obit isn't necessary?" he asked.

His partner, Peter Alexander replied, "Yes, but what did the Police Department decide?"

"I've talked with Laura Dodd, who indicated Helen Cooper was alone when she died of a heart attack. There aren't any questions about her death."

"All right, let's begin the probate process. What does the will indicate as far as the distribution of assets?"

George presented the details, noting "Helen Cooper had two requirements which must be met before any funds can be disbursed. I've made copies for your reference and would like your advice."

The will stated:

*IV. I direct sufficient funds shall be paid from my estate to accomplish the following:*

> *a) A professional genealogist shall be hired to research and write two reports:*

> *b) i) Identify actions by the Hale Gang which resulted in the unjustified confinement of my brother Fred John Cooper in the Mercy Hospital for the Insane and discover why the Oklahoma Bureau of Indian Affairs*

*took away his land. These events destroyed his*
*reputation and affected him for the next thirty years.*

b) ii) *Identify the family history of my parents to*
*determine why my mother always insisted my brother*
*and I should never marry.*

c) *When these two reports are completed and accepted*
*by the archives of the San Francisco Heritage*
*Association, I direct the residue of my Estate shall*
*become an anonymous donation to this organization.*

After their general discussion and astonishment about the stipulations, the partners agreed that Helen Cooper had an unusual will—yet, it was valid. They decided Helen Cooper's instructions should be followed for the benefit of the San Francisco Heritage Association.

"We need to make certain any reports given to the Heritage Association are factual because they will ultimately become public documents," Michael commented.

"Yes, we should have the two reports reviewed by our legal team before they are released," replied George.

"As President of the Association," said Michael, "I can talk with John Hawthorne and ask for a referral to a professional genealogist."

"Great idea," said Peter.

George asked, "Could you let me know his recommendation?"

"Sure, be glad to," replied Michael. The three attorneys talked a little longer about other matters and then adjourned their meeting.

Before leaving his office, George added a reminder note to the Cooper Estate file—must ask the genealogist to identify family secrets.

# The Genealogist

George Smoot was frustrated—time always seemed to stand still when he was anxious to start a new project. It had been three weeks since he requested the details and he couldn't hire a genealogist until he knew the dollar amount of the Cooper Estate. The rain and gray haze smothered everything, making his mood even worse.

"Mr. Smoot, your assistant is here to see you. Should I send him to your office?"

"Yes, certainly," he said, and went to the buffet cabinet to pour two cups of coffee.

David Calloway entered the office, sat down, sipped a little coffee and announced. "George, I have good news for you. I've received preliminary statements from the pension account, certificates of deposit, oil companies and other corporations. It looks like there will be about two million dollars. The photos and inventory list suggest Helen Cooper owned some valuable antiques. When these items are sold at auction there should be an additional amount of money."

"Great!" replied George. "Call Christie's and let them know we'll have some pieces for them soon." David scribbled a few notes and left.

Relieved at being able to take action, the attorney notified his secretary, "Jeanne, call Ellen O'Donnell and schedule an appointment with her as soon as possible."

∞∞∞∞

Two days later, the phone rang. "Ellen O'Donnell is here to see you."

"Good," he replied. "Please bring her to my office."

George Smoot stood to welcome his guest. A pleasant-looking older woman walked across the large, elegantly furnished corner office and shook his hand, "Hello, I'm Ellen O'Donnell." She had dark-brown hair and looked like she might be in her late fifties. A little overweight, but professionally dressed in a navy blue suit and pumps, Ellen's demeanor gave the impression she took her work seriously and would be a reliable person to hire.

His first reaction verified endorsements already received through his informal network—however George didn't want to hire Ellen without an official confirmation of her credentials. As administrator of the estate, he had due diligence and fiduciary responsibilities to ensure expenses were paid for a justified purpose. Besides, he also wanted to have some idea of Ellen's personality and her approach to solving problems in a timely manner. A meeting would validate her qualifications, identify if there might be any issues and establish the cost of fulfilling the terms of the Cooper will.

He asked Ellen to join him at the small conference table near the windows overlooking The City. "I want to thank you for coming here on short notice," he said. "Please tell me something about your research experience?"

Ellen wasn't at all surprised by his question; John Hawthorne, director of the San Francisco Heritage Association, had called last week to give her a heads-up about the situation. She understood this meeting was an official interview.

"I'd be glad to. As a detective for the San Francisco Police Department, I loved developing profiles and investigating problems. But, I was burned out from watching how crimes affected victims and their families, so I took early retirement. I've been a member of the Heritage Association for many years and have always belonged to the Genealogy Studies Group. A few months ago I completed coursework at the Samford University Institute of Genealogy in Alabama and received a certificate. Do you have a genealogy project that needs attention?"

"I'll try to explain the circumstances," said George. "Our office is handling the estate of Helen Cooper who died here in San Francisco about three weeks ago. Her will requires that a professional genealogist must complete two reports for the San Francisco Heritage Association. When these reports are accepted by the archives, they'll receive an anonymous gift of about two million dollars from the Cooper Estate."

Ellen gasped. "That's a lot of money!"

"Yes, which means we need to be very careful on handling everything," George replied. "Because it will be an anonymous gift, you should maintain strict privacy when talking with people or requesting records; the reason for your questions must remain a secret. The research also requires documentation in order to meet the terms of the Cooper Estate will."

"I can certainly understand your concern. We always had to follow confidentiality rules when conducting investigations, so I'm accustomed to working in those circumstances. Do you have any basic information about the family?"

The attorney handed her a bulky folder of documents and the 1888 journal written by Marie Klein. "Here's a copy of Helen Cooper's will. The two items, *IV a) i and ii*, will be your guideline for meeting requirements that benefit the Heritage Association. Helen Cooper identified family relationships in Addendum A. The genealogy charts scattered around the living room are also included."

As Ellen studied the pages, she considered the similarities between developing a profile for an investigation and developing a family history summary—in both cases, discovering details was a required first step to locating the answers.

After several minutes, she looked up and said, "There are some interesting circumstances that match my experience. My father was Irish Catholic, but my mother was Lutheran. About 1925, she emigrated with her family from Germany to San Francisco. Of course, we went to baptisms, confirmations and marriages on both sides of the family, so I'm familiar with the German dialect and Lutheran traditions."

She continued, "The information Helen provided in Addendum A, the genealogy charts and Marie's journal will be very helpful because they list the names, dates and places where her family lived. These details will become the basis for my research plan."

"*Item One*," she said, "appears to be a controversy over land, a connection to the Hale Gang, the Mercy Hospital for the Insane and the Bureau of Indian Affairs. Deed records are only available at the local county courthouse. I'm not sure how everything fits together; locating these answers will likely require a trip to Oklahoma."

Turning her attention to the next requirement, Ellen said, "There's a lot of missing information to verify before I can answer *Item Two*. San Francisco has excellent resources at the San Francisco Public Library, the

National Archives in San Bruno, and the Multiregional Family History Center in Oakland. If I can't find answers in their records, then a trip to Germany will be necessary. Most families have memories or stories; sometimes they have letters from relatives who've immigrated to America. A decision about Germany can be delayed until later."

While Ellen explained the research process, George reflected on his responsibility to monitor expenses of the Cooper Estate. "It appears that you have a good grasp of the overall project," he commented. "What is your billing rate?"

"I charge thirty dollars an hour plus library or courthouse fees, and travel expenses. I always record my billing hours and will enclose a progress report with an invoice."

George smiled. "You've been highly recommended by John Hawthorne so I believe we can proceed with arrangements. I'll draft a formal contract which outlines our discussion. If it is satisfactory to you, please sign and return a copy to our office. Of course, if there are any unusual travel expenses, they should be approved in advance. Is that agreeable?"

"Yes, here's my business card. I'm looking forward to working this assignment," said Ellen, and began placing the papers in her briefcase.

"There are a few other matters we should discuss," said George. "The apartment manager will probably know if Helen Cooper ever talked about her family. And, our firm also handled the estate of her brother, Fred John Cooper. I reviewed his will last week; if you need to look at those papers, just schedule an appointment.

"You might also be interested in the photos and documents the investigator found at Helen Cooper's apartment and the inventory of her premises."

Ellen perked up. "Definitely," she replied. "Tangible objects sometimes give hints about the family. Could I take everything with me?"

"Sure. We have an agreement in principle about your fees and how the project will be handled. The items can be returned to our office later."

"Okay, that will work," Ellen replied, as she signed a release document. She placed the journal, charts, copies of the will and addendum, as well as the photos in her briefcase.

With their meeting completed, George escorted her to the elevator. "I'm looking forward to your first report," he said.

While driving home, Ellen reflected on the importance of this assignment—it would be very interesting, there were lots of clues to track down and an extra paycheck would increase her savings account. Driving into the lower level garage of her Victorian Stick home, she walked into the basement office and placed her briefcase on a corner of the desk. The room was a mess; the desk held a jumble of scribbled notes, old IRS returns, legal pads with to-do lists in addition to file folders and books stacked everywhere. She sighed—the distraction interfered with being able to focus on solving problems—re-organizing the office would be her first priority.

Ellen closed the office door, went upstairs to the main level, picked up the mail, poured herself a glass of wine, kicked off her shoes and plopped down on the couch. On Monday she would begin concentrating on the Cooper Estate assignment.

# A San Francisco Interview

Leaving home on Vicksburg Street, Ellen drove past the San Francisco Botanical Garden and turned north on Twenty-Ninth Avenue. It was a neighborhood of wall-to-wall apartment buildings; there weren't any trees or landscaping, concrete dominated the scene. She circled the block a few times to find a parking space, then walked to the old three-story building, entered the small front hallway and knocked on the manager's door. Today, she was interested in learning more details about Helen Cooper and her family.

∞∞∞∞

"Hi, I'm Ellen O'Donnell. Could we talk about Miss Cooper, who died recently?"

"*Ja, Ja*, I didn't really know her," said Agnes Mueller. "You should talk to her neighbor, Miss Morgan. This morning, I asked her to meet you. Her apartment is on the third floor."

Ellen climbed the rickety stairs and knocked on Miss Morgan's door. It opened slowly.

"Hello, I'm Ellen O'Donnell. May I visit with you about Helen Cooper?"

"Yes, do come in, it's such a sad situation. Please call me Julia," she said, while leading Ellen into the living room. The older woman had beautiful silver hair, was dressed in dark wool slacks, a crème turtleneck sweater and brown loafers. Her only jewelry was a gold necklace.

Julia sat on the chintz couch and Ellen chose one of the Queen Anne side chairs opposite the couch, placing her briefcase on the other chair.

"I made cinnamon coffee cake this morning, would you like some? There's also coffee."

"That sounds delicious," said Ellen. "Yes, thank you."

Julia cut a slice of cake for each of them, placing it on a china plate. After pouring coffee into matching china cups, she handed the plate and a cloth napkin to her guest. Ellen was impressed by these elegant touches and old-fashioned manners.

Looking around the room, she observed that Julia collected Japanese Nippon china, had a few lithographs of architectural scenes and a collection of art books on the side tables.

"Your collection of Nippon looks very interesting, have you travelled much?" Ellen said.

"Not really, I inherited some nice things from my parents, and the china collection was one of them" replied Julia. "My friend Helen enjoyed antiques too. We always had a good time talking about antiques and family history when we met for coffee each week."

"I like genealogy too, so the request to locate information about the Cooper family is an interesting assignment. Do you mind answering some questions—we really don't know much and you might be able to help."

"Possibly," said Julia. "We were neighbors and good friends for years. What would you like to know?"

"One of my questions is where Helen lived before moving to this location."

"Helen moved here because her brother Fred died and she needed to leave the neighborhood on Geary Street," said Julia. "She first lived in San Francisco in 1930, but was gone for a few years to help her mother and brother in Oklahoma. She returned in 1935 and has been here ever since—my goodness—Helen lived here for over fifty years."

"Yes, that's a long time," Ellen commented absent-mindedly. Remembering the books about Native American crafts and genealogy charts, she then asked, "Did Helen have any hobbies?"

"We both liked history and genealogy, so we attended programs at the San Francisco Heritage Association," said Julia. "Mostly, we talked about genealogy; so, I learned quite a bit about Helen's family history. If I remember correctly, her mother, uncles and an aunt immigrated to the United States but one aunt remained in Germany. She had a sister who died at a young age and an older half-sister who lived in Nebraska." Ellen quietly jotted notes.

"I probably shouldn't say this, but she seemed a little eccentric about family history," Julia continued. "A few years ago Helen became very upset because she'd written several letters to the archives in Germany and they didn't reply. I recommended that she hire a professional genealogist to find the aunt who remained in Germany; she insisted that there wasn't any money to hire anyone. When Helen worked as an executive secretary at a private family investment company, the owner taught her how to choose stocks and she'd made successful investments. But, Helen was very tight with money and she'd only spend her pension and social security income for expenses. She refused to use any money from the investment accounts.

"While on that subject, I should also mention that Helen talked to a staff member at the Heritage Association about accepting the family history papers. He declined her offer because anything she submitted would be considered an amateur account based on verbal tradition. Then she asked if they would accept a professional genealogy report about her brother's experiences and their family history. The archivist turned her down again because it didn't fit their mission statement. Helen considered donating money to see if she could influence their opinion, but I don't know if she ever did anything further."

"That's very interesting," said Ellen, as she quickly made notes and changed the subject to avoid discussion about the Heritage Association.

"I wonder . . . did she ever mention her brother?"

"She was very protective about Fred John. Apparently he got into a lot of trouble when he was younger. Helen thought her brother was treated poorly because of unjust causes and said the Oklahoma events damaged his reputation. I never did understand it all."

"What about her mother. Did she ever talk about her?" asked Ellen.

"Yes, her mother emigrated from Germany and became a Translator in New York City. Helen told me she enjoyed looking at the shop windows in the fashion district and bought a few nice clothes once in a while. After she married, Marie didn't have a dime to call her own and she was often upset about not having any money.

"I think her mother's experiences must have influenced Helen's feminist ideas," Julia continued. "She read books about women's history and occasionally talked about the women's rights movement at Berkeley during the 1960s. She also seemed to be fascinated with anything related to Germany and hung a lace valance above her living room windows because her mother told her that everyone in Germany had lace curtains and red geraniums on the window sill."

"Helen's independent attitude raises a question for me," said Ellen. "Did she ever marry or confide in you about any relationships?"

"Only once did she ever discuss that subject. Apparently, her mother discouraged both Helen and her brother Fred from ever being married. She told them there were too many skeletons in the closet—but she wouldn't tell them anything else. Helen said her mother believed it was best to make your own decisions because a spouse couldn't be trusted. Helen followed her advice. She never married."

"That's interesting, and very unusual," Ellen commented. "Helen seems to have mostly talked about her mother and brother, what about her father?"

"I believe he was born in *Württemberg* but apparently never spoke about his relatives, so Helen didn't know if they remained in Germany or immigrated to Nebraska. Her father tried farming but wasn't very successful; they constantly moved from one house to another because he couldn't pay the rent. She rarely talked about him and didn't seem to know much about his family either."

"There's only one other topic that I can think of," said Ellen. "Did Helen ever talk about relatives in Nebraska or Oklahoma?"

"Not much," said Julia. "She tried to call relatives when her mother died but there was a bad connection and the phone went dead. There seemed to be a feud between Helen's mother and her brothers—Helen always changed the subject and wouldn't talk about her uncles."

Ellen glanced at her watch. "This has been very useful. I really appreciate the time you've taken to fill in some blanks," she said, while placing her notes in the briefcase.

"I'm glad to help," replied Julia.

"Here's my business card. If there is anything else that might be new information, I'd like to hear from you," said Ellen. Julia then escorted her to the door and they said "good-bye."

∞∞∞∞

Ellen walked down the worn stairs, returned to her car and drove to The Chocolate Croissant for lunch.  On arrival, she placed an order for spinach salad and coffee, and then pulled the notes from her briefcase. The interview with Julia had given tantalizing hints about individual personalities and family dynamics that she would never find in any document at a courthouse or library. She added a title page, *Reference #1 – Family Secrets*, and stapled it to her notes from the interview.

Ellen then retrieved the 1888 journal and Addendum A from the briefcase and compared them with her notes. She studied everything carefully and made a decision. She would focus research on the life of Marie Klein Cooper—the only person who played a role or was likely involved with every circumstance.

Marie was the direct link to answering questions posed by her daughter, Helen Cooper.

# *Altenkirchen, Germany*

A few minutes after nine o'clock, Ellen went downstairs to the garage and began her seventeen mile trip to the Family History Center in Oakland. Like most San Franciscans, she preferred to take the MUNI or a bus to her destination; however public transportation wasn't an option for this location. On the other hand, this important resource had offsetting benefits; because of their family focused philosophy, the volunteers were friendly and always willing to answer research questions.

Driving north from her home on Vicksburg Street, she merged east toward Bayshore Freeway, took Oakland Bay Bridge, passed through Yerba Buena Island, left McArthur Freeway and arrived at 4766 Lincoln Avenue. Lined with tall Canary Palm trees, Ellen glimpsed the main entrance of the Temple Complex for the Church of Jesus Christ of Latter-Day Saints (Mormon). On driving into the large parking lot, she found the Oakland Multiregional Family History Center located opposite the Temple and parked nearby. California Poppies were blooming next to the entrance.

She pushed the doorbell. A voice said, "May I help you?"

"Yes, I'd like to do family history research."

A volunteer opened the door and asked Ellen to sign the Visitor Register. "Could you help me identify where a certain village is located in Germany?" asked Ellen. "I'd like to order some microfilm records."

"Come over here and we'll look at the *Meyers Gazetteer of the German Empire*. This atlas identifies the villages in existence prior to re-districting after the wars. What is the time frame and the name of the village which you're looking for?"

"I need to find the *Altenkirchen* records from 1860 until 1902."

"Okay, the Gothic script of *Meyers Gazetteer* is a little hard to read, but we'll figure it out." The volunteer removed the heavy dictionary from the shelf.

"Here it is. Your village is in the province of *Württemberg* in southern Germany. *Altenkirchen* is a village of two hundred people about eighty kilometres north of *Stuttgart*."

"Great. Now I need to know if *Kirchenbuch* microfilm for the local Lutheran church is available. How do I find that information?" asked Ellen.

"Let's take a look at our catalog."

In a few minutes, she had an answer, "Yes, we have five microfilm records from the Lutheran church in *Altenkirchen*. Would you like to look at the descriptions?"

Reviewing the details, Ellen considered all of them important:

> *Taufen 1819-1884* (Birth Records)
> *Hieraten 1845-1933* (Marriage Records)
> *Tote 1842-1934* (Death Records)
> *Konfirmation 1809-1909* (Confirmaton Records)
> *Familienbuch 1852-1925* (A list of family members)

"This is exactly what I am looking for. How much does it cost to rent these films and how soon will they arrive?" she asked.

"You'll need to write one form for each order. The cost is three dollars each. We'll call you when the film arrives; it'll probably be about three weeks."

Ellen completed the order forms, wrote a check, and requested a copy of the microfilm descriptions for reference.

∞∞∞∞

She then re-traced her route via the Oakland Bay Bridge, drove through her neighborhood of two-story Victorian homes, parked the car in the basement garage and went upstairs to answer the door. The postman handed her a special delivery package from the office of Lardner, Alexander and Smoot. A contract from George Smoot included all the arrangements they talked about last week.

After lunch, Ellen went downstairs to her basement office. Located at the rear of the small room, her desk held an IBM Selectric III typewriter carefully balanced on the pull-out board above the left drawers. A cork bulletin board and shelf for reference books hung above the typewriter. On the opposite wall, the window featured a street-level view of a tiny patch of grass and the front sidewalk. Underneath it, a wrought-iron bookshelf which she'd found at a flea market, held stacks of gardening magazines and displayed pots of geraniums, begonias and African violets. On each side of the room, tall bookshelves were jam-packed with genealogy books, magazine boxes filled with family research folders, souvenirs, and her collection of hand-crafted pottery. Last week she had carefully placed the photos from George Smoot on one corner of her desk. Now, it was necessary to find a permanent space for them.

Looking at the reference shelf, Ellen removed all of the books except *German English Genealogical Dictionary* and *German Church Books – Beyond the Basics*. Then she arranged the Cooper Estate objects: a wedding photo of Katie and Chris, the framed 1902 death certificate of Sophia Katherina Klein, and the picture of Anna, *Vater*, and Fred. When placing everything on the shelf—one item was obviously missing—a photo of Marie Cooper was not found in Helen's apartment.

Next, she retrieved a three-inch notebook from her supplies drawer, then labeled dividers for the Klein family, the Kupper/Cooper family, San Francisco, Oklahoma, Nebraska, New York City and Germany. A blank Family Group Sheet for each family was added. Using the loose genealogy charts, the journal and the addendum as references, the unconfirmed information was written in pencil on each sheet. As a last step, blank pages were added behind each divider. The page title identified a specific library; underneath the title, the records to be found at each location were listed for reference.

Finishing these details, Ellen then reviewed the documents on hand. The journal entry revealed—Katie is four years old today, May 23, 1892—and the addendum disclosed—a daughter Katherine was born in Germany. Questions were added to her research notebook: Are Katie and Katherine the same person? If Marie left *Altenkirchen* when the baby was only a few weeks old, why did she leave so quickly?

It had been a good day. This morning, the first set of microfilms was ordered; this afternoon a list of missing documents had been itemized. Ellen filed all the research information in her briefcase and placed it in the car. Tomorrow, she would search for burial records.

# Cypress Lawn Memorial Park

On Wednesday morning there was a dense fog, but Ellen decided to go to Cypress Lawn Cemetery anyway; it was only twenty minutes from her house. She drove through the neighborhood on Dolores Street, then south on I-280 to Mission Street, where she took the exit toward 1370 El Camino Real.

Primarily known for its acres of cemeteries, Colma is called the 'City of the Silent'. Established in 1892, Cypress Lawn Memorial Park was a peaceful sanctuary. Tranquil lakes were scattered throughout the grounds, and thousands of trees, flowers, and statuary created by the leading sculptors of the era, were strategically placed to enhance the view. In 1912, San Francisco passed an ordinance requiring that all cemeteries within its city limits be moved to Colma. Subsequently, this cemetery became the last resting place for many famous Californians.

∞∞∞∞

Arriving at the cemetery, Ellen parked her car, walked to the Main Office and approached the reception desk.

"I'd like to speak with someone about Helen Cooper. She died a few weeks ago in San Francisco and was cremated at Cypress Lawn."

"Okay, I'll call one of our customer service representatives, please have a seat," replied the receptionist. A few minutes later, Deborah Elliott entered the lobby.

"Hello, please come to my office," she said. They walked down the hall to a cheerful room with views of the landscaped grounds; Ellen sat opposite her desk. Deborah asked, "How may I help you today?"

"My name is Ellen O'Donnell, here is my business card," she said. "George Smoot, the attorney who is handling the Cooper Estate, has asked me to complete a report about their family. I'd like to know if you have any records for Helen Cooper and if any other members of her family were buried here."

"I'll check our database," said Deborah.

"Here it is. Helen A, Cooper was cremated and placed in Section NE, Tier 15, Niche 80, which is located in the Lakeside Columbarium. Our records show that Helen made her own pre-arrangements."

"Interesting. I know her brother died about 1980. Was he buried here?"

"Yes, Fred J. Cooper died 16 April 1980 and he is in the same Niche 80. The funeral card states Helen Cooper paid for the cremation of Fred J. Cooper."

"That's a useful piece of information. What about Mary Cooper, their mother? I don't know anything about her," said Ellen.

"Mary Cooper died 09 February 1957. She was cremated and placed in Section NE, Tier 15, Niche 80. Our records indicate F. J. Cooper made the funeral plans for Mary Cooper. Since they're all in the same niche, they must be the same family," commented Deborah.

"Great! Helen had a brother Fred and her mother's name was Mary, but I didn't have an exact death date for either one. These are the first verifiable details," said Ellen. "Now that I have a date, I can order a death certificate; it might give more information about Mary Cooper.

"I'm also looking for information about Helen's father. Do you have any information about Fred or Frederick Cooper?"

Deborah re-checked her file, "No, he must have died in another state." Ellen jotted a note—check for Fred Cooper death records in Oklahoma and Nebraska.

"You've been very helpful but I have one more question," said Ellen. "Is there any file information about a funeral service or obituary for Fred J. Cooper or Mary Cooper? Obits sometimes list names of friends or organizations that might have other information."

"Here's a newspaper clipping which lists a private service for Mary Cooper on February 11, 1957, but the location of the funeral is not identified. If you check with the Carew and English Funeral Service, they might have more details. The clipping doesn't list any names of survivors or other details, so I'm not sure it will be of much help to you.

"I don't see any obit or funeral notice for her brother, Fred Cooper, but there is a reference to Pleasant Hills Memorial Park in Sebastopol, California. Perhaps they'll have more information. I'm sorry; I don't have any other records."

"On the contrary, these bits and pieces are quite helpful. Could I get a copy of your records and the newspaper clipping?" asked Ellen.

"Sure, I'll make copies now," said Deborah. "Would you like me to show you the Lakeside Columbarium?" she said.

"A map of the grounds would be helpful. I can walk to the columbarium myself," replied Ellen.

She took a few minutes to visit the Lakeside Columbarium, then re-traced her route to Noe Valley and stopped at the deli to pick up a sandwich, chips and a coke for a late lunch.

Afterwards, Ellen went to her basement office and began adding the new death record information to the Family Group Sheet for Fred and Mary Cooper, then placed the pages in her notebook.

# Clayton County and Adams County

When the alarm rang, Ellen turned on the radio; Noe Valley was sunny because the height of nearby Twin Peaks had blocked the dense fog. After breakfast and a quick look at the *Chronicle*, she picked up her briefcase and walked two blocks to the J-Church MUNI stop at Twenty-Fourth and Church Streets. The J-Church line travelled north past Dolores Park, with its skyline view of The City, then followed the subway tunnel at Duboce Avenue and continued to Market Street. Stepping off the streetcar, she walked to 200 Larkin Street.

∞∞∞∞

At the San Francisco Public Library, Ellen admired its impressive Beaux Arts architectural style. In the lobby, she took a few minutes to read several exhibit panels:

On April 18, 1906, a major earthquake demolished City Hall, which included the library. One hundred and sixty thousand books were destroyed. For city officials and residents alike, rebuilding their library was vitally important; however labor

31

disputes delayed new construction. The San Francisco Public Library didn't re-open until February 15, 1917.

Designed by George W. Kelham, the first level featured a rusticated stone foundation in the Italian Renaissance style, with garlands, fleur-de-lis and a central cartouche above the entrance doors. The second level displayed classical Greek Ionic columns and Roman arches. In the center of each arch, a statue represented Art, Literature, Philosophy, Science and Law.

Other exhibit panels described the *The Land* and *The Sea* murals by Gottardo Piazzoni. Displayed on the walls of the Grand Stairway, these murals distinctly represented California; one painting presented an eastward view of the land and the other painting displayed a westward vision of the ocean.

That's all very interesting, she mused; but, I must look for answers to my research questions. Ellen walked over to the Lobby reception desk to sign the Visitor Log.

"Could you please direct me to the Genealogy Department?"

"Yes, genealogy reference sources are located in the History Department, which is part of the Humanities Division, located on the second floor," the volunteer replied. "You may use either the Grand Stairway or take the elevator to reach all three floors of the library. The elevator is located in the hallway, to your right."

∞∞∞∞

Entering the second floor History Department, Ellen glanced at the surroundings. It was a typical library reading room with seating for eight patrons at each rectangular wooden table; tall shelves filled with books lined every wall. Men and women filled the straight-backed wooden chairs at every table; they were reading newspapers, magazines or consulting reference books.

The dark wood interior furnishings were balanced by soaring banks of windows which offered natural light for day-time reading while large cylindrical lamps lit the space during evening hours. Opposite the windows, a large painting by Frank Vincent Dumond was displayed; a nearby plaque gave details. In 1917, the mural *Pioneers Leaving the East* was installed in the History Department. On the same floor, located in an opposite room, his mural *Pioneers Arriving in the West* was hung in the Literature Department.

Ellen studied the painting for a few minutes, then realized she had gotten distracted again; she walked over to the reception desk.

"Good morning," she said, while signing their visitor log. "I'm here to look for family history records."

"Are you looking for local information or something from our special collections area?"

"I'm doing routine census research and also need to locate two county history books," Ellen replied, as she absent-mindedly picked up the Research Guidelines page. The Guidelines included a map of the shelves and microfilm drawer locations. Only one film could be checked out each time; it had to be returned before using a second film.

Walking into their Check Room, Ellen placed her briefcase and handbag in the locker and buckled a fanny-pack holding pencils and index cards around her waist. She picked up the Cooper Estate notebook, closed the door and slipped the key into her pocket.

Ellen returned to the research department and scanned the room to find an empty space. She selected a table near the window, sat down and opened her notebook to check the dates. Married in 1892, Fred and Marie Kupper should be listed on the 1900 and 1910 census.

At the Card Catalog cabinet, she pulled out a shelf for taking notes and copied citations for each source: 1900 census Soundex film, 1900 census microfilm, 1910 census index book, 1910 census microfilm, *History of Clayton County, Nebraska* and *Adams County Oklahoma History*.

Then, she found the 1900 Nebraska Soundex in one of the microfilm cabinets, checked it out at the reference desk and entered the elevator to the third floor.

In the Newspaper Department, Ellen loaded the film and cranked the handle. After reading thirty-five Soundex cards for every possible spelling variation of Fred or Friedrich and Kupper or Cooper, she found that Fred Kupper lived in Clayton County, Nebraska in June 1900. Ellen copied the ED page number, rewound the film and returned it to the second floor.

Next, she found the correct 1900 census microfilm for Clayton County, Nebraska, checked it out from the History Department and entered the elevator to the third floor Newspaper Department, again.

Returning to the same cubicle, Ellen threaded the film and scrolled through the pages to locate details. She discovered:

> Fred Kupper, farmer, renter, Arapaho Township, Farm Schedule 130, born September 1853, age 46, married 8 years. Born in Germany; both of his parents born in Germany. Immigrated 1889, a naturalized citizen. He could read, write and speak English.

Marie Kupper, wife, born September 1866, age 33, married 8 years, mother of three children, all living. Born in Germany; both of her parents born in Germany. Immigrated 1888. She could read, write and speak English.

Mary Kupper, daughter, born April 1893, age 7, attended school in 1900. Anna Kupper, daughter, born May 1895, age 5. Fred Kupper, son, born June 1898, age 2. All were born in Nebraska. Their parents were born in Germany.

It was the correct family—the 1900 census information matched Addendum A. Noting that Maria identified herself as Marie in 1900, Ellen copied the details on a census worksheet, then returned the film.

Time for lunch. Ellen placed everything in her locker, picked up her handbag and signed out. Needing a break from sitting on the hard wooden library chairs, she walked one block to the Market Street Café and ordered a sandwich, chips, a drink and cookies for dessert.

∞∞∞∞

On returning to the Library, she took the elevator to the History Department, then signed the visitor log and retrieved her research notes from the locker.

Instead of reading more microfilm, she found the county history books and checked each index. In the *History of Clayton County, Nebraska*, Ellen looked for Cooper, Kupper and Klein. No one with these surnames had contributed any family histories or photographs.

In reviewing the *Adams County, Oklahoma History* index, a search for the Cooper and Kupper names didn't find anyone either.

However, she found the Klein family! The list of names included Reinhard Klein, Sophia Katherina Kupper Klein, and their children, Katherina, Marie, Lena, Rosena, Caroline, Fred, John, George, Michael.

According to their oral history, the Klein family came from *Altenkirchen*. Their father traded a farm for a Mill, but he later returned to farming. Their oldest daughter Katherina Regina remained in Germany; Marie, George, John, Fred and Lena immigrated to Nebraska.

Ellen reviewed Addendum A—all of the names closely matched—it was the correct family. She printed copies of the relevant pages and then checked her watch.

Four o'clock, time to leave. Tomorrow, an appointment with George Smoot was scheduled. She decided to finish reading the 1910 census microfilm next week.

Retrieving everything from the locker, Ellen signed out, walked to the Market Street MUNI stop and boarded the streetcar. As it emerged from the tunnel near Dolores Park, the grassy median displayed clumps of daffodils nodding cheerfully. Spring weather would be arriving soon.

# The Phone Call

F riday, February 28, eight o'clock in the morning; rain drops were bouncing off the window panes. After her usual two extra cups of coffee, Ellen read the Klein family article that was discovered yesterday in the *Adams County, Oklahoma History.*

A closer review of the Johann Reinhard Klein story found the oldest sister, Katherina Regina, was married and remained in Germany. The next child was Marie. She could speak English, was employed as a Translator in New York City, sent passage money to each of her siblings and later married a Mr. Cooper in America.

Her brother George arrived in 1889; Fred and John arrived in 1891 while Lena emigrated in 1892. In reading the individual biographies of each sibling, Ellen discovered Fred Klein had a son named George. He was deceased, although his wife Gertrude currently lived in the same farmhouse where her husband was born. Ellen did some rough calculations. If George was born in 1903, and his wife Gertrude was roughly the same age, she would be eighty-three years of age now.

On a whim, Ellen retrieved the portable phone from the kitchen, then punched "O" and asked for the telephone number of Gertrude Klein in Adams County, Oklahoma. Astonished at receiving a working phone number, she immediately called.

"Hello?" an older woman answered.

"Hi, I'm calling from California and trying to find information about a woman named Marie Klein," said Ellen. "I came across your name in the *Adams County, Oklahoma History* book. I'm sorry to bother you—was your husband George, a nephew of Marie Klein?"

"Who are you?" the older woman asked suspiciously.

"I'm sorry," Ellen replied slowly. My name is Ellen O'Donnell and I live in San Francisco. I do genealogy research and a client has asked me to find the family of Marie Klein Kupper. The only information they know is Marie immigrated to New York City and left a child behind to be raised by her parents in Germany. It's possible her daughter came to Nebraska with her grandmother about 1901 or 1902. I've been asked to locate any family history and photographs of Marie."

"Okay, I'm Gertrude Klein and yes, those people were my husband's family. We have the same story about the grand-daughter in our family. Marie went to California during the Great Depression and we never heard from her again. In the 1950s, there was a phone call, but the line went dead. I'm not sure about family photographs."

"I'll be in Oklahoma City in a few weeks. Could I visit you?"

"I'll ask my daughters. We live in the country. You would have to rent a car to drive to our house."

"That's okay. May I call you again when I have the dates that I'll be in Oklahoma?"

"Yes, that's fine.

"Thank you so much," said Ellen. She hung up the phone, excited and amazed at her good luck in being able to contact a living relative.

# Naming Patterns

An hour later, Ellen placed an extra notepad, pencils and the Cooper Estate notebook in her briefcase, walked downstairs to the basement garage and drove into The City. Locating a nearby parking space, she took an elevator to the offices of Lardner, Alexander and Smoot. Ellen introduced herself to the receptionist, who in turn notified Jeanne of her arrival. A few minutes later, Mr. Smoot's secretary entered the lobby.

"Hello Ellen, how are you?" said Jeanne. "Mr. Smoot had an emergency and won't be able to see you until later. He asked me to help you in the meantime."

"Oh, thank you," replied Ellen. "I had asked about viewing the Helen Cooper death certificate and the will of her brother, Fred John Cooper. Did Mr. Smoot mention this?"

"Yes, I've placed everything in the small conference room so you can review the papers in a quiet space. I'll let you know when Mr. Smoot's other meeting is finished."

Ellen followed Jeanne into the conference room, removed the Cooper Estate notebook from her briefcase and began reading the legal documents.

First, she looked at the death certificate for Helen A. Cooper. The only unexpected piece of information was her date of birth. Identified as May 11, 1900—it conflicted with the census which stated she was five years old in June 1900. In fact, Helen A. Cooper was ninety years old when she died, instead of being eighty-five years old as recorded on the death certificate.

Next, she read the Last Will and Testament of Helen A. Cooper, dated April 12, 1981. It used fairly standard language, with the exception of the seventh clause which indicated there weren't any provisions for other persons, whether claiming to be an heir or not. This might be boiler-plate language or it could refer to an estranged family.

Ellen then reviewed the death certificate for Fred John Cooper. His date of birth was listed as June 14, 1902. It differed from the June 1900 census which stated he was born in 1898. Fred John Cooper was eighty-one years old, instead of being seventy-seven years old. Both Helen and Fred John claimed to be four to five years younger than their actual age.

Looking again at Fred's death certificate, she noticed an unusual detail. An investigation filed in Sebastopol, California on April 25, 1980 occurred two days after his death from acute myocardial infarction and acute coronary thrombosis. Cremation arrangements were handled by Pleasant Hill Cemetery in Sebastopol, with his ashes being sent to Cypress Lawn in Colma. Ellen added a note to her San Francisco research page: Decide whether to research the April investigation report.

Next, she read the Last Will and Testament of Fred John Cooper, dated February 13, 1953. It provided for the care of his eighty-six-year-old mother, who was a patient at the Garden Hospital, and left his railroad pension to his sister, Helen A. Cooper. An unusual clause directed that he be given a burial suitable to his station in life and another clause identified the possibility of estranged family members. Fred John Cooper stated he would give to any person who could prove that he or she was a relative of his, and entitled to share in his estate, the sum of One and No/100 Dollars ($1.00) and no more.

Several documents concerning his Railroad Pension were included in the file. Fred John Cooper lived on Geary Street in San Francisco; he was employed as a Tractor Operator in the Freight Department of the Southern Pacific Railroad Company on October 30, 1936. He retired thirty years later on October 31, 1966.

Pension documents also included a handwritten statement to the Railroad Retirement Board. In this letter, Fred indicated he was born June 14, 1898 in Stirling Township, Clayton County, Nebraska; nevertheless when employed by the S&P RR on October 30, 1936, he altered his age by four years and gave his birth date as June 14, 1902. Furthermore, his name was recorded with the German spelling of Johann Friedrich Kupper in the family Bible. Nevertheless, since childhood he used the Americanized spelling of Fred John Cooper.

The details about Fred John's date of birth were interesting. However, the statement about his correct birth name was important evidence about their family history. In Germany, families traditionally followed the practice of giving a son the same name as his paternal grandfather, which likely meant his grandfather was named Johann Friedrich Kupper.

It was also customary to give the infant an official, baptized name. Yet, in everyday usage, the child was usually known by his middle name. His parents were following German naming patterns; in their family, he was known as Fred or Fred John.

Elated at finding new information, Ellen filed her notes in the briefcase and stacked the documents neatly on the table. As she was thinking about her next steps, Jeanne walked into the conference room.

"Mr. Smoot is ready to see you now."

# Progress Report

George Smoot looked up from the papers on his desk, adjusted his glasses and rose to greet her. "Hello Ellen, how are you?" he said. "Let's sit over here by the window and talk about the Cooper assignment. I'm curious to learn what you've found."

"Thank you. It's been a good week and I've discovered several interesting items," said Ellen, as she removed her notes from the briefcase.

"First I should mention the German microfilms have been ordered and they will be here in about three weeks.

"On Monday I interviewed Helen's neighbor and she gave some fascinating insight into their family dynamics.

"I also visited Cypress Lawn and found the death date of Helen's mother, which means I can order a death certificate for Mary Cooper.

"Yesterday I went to the San Francisco Public Library. The 1900 census verified the Kupper family lived in Nebraska. However the 1910 census gave different counties for Marie and her husband Fred, so something happened to the family between 1900 and 1910. I'm going to the library next week to find more details about the 1910 census."

Referring again to her notes, Ellen itemized more information.

"I was pleased to find a Klein family biography in *Adams County, Oklahoma History*. All of the details matched the Addendum A that was provided by Helen Cooper.

"From this article, I learned that Mary's nephew George was deceased, but his widow is still living. This morning I called Gertrude Klein in Oklahoma.

"She confirmed Marie Klein was a relative. We had a good conversation and Gertrude might have family photos.

"A little while ago, when looking at the Fred John Cooper documents, I learned his baptized name was Johann Friedrich Kupper. This important piece of information will be very helpful in verifying family records in Germany."

"You've certainly made significant progress in only a few days," replied George. "What's next on your agenda?"

"First of all, I need to return this signed contract to you, everything looks fine with me."

"Thank you," replied George. "I'm glad it's agreeable to you."

"I've also been planning ahead a little and would like to ask about travel expenses. Although I still need to search for Marie's immigration records at the National Archives and read the *Kirchenbuch* records, the San Francisco research should be done by the end of March.

"In April, I'd like to retrace Marie's steps. In Nebraska, I need to look at courthouse records, check local church records or cemeteries and interview descendants of the Klein family.

"In Oklahoma, I can reconstruct land transactions at the courthouse, I should find information about the Hale Gang at the Oklahoma Historical

Society and I also need to review records from the Mercy Hospital for the Insane.

"After talking with Gertrude Klein this morning, it could be very helpful to meet her. If she has photos of Marie and her family, they would be a bonus.

"Altogether, an Oklahoma visit ought to identify information to complete *Item One* and a Nebraska visit should give details about the Cooper family history for *Item Two*."

Listening carefully, George scribbled notes on his legal pad; it was a customary habit he practiced when trying to make decisions about fiduciary responsibilities.

"You've already made substantial progress and I'm very pleased. However, it sounds like there's a lot of information that simply can't be found in San Francisco.

"I think you've given sufficient justification to make the Nebraska and Oklahoma trip," he said. "Go ahead with your travel plans, just turn in the receipts and a progress report later."

"Thank you," replied Ellen. "I'll check on reservations, the courthouse business hours and also decide who else I can meet while I'm there. If you don't have any other questions, I'd like to leave now, before rush hour ties up traffic."

"That's certainly understandable," said George. "Thanks again for helping us with this project and have a nice evening."

He then escorted Ellen to the elevator. It was still raining when she stepped outside and dashed to the car.

Ellen returned home to her Victorian house in Noe Valley. Driving into the basement garage, she dropped off the briefcase in her office and went upstairs to call her friends. She invited them to dinner at the La Roca restaurant the next evening and asked them to join her for the First Saturday Gallery Tour of the latest paintings by her favorite artists.

To celebrate the meeting with George Smoot, she then uncorked a new bottle of wine. It had been a successful first week of research.

# Family Relationships – 1910

Monday was beautiful weather, an ideal day for taking the J-Church MUNI streetcar into The City. Arriving at the Market Street stop, Ellen walked to the San Francisco Public Library and entered the imposing Beaux Arts building.

When the librarian finished helping another patron, Ellen said, "Hello, I'm back again. Is there any faster method to identify census details? I attended a conference about two years ago and a speaker talked about new search methods."

"Yes, we've also been told a massive database of all federal census information is being considered by a committee from the National Archives," said the librarian. "You know how bureaucracies work . . . it takes forever for a committee to study every possible detail and come to a conclusion. When they make a decision, it will really change how we search for information, but in the meantime we must continue using the old-fashioned methods. I'm sorry, we all wish this database would magically appear but I suspect it will be years before changes occur."

"Too bad. I was really hoping there would be a quicker method to search census records," replied Ellen. She placed her briefcase in the locker and took a seat at one of the library tables.

After checking her research notes, Ellen found Volume Three of the 1910 Nebraska census in *The Stacks* and brought the heavy book to the table. Marie Kupper and Anna Cooper were indexed for Clayton County. There wasn't any record of Fred Kupper in Clayton County; however in Douglas County, there were listings for Fred Kupper and Fred Cooper. Noting the 1910 citations on individual cards, she then located the 1910 census microfilm for Douglas County, Nebraska, checked it out and left the History Department.

In the third floor Newspaper Department, Ellen threaded the 1910 film, adjusted the focus and then scrolled through the pages until discovering an entry for Fred Kupper. He was divorced.

> Fred Kupper, Ward 2, City of Omaha, Douglas County, Nebraska. Occupation: servant and laborer for a Market Garden. Born 1853, age 57, divorced. Born Germany; both of his parents born in Germany. Immigrated 1889. He was a naturalized citizen.

Next, she looked at the entry for Fred Cooper:

> Fred Cooper, age 8, born 1902, St. Joseph Orphanage, Kentucky Precinct, Douglas County, Nebraska. The school attendance column was blank and other details weren't identified. (The list included 147 boys and girls.)

Fred wasn't living with either of his parents! Ellen quickly copied the details to her worksheet, then walked down the elaborate Grand Stairway and turned the film in at the History Department. Next, she checked out the 1910 Clayton County, Nebraska census microfilm.

Returning to the third floor, she chose the same cubicle and threaded the film. It didn't take long to find Marie Kupper:

> Marie Kupper, 1422 Main Street, Ward 4, Josephine, Clayton County, Nebraska. Born 1866, age 44, divorced; mother of three children, two living. Born in Germany; both of her parents born in Germany. Immigrated 1888. She could read and write English. Occupation: servant for a private family. Employer: Milton James, a real estate and insurance agent from New York.

Her status had changed—in 1910 Marie was divorced and one of her children had died. Marie didn't live with her family. She was alone.

Ellen checked her worksheet notes. Their son, Fred Cooper, age eight, lived in an orphanage in Omaha—not far from the address where his father roomed at his employer's house. But where was Anna? Reviewing the film again, she was found on a different ED page:

> Anna Cooper, 512 North 5th Street, Ward 2, Josephine, Clayton County, Nebraska. Born 1896, age 14, single. Born Nebraska; both of her parents born in Germany. She could read and write English. She did not attend school in 1910. Occupation: servant for a private family. Employer: Anna Miller, manager of boarding house, twenty-eight residents.

The family unit had dissolved. Anna was a servant. Her mother was a servant for a different family. Her brother lived in an orphanage. Her father lived in a boarding house.

Because of their parents' divorce, the children were separated. They couldn't live with their mother, who was a housekeeper for the Milton James family. They couldn't live with their father, who was a boarder in a

49

rooming house. Ellen added the census details and another comment to her worksheet—in 1910, Fred and Marie used the surname of Kupper, while their children used the Americanized surname of Cooper.

Glancing at her watch, it was time for a break. Ellen gathered her notes, walked down the marble steps of the Grand Stairway for the last time, returned the film to the History Department, removed everything from the locker, signed out and left the ornate library building.

∞∞∞∞

At the Market Street Café, Ellen sat at a window table and ordered lunch. While waiting for the salad to arrive, she tore a sheet of paper from the tablet and began writing: Why were Fred and Marie divorced? The photograph of Anna and Fred with their father had a studio label from Omaha, Nebraska—but their mother wasn't included. If the photo was taken while their father worked there and Fred lived at the orphanage, the children must've known about their divorce. But, Helen never mentioned it in the Addendum. Was the divorce a family secret? When were Fred and Marie divorced—before or after their daughter Mary died. When did she die? Why did she die? Where is she buried? How did Anna react to working as a servant in a boarding house? Where did Fred go to school? The orphanage was located in a metropolitan area and would've been a very different from living on a farm. How long did he live there? More questions—more mysteries.

Adding a title page, *Reference #2 – Family Relationships 1910,* Ellen stapled it to the 1900 and 1910 worksheets and filed them in her notebook. Afterwards, she re-traced her steps to the Market Street MUNI, took the streetcar to her neighborhood and walked home.

# Searching Immigration Records

The radio announcer reported another "marine layer" day in the bay area; it was fifty-seven degrees and foggy, with a visibility of four miles. Ellen opted to get dressed, have a leisurely breakfast, read the *Chronicle*, and then pack a lunch.

Leaving her home on Vicksburg Street, Ellen drove south, merged with I-280S, passed Lake Merced Golf Club and the Golden Gate National Cemetery, then took the Sneath Lane exit and arrived at 1000 Commodore Drive in San Bruno. Located near an island of huge redwood and eucalyptus trees, the parking lot was surrounded by misty fog. A landscape of naturalized English Ivy underneath smaller deciduous trees led toward the entrance to the National Archives; the setting displayed an attractive contrast to the stark exterior architecture.

∞∞∞∞

Entering the reception area, she asked for directions. "I'd like to look at emigration records of someone who left Germany in 1888."

"Please sign our register and place your handbag and briefcase in the locker, here's a key," replied the clerk in a brisk, efficient manner.

After writing her name in the register, Ellen placed everything except her research notebook, a tablet and pencil inside the locker.

Picking up a copy of their regulations, she slipped the locker key into a pocket and placed her research notes on an unoccupied table. A sign was prominently posted in several areas of the room: *Quiet Zone – Please Use the Patron Lounge for Discussions – Quiet Zone.* At the National Archives, there were rules governing access to all records; it was a business-like environment.

Returning to the reception desk, she softly said, "I'd like to look at any German emigration reference books first, then I'll need to look at microfilm of the ship manifest lists. Could you tell me where to find these materials?"

"I'll show you where everything is located," the clerk replied, then led her to the shelves of German reference books and pointed toward the wooden card catalog file, a wall of twenty microfilm cabinets, and a row of microfilm readers.

Before choosing one of the reference books, Ellen reviewed her notes. The title of Marie's journal implied that she arrived in New York in 1888 and her last scrawled sentence stated Katie was born on May 23, 1888. The addendum by Helen Cooper noted her mother, Marie Klein Cooper, was born in September 1866. These clues gave the basic details to begin searching for Marie's arrival date in New York City. Depending on whether she left Germany about June 1888 or if she left Germany after her birthday, Marie was probably twenty-one or twenty-two years old.

First, Ellen checked the *Württemberg Emigration Index.* There weren't any records for Maria or Marie Klein, Kleen, Klien or Kline. Frederick, Friedrich or Fred Kupper wasn't in the *Index* either.

However, if one of Marie's siblings could be found, their information might identify a different spelling or a port which Marie also used. After an hour of searching all name variations, there weren't any emigration records available for Fred, John or Lena. Yet, there was an entry for George Klein, born 10 August 1872, leaving *Württemberg* via the port of *Bremen* in July 1889. The details matched the *Adams County History*.

Yet—there must be an error—if George completed the emigration paperwork process, why didn't Marie, Fred, John or Lena? An answer was found in the Introduction to the *Württemberg Emigration Index;* these volumes didn't include anyone who left covertly or left before their papers were finalized. The *Index* identified the most common port of departure as *Bremen.* Although many emigrants left from *Antwerp, Rotterdam, Le Havre* or *Amsterdam*, these departure records were not available—a search of arrival ports was recommended.

This initial search for emigration details indicated Marie may have left secretly, left in a hurry before receiving official papers or else left from another region.

∞∞∞∞

Instead of beginning another intensive search procedure, Ellen stored her research materials in the locker, signed out and went outside to find a bench and have lunch. At one o'clock she signed in again, retrieved her research notebook and returned to the same table.

According to her notes, Marie's journal mentioned New York City—a search of the volumes titled *Germans to America* might give details. The index to each volume identified everyone in alphabetical order by surname, and then cross-referenced their name to a manifest.

First, Ellen tried to predict the earliest and latest month of Marie's departure. If Marie remained at home during the first month or so after her daughter was born, and it took about one or two weeks to travel from home to a port, then her earliest departure date would be July or August. Or, her latest departure date could have been October or

November, assuming she quickly found a job on arrival and sent money to her brother George in late December or January 1889. This analysis established search parameters of July to November, 1888.

Next, she created a chart. All spelling options were written in the left-hand column—Maria or Marie Klein, Kleen, Klien or Kline—and a heading of Volume 56–May 1 to November 30, 1888 labeled the next column. Each name was compared against each ship manifest page to identify the name, age and arrival date of each person named Maria or Marie, various surnames. Using the same process, she looked for Frederick, Friedrich, or Fred Kupper in Volume 57–December 1, 1888 to June 30, 1889. After comparing all records, Maria or Marie Klein, using the different spelling variations wasn't found. Kupper emigrants by the name of Friedrich, Frederick, or Fred weren't listed either.

Frustrated by the amount of time spent without any results, Ellen reviewed the Introduction of *Germans to America*. The volumes had strict selection criteria; they only indexed the manifest of ships which left Germany with at least fifty percent of the passengers departing from a German origination point. The directories didn't include German emigrants who left from *Le Havre, Antwerp, Rotterdam* or *Amsterdam*.

Census records indicated Marie arrived in 1888 and Fred arrived in 1889. Since neither of them was found in *Germans to America*, the missing information implied they might have travelled on ships which transported a conglomerate of emigrants from several countries or else they emigrated from France, Belgium or the Netherlands.

Four o'clock; she filed her notes, then removed everything from the locker, returned the key and signed out. Weary from a day of not finding any answers, Ellen returned to Noe Valley and reminded herself—this was the first setback. Tomorrow she would try again.

## SS Vaterland

After yesterday's disappointments, Ellen decided to fortify herself for another day of tedious research by having breakfast at The Chocolate Croissant. She listened to the weather report while getting dressed, picked up the newspaper and drove to her favorite café to order a Country French Breakfast. Following her usual two extra cups of coffee, she requested a lunch-to-go, then left for another day of research at the National Archives in San Bruno.

Taking the same route as yesterday, she parked in the same place; the distinct and refreshing minty-pine smell of the towering Eucalyptus trees drifted through the air.

Now familiar with the National Archives rules, Ellen signed in, left her briefcase, handbag and lunch in the locker and returned to the reference desk. While driving down the freeway, she had resolved to ask for advice about immigration records.

"Excuse me. I had such a frustrating experience yesterday in trying to find details in the *Württemberg Index* and *Germans to America*. Is there is any faster method of searching for emigration documents?"

The clerk looked up from his worksheet and said, "I'm sorry Ma'am, we're not allowed to help patrons individually. You'll need to do your own research."

Ellen politely answered, "I'm just wondering if there is a better method to look for information. Is there an immigration database on the computer?"

"No, we don't have such a system, although I agree it would really be nice for researchers. At the library conferences, they keep telling us about a new system—something called the World Wide Web—but no one has any idea when it will be available. The presenters tell us it will be a new way to locate information. I suppose it'll be several years before anything changes. At present, the names of emigrants are only available in the various index books."

"I'm sorry to hear that. I've tried looking in several volumes of *Germans to America*. Is there any other index I could use?

"You might try *Passenger and Immigration Lists Index,* by P. William Filby; his work references all emigrant names found in a published record. You could also check microfilm from the National Archives. I'm sorry I can't be of more help," said the clerk, as he pointedly began writing information on his worksheet again.

Resigned to another day of lengthy research, Ellen added the title to her notes, then went to the card catalog to locate the call number. She carried all of the volumes published between 1981 and 1985 to her table and began developing a research plan.

First, she created a chart of all possible spelling options in the left-hand column—Maria Klein, Kleen, Klien, Kline and Marie Klein, Kleen, Klien and Kline. At the top of the page, five column headings for each publication year were added; there were eight Klein names to review in five volumes.

The same procedure was repeated for the name combinations of Frederick, Friedrich, or Fred Kupper; there were three Kupper name combinations to be searched in the five volumes.

When searching all of the Filby volumes, a dozen Maria or Marie Klein names by various spellings were found. The women emigrated from Ireland, Germany or England, but none of them emigrated in 1888.

There were several Friedrich Kupper variations, but none of them matched an 1889 date. Another dead-end.

One o'clock, time for a break. Placing her research notes in the locker, Ellen took along the lunch-to-go, bought lemonade from the vending machine and went outside to watch the birds wheeling in and out of the tall Eucalyptus trees.

∞∞∞∞

After lunch, she removed her research notes from the locker and returned to the microfilm area. During the Great Depression, employees of the WPA (Works Progress Administration) developed a personal name index to ship passenger lists held by the Immigration and Naturalization Service. In reading ship manifests, line by line, they created an index card for each passenger.

The cards were later filmed by NARA (National Archives) under the subject title, *Passenger Lists of Vessels Arriving at New York, New York, 1820-1957.* These cards were the last resource where she could look for the immigration records of Marie Klein and Friedrich Kupper.

Ellen placed the "Kl" Soundex Roll on an empty spool and read each card; twenty-eight records were found. By comparing each card, all records of a Maria Klein, various spellings, of the wrong age, those who did not arrive in 1888 or originated from another country, were eliminated. There was only one woman who matched the search criteria:

> Marie Kleen, age 21, Germany. Departed Antwerp. *SS Vaterland*. Arrived Port of New York, October 4, 1888.

Great! Having information about Marie's arrival date meant a search of the city directory records in New York City might identify her occupation and address.

Elated at locating relevant details, she quickly copied the new information and then retrieved the next film, which listed ships arriving in October 1888.

A search for the *SS Vaterland* found:

> Marie Kleen, age 21, from Germany, 1 piece of luggage, assigned to Aft Deck D, intent Permanent Resident. The manifest list indicated she was alone (no one travelled with her) and was assigned to a second-class compartment along with other single women leaving Germany. Owned by the Red Star (Belgian) line, the *SS Vaterland* transported 80 first-class passengers, 60 second-class passengers and 1,200 third-class passengers.

"Hallelujah!" Ellen announced excitedly, and then remembered this was the microfilm area of a federal facility that emphasized silence. Oops.

After copying the new details, she threaded the "Ku" Soundex Roll and read forty individual cards. By careful comparison, all records of a Friedrich Kupper, various spellings, of the wrong age, those who did not arrive in 1889 or originated from another country, were eliminated. The only person matching the known information was:

> Friedrich Kupper, age 32, Germany. Departed Bremen, Germany and Southampton, England. Arrived Port of New York, May 11, 1889, *SS Evalena*.

More good news! This record identified a May arrival. According to the *Adams County Oklahoma History*, in July 1889 Marie sent her brother George to live with a friend in Nebraska. Marie's journal mentioned someone named Fritz. Since he arrived in May 1889, Friedrich Kupper may have been her friend in Nebraska.

Ellen copied the details, then located the next film. It identified ships arriving at the Port of New York in May 1889. A search for the *SS Evalena* discovered:

> Friedrich Kupper, age 32, from Germany, 1 piece of luggage, intent Protracted Sojourn. He boarded the ship at Bremen, travelling alone (no relatives travelling with him) and was assigned to a bunk in Steerage I (third class).
>
> Owned by the North German Lloyd line, this ship carried 125 first-class passengers, 130 second-class passengers, and 1,000 third-class passengers.

Finally! It had taken two days of research to discover valid immigration details for Marie Klein and Friedrich Kupper. Detail by detail, a family history profile was being created.

Ellen updated her worksheet and returned the film, then removed everything from the locker, walked outside to look for the towering trees and found the car. Although the immigration records search had seemed endless and tedious, it had been a triumphant second week of working on the Cooper Estate project.

Arriving home and walking into the basement office, she checked the answering machine. There was a message from the Oakland Multiregional Family History Center. Three rolls of microfilm were available for viewing on Monday.

# Discovering Marie's Family

Monday morning brought a week of blustery March wind. A few minutes after nine o'clock, Ellen left for the seventeen-mile drive to Oakland, exited at McArthur Freeway, then took Lincoln Avenue to the Multiregional Family History Center.

At the building entrance, she rang the doorbell and a voice asked "May I help you."

"Yes," she replied, "I'd like to do family history research."

When signing the visitor register, she said, "I'm hoping to find my family today. Can you show me where the films are located?"

The volunteer looked up from a visitor sign-in worksheet, smiled and pointed to the opposite wall, "The microfilm drawers are over there and the films are filed according to your name; just thread the roll on the machine, then turn the handle to read each page. If you need any help, please let me know."

"Thanks," said Ellen, as she glanced around the area. The small room included several shelves of genealogy reference books, a single work table with a few chairs, a wall of microfilm storage cabinets and several readers placed next to each other, without much space between them.

There weren't any windows because the glare would make it difficult to read faint transcripts.

After placing Addendum A and the Family Group Sheets on the narrow pull-out shelf, she wound the film on the empty spool, adjusted the focus knob for the best view, and began scrolling through several volumes. Each section listed marriages, baptisms, and deaths by year, then by date of the event; some pages were very faded, difficult to read.

Quickly scrolling through all the other categories, Ellen located the volume titled *Altenkirchen Familienbuch 1852-1925.* Turning the handle slowly, she reached the "K" section.

"I found it!"

The page included substantial facts about the Johann Reinhard Klein family. Most importantly, the volume title specified they were members of the church at *Altenkirchen* in 1882 and the page title revealed they lived in a settlement or village named *Mittelberg*. This new information was not mentioned in the *Adams County History*.

Johann <u>Reinhard</u> Klein and Sophia <u>Katherina</u> Kupper Klein had eleven children. The underlined names of Reinhard and Katherina signified the names by which they were usually known. Ellen compared all the children's names against Addendum A. It was the correct family.

She recorded the name, date and place of birth, baptism, and confirmation for the parents and each of their children on the Family Group Sheet page, then translated and highlighted a specific detail:

> <u>Maria</u> Magdalena Klein, born 02 September 1866, *Südbruch*, confirmed 1880, *Weißenfels*. Married Kupper in America. [A notation beside her name indicated Maria was assigned a separate family register.]

This entry gave important details about Helen's mother. Mary (Klein) Cooper, also known as Maria or Marie, was born in September 1866. The microfilm record identified her baptized name as Maria Magdalena Klein, as well as a date and place where she was born and confirmed. The record also verified that Marie married Kupper in America. Significantly—if the additional family register could be found—it ought to give more information about her child.

The background chatter was becoming louder as more people arrived; Ellen ignored the babble and concentrated on a final review of the copied information. A second reading of the baptism, confirmation and death dates listed on the *Familienbuch* page identified the Klein family lived in several villages and another child was born at each new location. Aware that most families lived in the same village for several generations, Ellen studied the dates and places where children were born or confirmed.

She decided to leave no stone unturned in her search for answers by requesting additional microfilm of the *Taufen (*Birth and Baptism Records) and *Konfirmation (Confirmation Register)* for each village: *Heideland (Südbruch), Martinshofen (Ehrenfeld), Unterharnsbach (Arnsberg), Hohenberg, Weißenfels,* and *Dorflingen.*

It was nearly two o'clock and her eyes hurt from concentrating on the handwritten script. Since the room was becoming more crowded by the minute, Ellen opted to search for Katherine Klein's 1888 baptism and confirmation records tomorrow. Placing the reference notes in her briefcase, she retraced her route to Noe Valley.

Arriving home, Ellen ate lunch and then checked for mail. Two answers from earlier queries had arrived:

> *California Death Certificate*: Mary Catherine Cooper, a widow, age 90 years; her father was Reinhard Klein from Germany. She died on February 9, 1957 at The Garden Hospital, San Francisco; funeral arrangements by Carew & English. Cause of death: Cerebral Hemorrhage due to Arteriosclerosis. Mary Cooper lived in San Francisco for twenty years. The information was provided by her son, Fred J. Cooper.

The most interesting detail from this death certificate identified that Mary used a middle name of Catherine in 1957, instead of her baptized middle name of Magdalena.

> *Social Security Application*: Helen Anne Cooper applied for a social security card on November 24, 1936. Birth date: May 11, 1900. She lived on Geary Street in San Francisco and was employed by the Canterbury Hotel.

In a fascinating memo attached to the application, Helen explained she was baptized as Anna, and named after her paternal great-grandmother. However, when leaving Josephine, she moved to Scottsbluff, Nebraska and changed her name to Helen.

This unexpected revelation answered the question of why Anna Kupper, born in 1895, was later known as Helen A. Cooper.

# Tracing Klein Family Records

After her usual breakfast and two extra cups of coffee, Ellen packed a lunch for another research day at the Family History Center in Oakland. On arrival, she punched the doorbell and a voice asked "May I help you."

"I'm here for more research," she replied. "Yesterday, I forgot to ask about printing microfilm records."

"Yes, that's possible," the volunteer replied. "First, you'll need to find each page number. After you've located all of your references, rewind the film and then position it on the microfilm copy machine. When you're ready, I'll show you how it works."

"Okay, thanks," said Ellen, as she removed the *Altenkirchen* film from the cabinet. Placing her briefcase on the floor beside the microfilm reader, she checked the reference notes. Today, her first priority was to locate a family register for Maria Klein. Secondly, she wanted to find Katherine's baptism and confirmation records. And, she hoped to identify Reinhard Klein's occupation on the confirmation and death records.

Ellen threaded the film. A few minutes later, she found the correct *Familienbuch* entry for Katherine, the daughter of Maria Klein:

Mother: <u>Maria</u> Magdalena Klein, born 02 September 1866, *Südbruch*, Emigrated to America 1888. Father: blank. Grandfather: Johann <u>Reinhard</u> Klein, *Tagelöhner, Mittelberg*; Grandmother: Sophia <u>Katherina</u> (Kupper).

Child's Name: Maria <u>Katherina</u> Klein, born 23 May 1888, baptized 17 June 1888, confirmed 14 April 1901. Immigrated to Nebraska with her grandmother, July 1901.

Amazing! This record verified that Maria Magdalena Klein emigrated in 1888 and Maria Katherina, born 23 May 1888, was the daughter named Katie—which Marie had scribbled in her journal and Helen also mentioned in Addendum A. It also verified that Katie emigrated with her grandmother, Sophia Katherina Klein, in July 1901.

Ellen added the Johann Reinhard Klein and Maria Klein family register pages to her printing list and jotted notes for future research: Official records identifying the name of Katherine's father are blank—a family secret? Ask descendants in Germany if there are any family memories about this event.

To look for an 1888 baptism record of Maria's daughter, she then checked the *Altenkirchen Taufen* (Baptism) dates on the box. Out of luck; the microfilm ended in 1884.

Since an 1888 baptism record wasn't available, Ellen retrieved the *Altenkirchen Konfirmation 1809-1909* film. The record of Maria Katherina Klein identified additional information:

*Confirmation 14 April 1901*: Maria <u>Katherina</u> Klein, born *Mittelberg*, 23 May 1888, baptized 17 June 1888. Confirmation completed before immigrating to America. Mother: <u>Maria</u> Magdalena Klein. Grandfather deceased: Reinhard Klein of *Mittelberg*, wife Kupper.

In reading the individual items, Katherine was age thirteen, although most of the children were fourteen years old. Because confirmation was a two-year cycle, her grandparents must have received approval to begin confirmation studies at the age of eleven. They probably wanted to be sure Katie was confirmed before she travelled to America.

Twelve o'clock, noon. Ellen noted the confirmation page on her printing list, rewound the film and returned it to the cabinet. Stacking her belongings on the chair, she signed out, found a bench in the courtyard and enjoyed the sunny weather while eating lunch.

∞∞∞∞

Forty-five minutes later, Ellen punched the doorbell.

A voice asked "May I help you."

"Yes, I'm back for more research," she replied. After signing in, Ellen picked up the *Konfirmation 1809-1909 and Tote 1842-1934* films and returned to her cubicle. According to the Reinhard Klein family register, Johann was confirmed in 1884, George in 1886, Magdalena in 1891, Karolina in 1894 and Rosina in 1897. Every document identified a common pattern: each child was fourteen years old and in each case, the father's occupation was a *Tagelöhner* at *Mittelberg*.

Next, she scrolled to the *Tote 1842-1934* title page. Organized chronologically by year, each death was recorded in sequence according to date. Ellen found death records for Karolina (1896), Reinhard (1900), and Rosina (1900); all died at *Mittelberg*. Each record also identified Johann Reinhard Klein's occupation as being a *Tagelöhner* in *Mittelberg*.

By three o'clock, the room was becoming crowded. The noise didn't seem disruptive now, since she merely had to follow a routine procedure. Ellen printed twelve documents: baptisms, confirmations, deaths, family registers.

While checking the *Konfirmation* lists, she also found *Kommunionen 1845-1904* records on the same film. Traditionally, each parishioner signed a register as they left the communion service. It identified who sat next to whom; relatives sat together, fiancées sat together, friends sat together.

The 1882-1888 years should identify when Maria lived at home and attended church with her parents. Or, if her name was absent, it then indicated when Maria left the area and immigrated to America. The 1882-1888 *Kommunionen* lists might give additional verification about her activities. Ellen printed the additional pages.

Her eyes were tired and her shoulders ached from leaning over the machine. At six o'clock, Ellen placed everything in her briefcase, returned the films to the cabinet, paid for the copies and returned home to Noe Valley.

# *SS Anna Luise*

At nine o'clock the next morning, Ellen drove a familiar route to the National Archives. Parking her car in the usual space, the tantalizing minty-pine smell of the towering Eucalyptus trees filled the air. Identifying the 1901 ship records for Sophia Katherina Klein and her grand-daughter Katie was the primary focus of today's research trip.

Entering the reception area, Ellen signed the visitor register, stored the briefcase and handbag in the locker and took along her research notes. After retrieving the alphabetical surname index created by WPA, she located a microfilm reader, threaded the film and began reading each faintly written card in the "K" category. She discovered:

> Catharine Klein, age 59, arrived 01 August 1901, Port of New York, *SS Anna Luise*. Katherina Klein, age 11.

Good news! This information identified the date of arrival and name of the ship. Ellen hurriedly copied the details and returned the film to the microfilm cabinet.

On reviewing a row of the films titled *Passenger Lists of Vessels Arriving at New York, New York, 1820-1957*, she located a specific film for the Port of New York-August 1901. Returning to her station, Ellen threaded it onto her machine and found more information:

> *Record of Aliens Held for Special Inquiry*: August 1, 1901, Port of New York, *SS Anna Luise.* Klein, Catherine & dau., widow, senility, released at 2:45 p.m., two meals.

Their situation must have felt traumatic. Catherine Klein and her grand-daughter arrived at Ellis Island, but were removed from the Registry Department processing queue and required to attend a hearing. Three judges decided their fate—whether they could enter the country or if they must return to Germany. Identified as "senile," Mrs. Klein had to show proof of financial support.

According to the Special Inquiry, the judges approved their immigration status that afternoon. They were then directed to the Exchange Office to convert *thalers* into American money. Next, they went to the Railroad Department to buy tickets, then to the Telegraph Department so they could notify relatives of their arrival.

Afterwards, Mrs. Klein and her grand-daughter collected their luggage and boarded a ferryboat from Ellis Island to a New Jersey railroad depot where they purchased tickets to Nebraska. They didn't know a word of English; an Interpreter would have helped them make arrangements. Most likely, since her grandmother was elderly, thirteen-year-old Katherine took care of everything.

Ellen copied the details; then she reversed the film to locate the title page and the correct manifest page:

> Norddeutscher Lloyd, Bremen. Manifest of Alien Passengers-B (Third Class), *SS Anna Luise*, from Bremen July 22, 1901. Arrived Port of New York, August 1, 1901.
>
> Kath. Klein, age 59, widow, nationality German, last residence *Waldberg, Germany*, destination Nebraska, passage paid by daughter, funds $30, senile.
>
> Katherina Klein, age 11, nationality German, last residence *Waldberg, Germany*, destination Nebraska, passage paid by mother.
>
> The *SS Anna Luise* left Germany with 227 first class passengers, 235 second class passengers and 1,564 third class passengers.

These details revealed Catherine Klein and her grand-daughter left *Waldberg*, travelling by wagon or carriage about four-hundred kilometres, north to *Bremen*. On arrival they would've waited in dormitory housing until being allowed to board the ship. Then, they were assigned a bunk in a dark, poorly lit room, along with 1,564 other passengers travelling in third class. Most likely Katherina was identified as younger on purpose; then she could remain with her grandmother.

An important association about the relationship between thirteen-year-old Katherine and her mother was revealed by this document. Although she'd left her daughter in Germany, Marie remained in touch; she sent them money for tickets and they were planning to live with her in Nebraska. Marie hadn't seen her daughter for thirteen years—yet she had not forgotten her.

Noting the new information, Ellen rewound the film and returned it to the cabinet. Removing everything from the locker, she then signed out and returned to Noe Valley.

∞∞∞∞

At home, she stapled all the immigration information for Marie (1888), Fred (1889), Catherine and Katherine (1901) to a title page, *Reference #3 - Immigration Details,* and filed it in the research notebook.

Next, she called Gertrude Klein in Oklahoma.

"Hello," an older woman answered.

"Hi, this is Ellen O'Donnell calling from California, how are you today?"

"I'm fine, the weather has been changeable, but it is nice outside."

"I'm making travel plans and would like to visit you on Saturday, April 12."

"I talked to my daughters and they said it would be alright for you come over" replied Gertrude. "They usually come to see me on Saturday. I'll write the date on the calendar and let them know."

"Wonderful! May I call you the day before and get driving directions to your house?"

"That's a good idea. I'll have Barbara write down the highway and road directions."

"I'm really looking forward to meeting you and your daughters," said Ellen.

"Me too, thanks for calling," Gertrude replied, and hung up.

Ellen was glad to have the appointment with Gertrude confirmed and crossed that item off her list.

Next, she began reviewing the 1882-1888 *Kommunionen* pages and listed Maria's attendance:

> *Adventfest* (Advent), on 20 November 1884, with her parents.
>
> *Pfingstfest* (Pentecost), 10 May 1885, with her sister Rosina.
>
> *Trinitare Sonntag* (Trinity Sunday), 17 May 1885, with her parents.
>
> *Dankfest* (Thanksgiving), 22 November 1885, with her sister Katherina Regina.

This comparison suggested Maria probably left her parent's home after Christmas 1885; she didn't attend any *Kommunionen* services in 1886, 1887, or 1888. However, some possibilities could be read between the lines; she wasn't living with her parents in 1886, her daughter would've been conceived about September 1887 and she returned home for the birth of Katherine in May 1888.

With this final review, the first round of research to locate family history facts and add new details to the Family Group Sheets was finished. Now, she could concentrate on solving the unknown questions.

Ellen suspected the trip to Nebraska and Oklahoma would uncover additional interesting information. And, she was looking forward to meeting Gertrude Klein.

March 24, 1986

Mr. George Smoot, Partner
Alexander, Lardner and Smoot
330 Powell Street, Suite 1400
San Francisco, California 94102

Dear Mr. Smoot:

As we discussed earlier, I am enclosing an invoice for my time and expenses to date. I have completed all research at the San Francisco Public Library, the Multiregional Family History Center in Oakland and the National Archives in San Bruno. These activities have resulted in the following details which will be incorporated into future reports:

- An interview with Julia Morgan offered valuable insight into the Kupper family dynamics and suggested significant clues.
- A *Familienbuch* register of the Reinhard Klein family and of Maria Klein, including a record of her daughter Katherine, was found in *Altenkirchen, Wüerttemberg, Germany*.
- Ship manifest documents for Marie Klein (1888), Friedrich Kupper (1889) and Marie's daughter and mother (1901) confirmed they left Germany and immigrated to Nebraska.
- The 1900 and 1910 census records for Fred and Marie Kupper have been found.
- The *Adams County, Oklahoma History* book included the Reinhard Klein family and their descendants; an interview with Gertrude Klein is scheduled for April.

I will be leaving for a research trip to Nebraska and Oklahoma on April 2nd. After returning, I will complete a summary report and meet with you to talk about the new information I've found during this trip.

Thank you for the opportunity to work on this interesting project.

*Ellen O'Donnell*

# NEBRASKA

# Locating Orphanage Records

Wednesday, April 2. Ellen sleepily climbed aboard the shuttle bus for the twenty-minute trip to the San Francisco International Airport; her flight left at 5:30 a.m. In Denver, she changed planes and continued toward Eppley Airfield. It was a routine flight until they reached Omaha, where the Boeing 757 began circling and waiting for a break in the driving thunderstorm. Twenty minutes later, they began the bumpy descent through the clouds.

Glad to be on the ground again, Ellen took an escalator downstairs to the baggage carousel, lifted her heavy suitcase off the rack, found a luggage cart and looked outside at the steady downpour. She didn't have an umbrella and didn't want to drive in an unfamiliar city during a rainstorm. At a news stand, she bought the *Omaha World-Herald* newspaper, road maps for Nebraska, Kansas and Oklahoma, a jacket and umbrella. After finding a restaurant and ordering lunch, she read the local news and checked the weather page for the latest forecast.

By one o'clock the sky was clear again. Ellen found the Hertz Rental Car agency, signed the papers, picked up the keys to a Ford Taurus sedan and asked, "Could you tell me how to find the Omaha Public Library?"

"Sure," the clerk said. "When leaving our parking lot, go north on Abbot Drive, make a U-Turn, continue south and turn right on South Fifteenth Street. There is a public parking garage a block north of the library, across from Central Park Plaza."

"Thanks," replied Ellen, as she gathered everything together. Twenty minutes later, she parked, took along her briefcase, walked to 215 South Fifteenth Street and entered the W. Dale Clark Main Library.

∞∞∞∞

Exiting the elevator, Ellen noticed display panels with photographs and a story about the Union Pacific Railroad. Established as the primary western route from Omaha, Nebraska Territory, it connected with the Central Pacific Railroad at Promontory, Utah in May 1869. Although an interesting bit of historical information, reading the exhibit was a distraction; it had delayed her primary reason for visiting the library. She walked to the reference desk.

"Hello, I'm Ellen O'Donnell. Do you have any files on St. Joseph Orphanage in Kentucky Precinct? I'm doing research about Fred Cooper, who was eight years old. According to census records, he was living at the orphanage in 1910."

"Yes, I believe we have some newspaper clippings about St. Joseph's. Please sign our register with your name, address and research topic. I'll bring the file to you. Wait over there," said the librarian, pointing to a table.

Ellen sat down, opened her briefcase and removed a copy of the 1910 census. A few minutes later, the librarian brought her a manila folder titled *St. Joseph Orphanage, Omaha*. She read the minutes and all the clippings, and then abstracted a few notes:

*Sisters of Charity:* They accepted children of all faiths prior to the 1940s. A large three-story brick dormitory building was built in 1890 and replaced in 1914. Children from the orphanage attended Rosemont Elementary School.

*Admission:* A child had to be less than twelve years of age, whose parents were deceased or unable to provide housing, food, health care, and schooling. At the age of twelve, or graduation from the eighth grade, the child was adopted or released to their parents. If the child was released, their records were destroyed.

*Records:* If the child was adopted by another family, the records were kept. The attached list of adopted children's names had a brief notation beside each name—see Guardianship records at the courthouse.

Ellen checked the list for Fred Cooper, age 8-12. He was not included; Fred must have been released to his father, who was also living in Omaha, Nebraska. She jotted notes on her reference pages and returned the folder to the librarian.

"Do you know if the Omaha Public School system has any enrollment records for children who attended Rosemont Elementary School between 1910 and 1914?"

"I'm not sure," the librarian replied. "But you could call their office and ask. There is a public phone booth on the first floor of the library."

"Thanks." Ellen filed the notes in her briefcase, signed out, then returned to the first floor and dialed the number.

"Hello, my name is Ellen O'Donnell," she said. "I'm trying to identify if enrollment records are available for Rosemont Elementary School in the years 1910 through 1914."

"We might have those records," the receptionist answered. "But, they're filed in the lower level of the administration building and are not available for privacy reasons."

"Could I make an appointment to search the records? I've been hired to conduct research for the Cooper Estate," Ellen said.

"No appointments to search records are allowed. Those records are closed to the public," the receptionist answered firmly.

Disappointed, Ellen hung up the phone and returned to her car. Before leaving the parking garage, she added a note to the Nebraska research page: According to St. Joseph Orphanage records, Fred Cooper may have attended Rosemont Elementary School between 1910 and 1914. Unable to confirm, access denied.

∞∞∞∞

Checking her watch, she looked at the map. It might be interesting to take the "antiquing route" following U.S. Highway 75 from Omaha through the small towns located along the western side of the Missouri River. However, there wouldn't be any time for shopping; it was a two hour drive to Josephine. Instead, she left Omaha, took Interstate 80 and crossed the Platte River, driving south.

The landscape was completely different from her familiar neighborhood in San Francisco. It seemed isolated—no houses, mostly flat fields of unfamiliar crops starting to show a little green, a few old trees here and there, and huge billowing clouds in every direction. Now she understood why this region was known as "The Great Plains".

Ellen watched the sky and considered how to begin conversations with people who didn't know her. She realized that she'd easily be identified as a stranger because of her clothing style and accent. While driving, she thought about the questions to be answered in Nebraska.

At six o'clock, she parked under the Holiday Inn portico and walked into the Lobby.

"Hi, I'm Ellen O'Donnell. I have a reservation for the next eight days."

"Yes, everything is ready for you," the receptionist replied. "Please sign this form for our records. You can park directly outside your room."

"Thanks. I'd like to know where there is a good restaurant, so I can have something to eat after I unload my car."

"Josephine is a small town and there aren't many places to eat. There is the Elk's Lodge, the VFW and the American Legion but they're only open for members. We have a McDonalds, Kentucky Fried Chicken and the Runza café, all on Fourth Street. The Black Raven is a fancier restaurant in the older part of downtown but it requires a reservation in advance. We do have a small restaurant here at the Holiday Inn; it closes in thirty minutes so you might want to have something to eat first and then unload your car."

"Okay, thanks for letting me know. I'll park my car and come back to your restaurant for supper," she said.

On returning to the nearly empty restaurant, Ellen scanned the menu and ordered a home-cooked meal of meatloaf, mashed potatoes, green beans, a roll and Lemon Meringue pie. Next, she unloaded the car. Inside, the motel room brought memories of travelling with her parents twenty years earlier; the décor featured brown shag carpet, with wallpaper and drapes in an olive-green and beige pattern. Two double beds, a small desk and chair, a four-drawer dresser with a mirror, a television set and rotary telephone on the night stand completed the furnishings. The picture window offered a view of the parking lot. Placing her suitcase on one of the beds, Ellen hung her clothes in the tiny closet and put toiletries in the bathroom. The furnishings were out-of-date, but the room was clean.

On her nightstand, Ellen placed an alarm clock and the books she intended to read in the evening hours—*My Antonia* by Willa Cather and *Old Jules* by Mari Sandoz. She hoped these novels would help her understand the community where Marie and Fred Kupper lived.

Tomorrow would be her first day of looking for documents in Clayton County. With a bit of luck, she would find naturalization records, a Klein-Kupper marriage record and details about the Kupper divorce.

# Clayton County Courthouse

On Thursday morning Ellen woke up disoriented until she recognized the furnishings of the Holiday Inn. She looked at the clock; there was time for breakfast before going to the courthouse.

Taking her umbrella, Ellen walked over to the restaurant in the steady downpour. After a continental breakfast and two extra cups of coffee, she asked the waitress, "Could you tell me how to find the courthouse?"

"Oh, that's easy. All you have to do is turn left and continue on the same highway. When you're driving through town, the north-south street is called "Fourth" and the east-west street is known as "Main." Stay on Fourth until you reach Lincoln Street, where you will see a large limestone courthouse on the southeast corner.

"Here's a brochure. Our courthouse was built in the Richardsonian Romanesque style in 1892 and has a fantastic clock tower. There used to be a large post office building of the same style and time period; a bank bought the property during the 1960s and demolished it because they needed a larger parking lot. It seems like most of the local people are more interested in new construction instead of saving historical buildings. The preservationists stopped the destruction of the courthouse. Everyone is proud of it now."

"Very interesting," replied Ellen. "I'm from San Francisco and we have a strong tradition of preserving old buildings. I'll be at the courthouse most of the day and see you again tonight."

Returning to her room, Ellen picked up her briefcase, then drove to Fourth and Lincoln. She parked the car and added three dollars of quarters to the meter. A large bronze canon was located midway to the entrance doors—it pointed south—a plaque included names of the men from Clayton County who served the Union cause during the Civil War. Tulips were blooming in the flowerbed beneath the memorial.

∞∞∞∞

Inside, Ellen checked the building directory and elected to begin her search in the District Court office. Since the elevator wasn't working, she climbed marble steps to the third floor and found their office in the west wing of the building.

"Hello, I'm Ellen O'Donnell. I'm from out-of-town and am hoping to locate information about the Klein and Kupper families. Does your office have naturalization records?"

"We have some naturalization records but they're not indexed and you'll need to search several of the large ledger books. They're organized by year, then alphabetically by last name. Do you want to look at the books?" asked the clerk.

"Definitely, I'd like to check the 1889 records. According to National Archives, Friedrich Kupper arrived in 1889 and the census records show he was married in 1892."

"Okay, come around the front counter and you can look at the books in the vault," replied the clerk. Ellen entered the musty room where the

86

large legal books were kept, placed her briefcase and handbag on a nearby table and began searching. Thirty minutes later, she found:

> *Naturalization Record, State of Nebraska, Clayton County*: Fred Kupper, native of Germany, renounced all allegiance and fidelity to the King of *Württemberg* of which he was heretofore a subject. Signed: Fred Kupper, August 24, 1889.

Ellen checked her notes. A record from the *SS Evalena* identified Friedrich Kupper, arriving at the Port of New York, on May 11, 1889. This Clayton County record indicated Fred Kupper filed his *Intent to Naturalize* papers on 24 August 1889, about three months after his arrival. The document was consistent with the immigration details.

She placed her pencil on the page as a bookmark and returned to the District Court office. "I found the record I need. Could I get a copy?"

"Sure," said the clerk. "Bring the book over here, copies are 15 cents each." A few minutes later, Ellen placed the page in her briefcase and walked down two flights of stairs to the County Clerk's office.

∞∞∞∞

"Hi, I'm Ellen O'Donnell. I'd like to check on an 1892 marriage license. Am I in the correct office?"

"Yes. If you know the name of the groom or bride, you can locate their license in the cardex file," the clerk said, pointing to a wall. "Just copy the volume and page number, then I can look up the record."

Ellen began scanning the "K" names until she found the correct reference. She gave the citation to the clerk, who then found the original document:

Marriage License: 15 June 1892.
Groom: Fred Kupper, age 39, Germany.
Father: Fred Kupper. Mother: blank.
Bride: Mary Klein, age 26, Germany.
Father, Rinehart Klein. Mother: Katherina Kupper.
Witnessed: 19 June 1892. Fred Klein and Mary Pfarer.
Signed [illegible], Minister of the Gospel.

Another lucky discovery—everything matched with the Addendum. Paying for a copy of the record, she then said, "I'm also looking for birth records in 1893, 1895 and 1898. Where would I find those documents?"

"I'm sorry, we can't help you. The State of Nebraska didn't require a doctor or a midwife to register the birth of a child until 1904. A substitute record could be a baptism certificate or a school enrollment record. But to search for school enrollment, you'll need to know the township and district where the children lived."

"Okay, according to the 1900 census, they lived in Arapaho Township. But, the record shows the Kupper family as tenant farmers, not owners."

"You might check the deed records to see if he bought land sometime after 1900. They are kept in the Register of Deeds office on the east wing of the first level. I'm sorry the elevator isn't working but at least you'll be walking down the stairs instead of climbing stairs."

"That sounds like my next stop," replied Ellen. She filed the latest information in her briefcase and left the County Clerk's office.

∞∞∞∞∞

On the lower level, she found the door marked Register of Deeds and entered the office. "Hello, I'm Ellen O'Donnell. I'm looking for deed records of land owned by Fred Kupper but I'm not sure about a date. According to the 1900 census, he lived in Arapaho Township."

"First, you'll need to find his name in the *Grantor and Grantee Index*, which identifies all deed transactions," said the clerk. "If you find a record, it will show the volume and page number; then, we can identify the legal description of where his land was located."

"Great. Where do I begin?"

"Here's the *Index*. The Grantor is the seller and the Grantee is the buyer. Write down the *Index* entry that you'd like to review. The original documents are kept in the vault."

Twenty minutes later, Ellen noted the entry for Fred Kupper:

> Grantee: Fritz Kupper
> Section 1-3-6 NW #2 (1.5 acres)
> Warranty Deed $800. 20 Feb 1903

She scanned other entries for the same land and found:

> Grantor: Fritz Kupper and wife
> Grantee: Tom Hawkins
> Mortgage $800. 20 Feb 1903

> Plaintiff: Tom Hawkins
> Defendants: Fred Kupper and Marie Kupper
> Decree in favor of the Plaintiff, 11 June 1908
> Foreclosure, Section 1-3-6 NW #2

The records revealed that Fritz and Marie Kupper lived on the acreage for five years, missed payments and lost their property to foreclosure.

"This is very interesting," she said. "Do you know how to locate the school district where the children were enrolled?"

"According to the plat map on the wall, their land is in Section 1-3-6 NW #2, which is in Arapaho Township," the clerk said. "The children would've attended School District 105."

"That's good news. Could I have a copy of these land records from 1903 and 1908? Are there any copies of this plat map?"

"I can make copies of the deed records, but unfortunately we only have the wall map," the clerk replied. "If you draw a diagram, then I'll show you where the school and the land are located. I'll also add the current roads, so you can drive to the acreage and see where they lived."

"Okay, that should work."

After sketching a map, and having the deed and school locations identified by the clerk, Ellen paid for the copies, put everything in her briefcase and walked out the door. One o'clock, time for lunch.

# A Stunning Discovery

Earlier that morning, Ellen had noticed a small lunch room on the lower level of the courthouse. However, before she could grab a sandwich, she must return to her parked car and add coins. Or else, the meter maid would write a ticket.

On entering the courthouse again, she walked into the tiny café, checked her watch and went to the counter.

"I hope you're still serving lunch," said Ellen, while looking at the overhead menu board. "I'd like a tuna sandwich, some chips and a Pepsi."

"Yes, you're just in time," the owner answered. "That'll be two dollars, please."

"I'm starved. Do you bring everything to the table or do I come to the counter to pick things up?" she asked.

"Oh, I'll bring everything to you, this is a small place and we do things the easy way."

Ellen sat at a nearby table, retrieved her notes from the briefcase and added new questions: The District Court naturalization papers stated Friedrich Kupper emigrated from *Württemberg*. Marie Klein also left from *Württemberg*. Did they know each other, prior to emigration? A comparison of the 1892 marriage license with the Addendum found that

Fred Klein was Marie's brother but the other witness was unknown. Was she a relative of the groom? A man named Fritz was listed in Marie's journal and Fritz Kupper was named on the Arapaho Township deed. Did these names identify the same person?

After lunch, Ellen placed her notes in the briefcase, then checked the building directory and walked upstairs to the third floor.

∞∞∞∞

In the District Court office, Ellen said, "Hello, I'm back. Now, I'd like to look for divorce records."

"Okay, if you know the name of the plaintiff or the defendant, we can find it on the index. I'll pull the file and you can read the various proceedings," the clerk replied.

It didn't take long to find the correct citation; the clerk handed a large packet of information to Ellen and she read the introduction:

> 20 July 1904. Marie Kupper filed for divorce from Frederick Kupper. The defendant was guilty of extreme cruelty toward the plaintiff without any cause or provocation on her part.

Stunned by the new information, Ellen said, "It looks like there are about forty pages here. Could you make copies of these divorce papers? It's four o'clock now and I still need to see the County Clerk's office about school records. I can pick them up tomorrow morning."

"Sure," replied the clerk. Ellen paid for the copies and hurried downstairs to the County Clerk's office on the second floor.

"Hi, I'm still looking for more information. The Register of Deeds office identified the Kupper children attended School District 105 in Arapaho Township. I'm hoping you have school enrollment records."

"Okay, you can leave your briefcase and handbag on the table behind the counter. Come with me and we'll look for the school records; they're in another room."

Walking down a long hallway, the clerk unlocked the outer door to a former women's restroom, next unlocked a closet door and then unlocked one of the file cabinets holding school enrollment records.

Opening the file drawer, the clerk said, "School records are filed by district number, then alphabetically. If the father's surname was Kupper, what was his first name?"

"It should be listed as either Fred or Frederick," replied Ellen.

"Here it is. This school enrollment record shows two Kupper children attending School District 105. Their names are Anna and Fred. The registration is dated 10 July 1904 and the page identifies children enrolled for the Fall 1904–Spring 1905 academic year."

"Wonderful. Does the record give their birth dates by any chance?"

"Yes, Anna was born 11 May 1895 and Fred was born 14 June 1898."

"That's very good news! The 1900 census stated they were born in 1895 and 1898 but I didn't have an exact date of birth for either of them. Could I have a copy of the records?"

"Sure. The court allows school or baptism records as proof of birth before 1904, so we sometimes have a request for enrollment records."

"While you have the files open, could you check if Anna and Fred attended school at District 105 in 1905 and 1906?"

The clerk carefully checked other years for the same school district, then said, "I'm sorry, Anna or Fred Kupper aren't listed. I guess we're lucky to find them in the 1904-1905 records."

"That's a disappointment, but I just learned the parents divorced after July 1904. This record suggests they intended for Anna and Fred to be enrolled at District 105 in September 1904, but the children must have lived somewhere else in 1905 and 1906. I'll add it to my files as another piece of the family history. I'm very pleased about finding their birth dates."

Glancing at her watch, Ellen asked "Do you have an index for probate records?"

"Yes, let's go to the office." Taking the school enrollment page with her, the clerk locked the file cabinet, closet door, and restroom door.

Returning to the County Clerk's office, she said, "Take a look at the cardex on the wall, over there. If you find the name you are looking for, just copy the date, volume and page number. I'll look up the original document."

Ellen looked for Fred or Frederick Kupper in Clayton County. There weren't any probate records for the husband of Marie Klein Kupper. He must've died in Oklahoma.

Next, she looked for Maria, Marie or Mary Klein or Kupper or Cooper. An entry for Mrs. Mary Cooper, was cross-indexed to the probate record for Mary Klein (Mrs. George Klein). Ellen checked the Addendum; George Klein was a brother of Marie Klein Kupper and he lived in Clayton County, Nebraska. She excitedly asked the clerk to pull the probate file, then scanned the details and abstracted the main points for her file:

Mrs. Mary Klein, widow of George Klein, died 11 March 1943 at the home of her sister in Josephine; she didn't have any children.

Her Will, dated 27 June 1932, was filed 15 March 1943: Mrs. Mary Klein left $1,000 to Katie, the niece of George H. Klein, and 1/10 of the remaining estate to . . . and Mrs. Mary Cooper . . . but if said person shall predecease me then in lieu of said 1/10, her children, Fred Cooper shall receive $495 and Anna Cooper shall receive $495.

10 August 1944 Petition by Executor: The said Mary Cooper sent a letter to her daughter Katie about nine years ago, which stated that she and her son Fred Cooper were going to Pasadena, California where her daughter Anna already lived.

08 November 1944 Testimony from the attorney: It appears that Mary Cooper if living would be very aged; so the fact of her not being heard from by any known relative for nine years adds to the presumption of her death. Apparently, Fred Cooper was at one time committed to the asylum in Oklahoma, a probable indication of some affliction which would cause his early death. Further investigation indicates that Anna Cooper has not been heard from since 1935.

08 November 1944 Decree: The said Mary Cooper, Fred Cooper, and Anna Cooper have not been heard from by relatives for many years; that said persons were deceased prior to the death of Mary Klein on 11 March 1943. The provision for these persons has lapsed; therefore, the money belongs to the estate of Mary Klein deceased and should be distributed therein to the other beneficiaries.

Ellen studied the unexpected details. This was the first reference to Fred Cooper being placed in an asylum. The attorney evidently followed instructions from relatives and searched for Mrs. Mary Cooper in

Pasadena, California. In fact, Anna had changed her name to Helen and they all lived in San Francisco. Mary Cooper and her children never knew about their inheritance.

She looked at the clock; the courthouse closed in fifteen minutes. "Could I pay for copies of this packet and pick them up tomorrow?"

"Yes, we can have everything ready for you," the clerk replied.

Ellen placed her notes in the briefcase, carried it down two flights of stairs for the last time and returned to the Holiday Inn restaurant to order an evening meal.

She was very pleased with the new information, but was also dog-tired from the upstairs and downstairs routine at the courthouse.

# Locating Church Records

Friday, a second day of research in Josephine, Nebraska. Ellen looked out the window—rain and fog—but she couldn't stay in bed any longer. She took a shower, pulled on khaki slacks and an olive green shirt, then grabbed the umbrella and walked to the restaurant.

"Good morning," said the waitress, "How are you today?"

"Oh, still a little sleepy," answered Ellen. "I'll have some breakfast and then start on my list of things to do. I'd like to order an omelet, toast, orange juice and coffee." She retrieved a newspaper from the vending machine and read the local news.

At nine o'clock, Ellen picked up her briefcase from the room, drove to the Clayton County Courthouse, parked on Lincoln Street and added a quarter to the meter. She went upstairs to the third floor District Court office to collect the Kupper divorce documents and to the second floor County Clerk's office to pick up the probate records of Mrs. George Klein.

"Thanks for making the copies. Now I need to find the public library. Could you tell me where it is located?"

"Of course, turn left on Fourth Street and drive four blocks until you reach Ella Street. Turn right on Ella, which is a one-way street, and turn right again on Third Street. Our Library is about a half-block on your right side; it's a Beaux Arts style building. Here's a brochure with a photo of the building. Just park in front of the library and be sure to put some coins in the meter."

"Thanks," said Ellen. She walked down the courthouse stairs and hurried to the car, then followed directions to the Library. Plugging the meter with quarters, she grabbed her briefcase and dashed up the entrance steps. Inside, marble steps led to a large room with a reception counter. A series of bookshelves radiated from each quadrant of the octagonal room; tall, narrow windows overlooked a nearby park.

∞∞∞∞

Introducing herself at the front counter, she said, "Hello, my name is Ellen O'Donnell. I'm looking for a burial record of Mary Kupper. I know from census records that Mary was born in 1893 and died sometime before 1910."

"Our genealogy and local history records are over here," the librarian replied, pointing to a reading room on the right side of the counter.

"Let's check, I believe we have a book listing burials at Rosehill."

The librarian located *Rosehill Memorial Cemetery Index, Clayton County, Nebraska* and handed it to Ellen. She found the correct page:

> Mary Magdalen Kupper
> Rosehill Memorial Cemetery
> February 9, 1901

Mary must've been named after her mother, Maria Magdalena (Klein) Kupper. Ellen copied the reference entry and cover page of the book, then re-shelved it and returned to the reception area.

"I've had good luck. Do you happen to have any Josephine City Directories for 1904 through 1912?"

"No, we don't, but the Clayton County Historical Society might have those years. They're located west of downtown in the old train depot, near Main and Burlington Avenue. Before crossing the Big Muddy Bridge, you'll see it on the right side of the street."

"Okay, I also need to visit the Rosehill Memorial Cemetery and St. Luke's Lutheran church. Can you give me directions?"

"Sure, for the cemetery, you drive east on Main Street for about two miles, until the edge of town. It is on the left side of the road.

"To find St. Luke's, drive north on Third Street until you reach Washington Street, then cross the intersection, look for a parking lot and you'll see the side entrance to the church."

"Thanks for helping me," said Ellen. She returned to her car and drove to St. Luke's Lutheran church. Taking her briefcase along, she walked into the building and followed the hallway signs to the office.

∞∞∞∞

"Hello, I'm Ellen O'Donnell. A little while ago, the librarian told me about St. Luke's. I'm trying to find information about an 1892 marriage for Marie Klein and Friedrich Kupper and if there are any baptism records for their three children."

"Do you know if they were Lutheran?" asked the secretary.

"Yes, the bride belonged to the Lutheran church in Germany."

Glancing at the clock, the secretary said, "We close in sixty minutes for lunch. Here's our published list of marriages, baptisms and deaths. The index is arranged by category, by year, then alphabetically. If you find the people you are looking for, write down the date and type of event as well as the person's name.

"I can check to see if the pastor recorded the information in the official *Kirchenbuch*. In 1892, the marriage and the funeral would've taken place at the old St. Luke's church. It's located at Second and Market Street and is now the Salvation Army building."

"Thanks, this won't take very long since I know the years and names."

Ellen sat down at a nearby table and scanned the index pages. In 1892, she found the marriage record of Friedrich Kupper and Marie Klein. Next, she checked 1893, 1895 and 1898 for a baptism record of Mary, Anna and Fred—no luck, they weren't baptized at St. Luke's. She also looked for a 1901 death record of Mary Magdalen Kupper. Returning to the secretary's desk, Ellen asked to view the original documents.

"Alright, I'll get the old *Kirchenbuch* from the vault," replied the secretary. A few minutes later she returned with the ancient volume. The worn binding barely held everything together; fragile pages displayed records in a faint hand-written script.

The *Heiraten* (Marriage) record for 1892 identified:

> Friedrich Kupper and Marie Klein, married June 19, 1892, St. Luke's Lutheran Church.

The *Tote* (Death) page for 1901 included:

> Mary Magdalen Kupper, age 7. Parents: Friedrich Kupper and Marie (nee Klein) Kupper. Funeral February 9, 1901. St. Luke's Lutheran Church.

Looking over Ellen's shoulder, the secretary commented, "The pastor entered a cause of death for Mary, but it's written in the old German script. I don't know what it means."

"It's alright. I'm happy to find an official record. Could I have copies of these pages?"

"No, I'm sorry. The *Kirchenbuch* is our official record. It's heavy and so fragile that we cannot place it on the copy machine anymore because it would cause even more damage to the spine and the pages. You can manually copy the original text of the entries though."

After copying the details, Ellen returned the old book to the secretary's desk.

"Thanks for allowing me to look at the original records. I didn't find any St. Luke's baptism records for their children, which seems a bit unusual; maybe they married at St. Luke's but lived somewhere else. Fred was a farmer. Do you know if there is a Lutheran church in a nearby rural area? I'd like to check if they were members of a different congregation."

"Yes, that's likely. Our church was established by a group of German farmers who moved into town when they retired. There is a strong Lutheran community of German immigrants who settled in Stirling Township. I'd recommend checking with First Lutheran. It's located about eight miles from Josephine."

"That's very good news. From pension records, I know their youngest child, Fred John Cooper, was born in Stirling Township. First Lutheran might have his baptism record. Could you give me directions to the church?"

"Sure," said the secretary. "The church secretary is my cousin and she's usually in the office on Friday. The main sanctuary entrance is on the east side, but if you park on the north side, you will see the door to the church office. Just knock and go inside. I'll call her when I return from lunch and let her know that you'll be visiting this afternoon. Here's a rough map of how to find the church."

"Thank you, this is very helpful," said Ellen. She placed her notes and the map in her briefcase, then left the church.

∞∞∞

Driving to the Runza café, she went inside and ordered a sandwich, French fries, and a Root Beer soda. Afterwards she left town, drove east past a one-mile windbreak of large fir trees, turned north on the first gravel road, followed it by curving east, then north again. On a hill in the distance she saw twin spires—it was her first sight of the impressive church.

A few minutes later Ellen reached her destination, parked the car and walked to the western edge of the property. Around her, large fields of winter wheat were beginning to turn green, a group of trees outlined a winding creek and billowing clouds reached downward to the horizon. From this hilltop view, she could see the water tower of Josephine in the distance.

Ellen returned to the car, picked up her briefcase, then knocked on the door and entered the small office. "Hi, I'm Ellen O'Donnell. Your cousin said I might be able to look at the church records for First Lutheran."

"Yes, she called me a little while ago. Our *Kirchenbuch* is very old and we usually don't allow people to leaf through it. We do have a published list of marriages, baptisms, confirmations and death records which might help you. I've put a copy on the table over there."

"Thank you, I appreciate it," Ellen replied. She checked the Kupper Family Group Sheet for reference dates, then began looking for baptism information on the three children. None were baptized at First Lutheran.

On a whim, she looked for the marriage of "Chris and Katie, 1908."

"This is great news. I didn't find any baptism records for the three children; however the index has a marriage record for Christ Zimmermann and Katherine Kupper in 1908. Could I see the original information?"

"The 1908 records are in better condition, so I can look for it. She checked the official marriage register at First Lutheran and found:

Christian Zimmermann and Katherine Kupper,
March 26, 1908

Excitedly, Ellen flipped through the pages of her notebook and said, "Here, I can show you a copy of their wedding photo."

"Her dress is very nice, such fine hand-stitching," commented the secretary. "Did you know Chris was the grandson of the man who built our first church? Their family was very well-known in our community."

"No, I had no idea. Are any of their children still living?"

"Most have moved away, but I believe one or two of them still live here. If you'd like to attend ten o'clock services on Sunday, you're certainly welcome. I can ask if any of our older members remember Chris and Katie. They might be willing to talk with you."

"It would be nice if I could meet some friends or relatives," said Ellen. "Thanks so much for helping me. I'll plan on being here Sunday."

Ellen gathered everything together, returned to Josephine, stopped at Kentucky Fried Chicken to pick up supper. Then she drove to the Holiday Inn, parked her car and brought everything into the room.

Today, she had learned only a few pieces of new information, but they were important. When beginning her journey, Ellen never imagined that she'd find a connection to the 1908 marriage photo. It was an unexpected discovery.

# Nebraska Photographs

When the alarm buzzed, Ellen reached for the remote and turned to the local weather channel. It was Saturday, fifty degrees and sunny—a perfect day for taking photos—but there wasn't any need to hurry. She pulled the covers over her head and went back to sleep. Later, she walked over to the restaurant and dropped a quarter in the slot to buy the local newspaper.

"Good morning, how're things going today?" the waitress asked.

"It's great to have sunny weather again, so it will be a good day." said Ellen. "I'll have some French toast, crisp bacon, orange juice and coffee."

After breakfast, she returned to her room and listed directions for St. Luke's Lutheran church, Marie Klein's residence in 1910, the Rosehill Memorial Cemetery, and plat map locations for the one-room schoolhouse and the Kupper property. Taking along her camera, handbag, and a tablet, Ellen drove four miles south to Josephine.

∞∞∞∞

This was her first trip into the old downtown area—the architecture reminded her of an Edward Hopper painting. A few of the buildings in the six square blocks of Main Street and Fourth Street were boarded up and abandoned. However, by looking at the carved columns, pediment-trimmed windows and an occasional cartouche emblem above a door, it was obvious that Josephine had initially been a prosperous community.

The town included several well-known retail names and some local establishments—Woolworth's Five & Dime, Sears, J.C. Penney, Jones Drugstore, Brown's Shoes, Schmidt's Clothing, Gale's Photographs and Gifts, Hill's Furniture, and the *Daily Monitor* newspaper. When she checked the telephone directory earlier, she had found Lutheran, Catholic, Methodist, Christian and Presbyterian churches; there weren't any Jewish, Unitarian, or Baptist congregations.

Josephine had a population of 10,800 residents. In addition to its Police Department and Fire Department, there were four elementary schools, one junior high school and one senior high school; the Catholic and Lutheran churches offered private elementary classes. There were also three public parks, one public swimming pool and a private country club. Local entertainment venues included the Granada Theatre, the Little Bar, the Office Bar, the Railhead Bar, Ralph & Sadie's Tavern, and the Johannes Pool Hall.

Overall, it appeared the downtown may have reached its highpoint in the 1890s, although many well-known merchants arrived later. An emphasis on schools and religious buildings implied Josephine was a traditional, family oriented town. On the other hand, the number of bars alluded to a community that tolerated alchoholism.

∞∞∞∞∞

Circling through old downtown for a few blocks, Ellen found the former St. Luke's Lutheran church building. She drove into their parking lot, snapped a few photos of the white frame building with its bell tower steeple and noted the film numbers for *St. Luke's Lutheran – 1892 marriage of Friedrich Kupper and Marie Klein.*

Referring to her list, she then drove to 1422 Main and parked across the street. In 1910, Marie Kupper worked for the Milton James family at this address. The original house had been demolished and replaced with a gas station. No photos.

Next, she drove to the eastern edge of town and found Rosehill Memorial Cemetery. It was a large old cemetery, with trees outlining the road and many tall, impressive headstones. Ellen knocked on the door of the Sexton's office; no one answered. Nearby, a map of the cemetery plots could be viewed in a glass display case—Mary Magdalen Kupper was buried in Lot 29, Block 48.

Ellen sketched a map, returned to the car and then followed a narrow lane through the cemetery until finding the southernmost quadrant. She parked the car and walked over to the small plot.

Mary's tombstone was white marble and covered by an olive-brown moss yet the letters remained legible. Nearby, fragrant yellow flowers were blooming. After taking a photograph of the tombstone, Ellen broke off a small branch of Forsythia and placed it on Mary's tombstone. It seemed forlorn, as if no one had visited for many years.

She then studied the surrounding countryside. To the west, a row of rooftops defined a small housing development. Toward the north, tall oak and maple trees outlined each section of the cemetery. Looking east, there were wheat and corn fields, with distant views of a creek, fluffy clouds and a vast sky descending to the horizon line. To the south, she noticed a small schoolhouse.

Returning to the car, Ellen checked the roughly drawn courthouse map—the cemetery, schoolhouse and Kupper home were located on the same road. Following the asphalt lane that led out of the cemetery, she turned south, crossed over Main Street and turned left into a former one-room school parking lot.

A wood frame building with tall windows on each side and a bell tower above the entrance occupied the center of a one-acre lot. Steps led to two doors of the enclosed porch; one door was an entrance for boys and another separate door was designated for girls. Fragments of a rusted swing set and two dilapidated outhouses could be seen at the rear of a playground area filled with knee-high weeds.

Apparently, the property was sold when all the one-room schools merged with consolidated elementary and high school districts during the 1950s. Currently used as a woodworking shop, the former school building was painted light gray with white trim and the bell tower opening was covered with boards to prevent birds from building nests inside. After taking photos, she studied the plat map again.

∞∞∞∞

Leaving the schoolhouse parking lot, Ellen turned left on an abandoned one-lane road. Driving slowly, she compared her surroundings with the rough courthouse sketch. According to the plat map, the Kupper family lived on the east side of the road. Looking at the fence, which defined property lines, and reviewing the distance she had driven, Ellen thought this site was the correct location. The Kupper family lived about three-fourths of a mile south of the schoolhouse. She pulled off to the west side of the gravel road and parked the car.

The surroundings were eerily quiet. Birds chirped somewhere in the underbrush. Taking along her camera, Ellen carefully walked across the uneven road and cautiously ventured into the ditch on the east side. She didn't want to fall down out here in the middle of nowhere; on the other hand, she wanted to study their plot of land and take photos.

The only indication of a former homestead was the faint outline of tire tracks leading up a slight hill to the east and a group of cottonwood trees that sheltered a small creek. If a house had been there originally, it had fallen apart many years ago; the lumber hauled away for another use. There weren't any fences, old-fashioned Iris flowers or tall Lilac bushes to mark the site of a former home.

Although, there wasn't any distinct physical evidence, the location felt intuitively correct. She took photos of the trees, the worn path leading slightly uphill and the tall prairie grass that had overtaken the original homestead.

Returning to her car, Ellen jotted down the film numbers and some notes that compared the abandoned site with the courthouse map. The unusual field trip had been very worthwhile but it was time to return to Josephine.

Edging her car onto the main track of the gravel road, she drove south, until reaching an intersection where she could turn the car around. Then she drove north, leaving the Isolated area.

∞∞∞∞

Reaching the Main Street intersection, Ellen recognized the large cemetery across the road; she was in familiar territory again. She drove west on Main Street, turned right on Fourth Street, noticed a McDonald's sign and stopped for lunch.

Afterwards, Ellen returned to her motel room, removed a large stack of papers from the briefcase and began reading. She wanted to identify how the divorce proceedings affected Marie Kupper.

# Kupper vs. Kupper

In July 1904, Marie Kupper asked a neighbor to take herself, two children and their trunks to the railroad station in Josephine; she was leaving to visit her sister Lena.

A few days later, she met with a local attorney and filed for divorce; an additional record was filed at the Clayton County Courthouse.

The documents gave significant details that described Marie's predicament:

> Marie Kupper, Plaintiff. Frederick Kupper, Defendant: Friedrich Kupper and Marie Klein married 19 June 1892 at Josephine, Clayton County, Nebraska.
>
> The defendant is guilty of extreme cruelty toward the plaintiff without any cause or provocation on her part. On March 19, 1904 or thereabouts the defendant while in a great rage cruelly and willfully struck the plaintiff on the neck with his clenched fist and knocked her over on the stove and it greatly bruised and maimed her so that she was sore and lame therefrom for a month thereafter.

The defendant for the last six years has compelled the plaintiff to work in the fields like a man and to do a man's work when on account of poor health she was wholly unfit for such hard work and by such violent labor her health has been much impaired.

Plaintiff states that for six years she has not had a fit dress or other clothes to attend church or visit her friends and has been compelled to go without underclothes in both winter and summer, all of which suffering and neglect has been brought about by the neglect and cruelty of the defendant towards the plaintiff.

Plaintiff states that during their married life the defendant has been insulting, coarse, brutal and cruel to her.

Two children were born to the parties to this action to wit: Anna, aged nine years, and Frederick, aged six. Defendant by reason of his habits of brutality, improvidence and vulgarity is wholly unfit to have the care, custody or education of said children.

Defendant has real and personal property of about $500.00. The plaintiff prays for a divorce from the defendant and for the care, custody, control and education of said children, and for such other relief and permanent alimony as may be just and equitable.

The lawsuit was quite lengthy, including several pages of later charges and counter-charges. On December 31, 1904, the judge ruled in Marie's favor and awarded alimony in the amount of $200 and custody of the children.

Fred ignored the court order. Marie hired a different attorney and filed suit again in 1908 and 1911. In 1908, Fred also hired a new attorney. He refused to honor a 1911 summons.

Ellen was initially shocked at how Fred responded to his wife and the court, but then recognized she was reading the actions and decisions from a 1986 point of view. To place everything into a 1904 context, she reviewed the documents again:

*Marie:* When she filed for divorce, Marie felt there was sufficient cause. She had supported herself while living in New York City and had encountered the polite social relationships of her friends and fellow workers. When she married Fred in 1892, they were happy during the early years—three children were born between 1893 and 1898. Marie tolerated the later years of marriage. Even though divorce was rare and frowned upon in her isolated rural community, she was aware of women's legal rights from her New York City experience. She knew women could independently talk to a lawyer, that she likely had adequate cause, and divorce was possible. Marie was counting on receiving money from Fred to take care of the children.

*Fred:* Apparently he had a drinking problem and squandered money on alcohol instead of supporting his family. Over time, expectations changed. Fred became verbally abusive, his wife worked in the fields and money became scarce. When Fred became violent, Marie fled with the children and filed for divorce. Fred denied all allegations of domestic violence and presented himself as a hard-working farmer; he had done nothing wrong. He and his neighbors expected Marie to be a good wife—defined as doing any work necessary to help her husband, to not complain about money, his abusive behavior, drinking and violence. When Marie filed for divorce, Fred and his friends considered it dis-respectful, an audacious act. Marie had embarrassed Fred by calling attention to his problems; she refused to quietly accept an unbearable situation any longer. Tom Hawkins and two other neighbors testified in court on behalf of their neighbor. They characterized Marie as mentally unbalanced and unfit to have custody of the children.

*The Decree:* Fred was found guilty of extreme and inhuman cruelty on December 31, 1904. The Judge awarded $200 alimony and custody of the children to Marie.

*Fred:* He felt if Marie had the nerve to abandon him and file for divorce, then she was on her own. It didn't matter what the court said; he refused to make any payments.

*The Sheriff:* When Fred refused to pay alimony, the Sheriff tried to collect $200 from the sale of jointly owned property, as settlement for the divorce. Tom Hawkins intervened and stopped the collection attempt. He held the first lien.

*Fred:* He claimed he was not at fault for failure to make mortgage payments on the land and small house which they jointly purchased in February 1903.

*Marie:* She questioned Hawkins explanation. Marie admitted payment was due but requested a written audit to show the correct amount. She also petitioned for her share of the dollars that had already been paid, as compensation toward alimony.

*Fred:* A motion filed by a new attorney on June 6, 1908 required Marie Kupper strike from her answer and cross-petition all portions of testimony, for the reason that 1) said Court has no jurisdiction to make an order against Fred Kupper and, 2) said cross-petition does not state sufficient facts to constitute a cause of action against Fred Kupper nor to entitle Marie Kupper to the relief requested.

*The Sheriff:* Foreclosure occurred in August 1908. The property was sold to Tom Hawkins for the outstanding amount due. There wasn't any extra money for Marie.

*Marie:* In 1911, she tried to collect $200 by garnishing Fred's wages.

*Fred:* He did not reply. Other documents were not found.

This analysis revealed that Marie received custody of the children; however Fred refused to pay any alimony.

Marie, Anna and Fred returned to Clayton County in the fall of 1904. Marie knew the children should be in school. But, Fred wouldn't allow his wife and children to live in their former home. She found work as a housekeeper, but the children couldn't live there. According to school enrollment records, Anna and Fred must have lived with their father during 1904-1905. The school records suggest custody of Anna and Fred was assumed by their father, regardless of the court decision.

After reviewing the divorce records a second time, it appeared that Marie made a decision based on legal advice and her understanding of the law, but it didn't make any difference. Fred refused to pay alimony. The court didn't enforce the divorce decree or punish him.

Ellen scribbled a reminder—must schedule a meeting with the Historical Society Director to ask about 1904 attitudes and behavior toward women.

She added a title page, *Reference #4 - Kupper vs. Kupper*, stapled it to her notes, and then filed the pages in her notebook.

That evening, Ellen celebrated a remarkable week of research by dining at the Black Raven, an upscale white-tablecloth restaurant in the historic district of downtown Josephine.

# Clayton County Historical Society

Monday morning. Ellen was anxious to begin locating a few more details about the Kupper family, but the Historical Society didn't open until ten o'clock. With time to kill, she watched the morning news and then walked over to the restaurant for breakfast.

"Hello," the waitress said. "Did you find your family at the Courthouse?"

"Yes, I found some very interesting details," she replied. "I'd like to order a bowl of oatmeal with berries and nuts, whole wheat toast, orange juice and coffee. Today I'm going to the Clayton County Historical Society to see if they have more information."

After breakfast, Ellen returned to her room, picked up her briefcase and handbag, then left for Jospehine. She drove south on Fourth Street until she reached Main, turned right and continued toward the Big Muddy River. Before the bridge, she turned right again and parked in the driveway of the old train depot, now occupied by the Clayton County Historical Society.

∞∞∞∞

Entering the historic building, she walked to a ticket window. Behind the grill, this space was currently used as an office. "Hello, my name is Ellen O'Donnell and I'm from San Francisco. I'd like to know if you have any old City Directories."

"My goodness, you've come a long way," said the Director. "Do you know which years you are looking for?"

"Yes, I'm trying to find information about Marie Kupper and her husband Fred or Fritz Kupper. They divorced in 1904. The 1910 census indicates Marie was a housekeeper in Josephine. I'm hoping the City Directories might list her name in years 1905 through 1910. They also had a daughter named Anna."

"Okay, I'll bring you the Directories that we have on hand. Since we rely on donations, all the years aren't available, but maybe you'll find some hints about the family."

Pauline Grunewald brought a stack of City Directories to the table and Ellen began looking through each one, systematically checking for Kupper and Cooper entries. She found:

*1903*      Fritz Kupper, Arapaho Township, RFD 4

*1904*      No City Directory available

*1905*      No entries for Fred, Fritz or Maria, Marie

*1906*      No entries for Fred, Fritz or Maria, Marie

*1907*      Maria Kupper, domestic, 910 North Seventh Street. This large three-story southern plantation style home was owned by H. B. Adams. The historical society has a photo; the home was demolished in 1956.

*1908*      No entries for Fred, Fritz or Maria, Marie

*1909*      Mary Cooper, no street address, a Saleslady.

*1910*      Mary Kupper, domestic, 1422 East Main Street.
No photo; this house was demolished.

Anna Cooper, domestic, 512 North Fifth Street. The historical society had a 1950s photo of this boarding house; it was later demolished.

*1912*      Mary Kupper, domestic, 1422 E. Main Street.
The same address as 1910.

Anna Cooper, operator, Nebraska Telephone Company, rooms 1221 North Ninth Street. The telephone company was located at 106-1/2 North Sixth Street. The Historical Society had a 1920s photograph of the entire downtown block; they didn't have any clipping files about the telephone company. They weren't any 1912 photographs of the 1221 North Ninth Street house, although a 1950s photo found the home had been remodeled.

*1913*      No City Directories available 1913-1919.

This summary revealed an interesting coincidence. In 1912, Anna was sixteen years old and evidently ambitious enough to look for a better job. She found another room to rent instead of staying at the boarding house. This decision was an early sign of independence by Anna Cooper.

Reviewing her list, Ellen asked for copies of each City Directory page and of the three photographs: 910 North Seventh Street, 512 North Fifth Street, 106-1/2 North Sixth Street. While waiting for them to be printed, she walked through the Society's exhibits. The surrounding communities were located on a FM or Farm-to-Market Road, about ten miles apart. Each village had its own church, primarily Lutheran, and was very proud of their school and sports team. Many of the displays included examples of earlier clothing styles, household equipment and photos of one-room schools. Josephine and the surrounding towns were interdependent—farming and grain elevators dominated the region—while each community emphasized their local church and school.

Returning to pick up the copies, Ellen asked the Director, "I have one more favor to ask—I'd like you to be my guest at the Black Raven for lunch on Wednesday. I'm hoping you can tell me a little more about the German community of Josephine."

"I'm not sure if I know anything about your family," Pauline replied.

"That's okay. I always try to spend time with a local historian. Could we meet about noon at the Black Raven?"

"Okay, I don't have any other plans. I can be there."

"Thanks so much," said Ellen. "I'll see you then."

∞∞∞∞

Leaving the Historical Society, Ellen stopped for lunch at the Runza café, and then returned to her motel room. She looked up the phone number for the Black Raven and made a reservation for a party of two, lunch on Wednesday.

Next, she checked the maps of Nebraska, Kansas and Oklahoma. Stillwater was the best location in relation to the other research sites; she walked across the parking lot to the motel office.

"Hi, I need to make a reservation for the Holiday Inn in Stillwater, Oklahoma. I'll arrive on Thursday evening, April 10 and leave on Wednesday morning, April 16. I'll also need a reservation at the Holiday Inn in Oklahoma City, arriving Wednesday evening April 16 and leaving Friday morning, April 18."

After an early supper at their restaurant, Ellen read *My Antonia* for the remainder of the evening.

# Updating Research Files

Yawning, Ellen looked around her motel room. She needed to do laundry, so she could pack the suitcase tomorrow and be ready to leave on Thursday. She placed her dirty clothes inside a pillowcase, ate breakfast at the motel and then drove to Josephine. Yesterday, she had noticed a Laundromat on Main Street.

Entering the building, Ellen placed her briefcase near one of the plastic chairs lining the walls, then chose two nearby washing machines, sorted her clothes, bought some detergent, and added quarters to start the machines. Spying another vending machine across the room, she bought a cup of coffee and sat down to review her research notes.

Everything was mostly up-to-date and filed correctly, but there weren't any comments about attending services at First Lutheran. Ellen tore a sheet of paper from the tablet and started writing:

*Sunday, April 6:* I attended ten o'clock services at First Lutheran, located about eight miles northeast of Josephine. Known as the "mother church" because it sponsored five other congregations, First Lutheran was established in 1874.

The two-story building was a brick imitation of early Gothic architecture with twin towers and arched trefoil windows. Each steeple had its own entrance door, originating from the custom of men sitting on one side of the church and women sitting in separate pews on the other side. By the time I arrived, the bells were ringing, calling everyone to worship.

Sunlight filtered through the stained-glass windows. An elaborately carved white altar, trimmed with gold, beckoned all eyes toward the front. Above the altar, a carved statue of Jesus Christ faced the congregation, while a gilded baptismal font was prominently placed nearby

A white and gold-trimmed lectern was located at a higher level, so everyone could hear the sermon in a space that didn't have loudspeakers. Sitting at an old pipe organ, the organist played hymns while everyone sang enthusiastically. The service brought memories of attending baptisms and confirmations with my parents.

Afterwards, the organist played a final hymn while ushers stood beside each row of pews, alternately giving permission for parishioners to leave the sanctuary, until the church was empty. Everyone gathered outside to visit with their neighbors.

While standing on the steps, and trying to decide what to do next, the church secretary introduced me to Mrs. Daubendieck. I asked her about Chris and Katie; she said they were highly respected by their neighbors.

Chris was a farmer, served on the church council and was a trustee of their one-room school. His wife, Katie, was a kind, gentle person; she didn't speak much English.

Mrs. Daubendieck did not know anything about Katie's mother, Marie Kupper. She said Katie never talked about her parents. They were not members of the church.

She introduced me to a young woman and told her I was researching Chris and Katie Zimmermann. Jennifer was their grand-daughter. I asked if anyone in the family ever talked about Katie's mother. She didn't recall ever hearing anything about Marie or her husband Fred.

I wasn't able to discover any new information; however it was very interesting to visit the church and its community.

While concentrating on writing, Ellen hadn't realized the washing machines stopped. Belatedly, she jumped up to remove the clothes, take them to the dryer, adjusted the heat, added quarters, started the machine and returned to her chair.

Due to new information, she next developed a chronology of events:

*June 1892*    Marie Klein married Friedrich Kupper in Josephine, Nebraska.

*Apr 1893*     Their daughter, Mary Magdalen, was born.

*May 1895*     Their daughter, Anna, was born. She later changed her name to Helen.

| | |
|---|---|
| *June 1898* | Their son Johann Fredrick was born. He was known as Fred John. |
| *Feb 1900* | Marie's father, Johann Reinhard Klein, died in Germany. |
| *April 1900* | The 1900 census indicated they rented property in Arapaho Township. |
| *Feb 1901* | Their daughter, Mary Magdalen, died. |
| *Aug 1901* | Marie's mother and daughter, Katherine Klein, arrived from Germany. |
| *Apr 1902* | Marie's mother, Sophia Katherina Kupper Klein, died in Nebraska. |
| *Feb 1903* | Fred and Marie Kupper bought a small acreage in Arapaho Township. |
| *Jul 1904* | Marie Kupper filed for divorce from Fred Kupper. The Decree awarded her alimony and custody of the children. Fred ignored the court order. |
| *Jan 1907* | Maria Kupper was a domestic servant, living at 910 North Seventh Street. |
| *Jan 1908* | Marie Kupper filed for alimony from sale of the acreage property. |
| *Mar 1908* | Marie's daughter, Katherine, married Christian Zimmermann. |
| *Aug 1908* | The acreage sold at Sheriff's Auction. Marie received zero dollars. |

| | |
|---|---|
| *May 1910* | Mary Kupper was a domestic servant, living at 1422 E. Main Street. Her former husband, Fred Kupper, lived in Omaha, Nebraska. Her daughter, Anna Cooper, was a servant for a boarding house at 512 North Fifth Street, while her son, Fred John Cooper, lived at an orphanage in Omaha, Nebraska. |
| *Aug 1911* | Marie Kupper tried to garnish Fred Kupper's wages in Omaha, Nebraska. He never replied. |
| *Jan 1912* | Mary Kupper was a domestic servant, living at 1422 East Main Street. Her daughter Anna Cooper, living at 1221 North Ninth Street, was an operator for the Nebraska Telephone Company. |
| *1913* | Other records were not found at the Clayton County Courthouse or in the City Directories of Josephine, Nebraska, 1913-1919. |

From this review, Ellen verified the Kupper family had lived in Josephine for twenty years. Yet, two generations later, no one could recall anything about them. Something must've happened during the intervening years.

The dryer buzzer was ringing. She placed her notes in the briefcase, then folded the clothes and placed them in the pillowcase. Putting everything in the car, Ellen locked it, and walked over to the Dairy Queen to order a hamburger, fries and chocolate shake.

Afterwards, she decided to give herself a break and drove to the downtown historic district to visit the local antique stores.

Returning to her motel room, Ellen filed her comments about First Lutheran and the twenty-year chronology in her notebook. She then walked over to the motel restaurant for an early supper and spent a quiet evening watching movies on television.

Tomorrow would be her last day in Josephine, Nebraska.

# A Nebraska Interview

Wednesday morning. Ellen woke up earlier than usual, checked the clock and decided to read for an hour before getting dressed. At nine o'clock she walked over to the restaurant.

"Good morning," what would you like to order today?"

"It's chilly outside, so I'm going to have hot oatmeal with all the toppings, an English muffin, orange juice and coffee," Ellen replied. Returning to her room, she finished reading *My Antonia*, then left for her lunch meeting at the Black Raven.

"Hi, I have a reservation. Could I sit near the front window?" The waitress escorted her to the table with a view of historic buildings across the street.

Pauline walked through the door and over to her table. "Hello, sorry I'm late," she said.

"No problem, I only arrived a few minutes ago. Let's decide what to order and then we can visit." They each ordered Spinach Salad with Dried Cranberries and Gorgonzola Cheese Crumbles, Homemade Rolls, Raspberry Iced Tea and Cheese Cake Supreme for dessert.

"I'm so glad you could meet me today," said Ellen. "Although I'm from a large city, I love visiting small towns. I especially like the variety of architectural styles."

"The architecture is what attracted me to the area also," replied Pauline. "I'm originally from the capital city of Lincoln, Nebraska. When I was a sophomore at the university, my art history class assignment was to write an essay about the architecture of any small town within fifty miles of the university. I happened to decide on Josephine as my subject."

"Did you realize at the time that you might be living here someday?" Ellen asked.

"Not really. My first major was Architecture; but I later switched to Art History and minored in Sociology. During my junior year, my sorority sisters and I went to a dance sponsored by one of the fraternities and I met my future husband. His parents thought he should get a college degree as a backup plan; but when he graduated, they insisted he return to farming. We married twenty years ago and are now living on the family land near First Lutheran."

"What a coincidence, I visited your church on Sunday morning and talked with Mrs. Daubendieck. I'm curious though, since you lived in a larger city and moved to a rural community, was it a difficult transition?"

"Yes, at first. That's why I accepted the position of Director for the Historical Society. I like developing the displays and attending meetings of the Main Street Historical Preservation Society. The sociology minor was good background though; I've used this training to understand the German community and its expectations."

"That's an interesting connection," said Ellen. "The woman I'm tracing is Marie Kupper. She filed for divorce in 1904 because of her husband's alcoholism and domestic abuse. The judge agreed Marie had

128

sufficient cause for divorce, awarded her alimony and custody of the children. However, when reading their divorce papers, I was shocked. The neighbors criticized her and her husband plainly ignored the court orders. Was his behavior considered acceptable?"

"Oh, my," replied Pauline. "I'll try to explain how her community reacted. The Germans are good people, but they can be very insistent about obligations to family members.

"First of all, they considered divorce a sin. It wasn't tolerated for any reason.

"Second, alcoholism was commonplace. In 1904, her brothers and sisters, her friends and neighbors—all of them would've expected Marie to stay with her husband—even if he punched or slapped her and was falling-down drunk all the time. They likely claimed his behavior was "her fault" and told Marie that she must stay with him, do whatever he wanted, without question.

"Third, they probably criticized Marie because of the publicity. When the *Daily Monitor* published the legal proceedings, it embarrassed her husband and her family. People gossiped.

"Another reason for disapproval would've been taking individual actions. In other words, Marie made a choice on her own initiative; she didn't obey the typical practice of all decisions being made with the advice of her immediate family.

"By filing for divorce, Marie aligned herself with the American legal system instead of following traditional German customs. Her family probably didn't like her decision to divorce Fred and showed their disapproval by ignoring or shunning her. If she was always absent from family or church activities, any memories of Marie were forgotten."

"I had no idea," said Ellen. "Living in a small community must've been very different from living in a larger town where divorce was acceptable. On Sunday, I was surprised that Marie's relatives didn't know anything about her. Your explanation might be the reason."

"I do have one other question. The records show the divorce decree was in her favor, but her husband ignored court orders and refused to pay any alimony. There are some clues suggesting he had custody of the children, regardless of the court order. Have you heard of any other situations like this?"

"No, but I'm not surprised," said Pauline. "We're thinking in 1986 terms. Marie lived in an isolated rural area dominated by old-fashioned rules—men made the decisions—women followed traditional roles. The men likely talked among themselves and agreed to help their friend. Marie was probably battling an early version of the "good old boys club." The men didn't feel obligated to comply with any laws that benefited a woman.

It had been a long-winded conversation, but Ellen was pleased to learn the details that Pauline depicted. The waiter brought their dessert, and Pauline resumed her explanation.

"Perhaps, I should give you an example. The best way to understand their environment is to explain how the German community identifies everyone," Pauline said.

"Among the older generation, men are known by their given name and women are identified by association with their husbands. For instance, a wife is always known as "Henry's Emma" or "John's Grace," instead of being recognized individually as Emma or Grace.

"This tradition is dying out among the younger generation, but it is still used by the older folks. My mother-in-law doesn't refer to me as Pauline; instead she identifies me as "Don's Pauline" whenever she mentions my name to someone else. It's an unusual naming pattern; but, that is how the old German families describe women."

"I wonder—did Marie continue being a bit independent? Without alimony she probably had a difficult time supporting herself."

"That's a fascinating question," replied Ellen. "From information I found at your Historical Society, I learned she was a housekeeper for at least two families in Josephine, so I'm assuming she had a place to live. But, I'm not sure what happened with the children. I should learn more about Fred and Marie Kupper when I talk with Gertrude Klein."

Pauline checked her watch; the lunch hour was over. "I've really enjoyed being able to talk about social history," she said. "Thank you for inviting me. It's wonderful that you can concentrate on genealogy research."

"Yes, it's nice to have an assignment," replied Ellen. "I'll be in Oklahoma next week, then returning home to San Francisco. You've been very helpful and given me a great deal of new information." With the conversation at a close, they said "good-bye" and walked out the door.

By the time she'd driven four miles to her motel room, Ellen had identified the significance of this meeting—the nuances of local expectations couldn't be found in the dry details of an official document—reactions by Marie's community could only be understood by talking to a local resident. It was a very important meeting.

On arriving at the motel room, Ellen sat at the desk, tore off a sheet of tablet paper and began writing notes about everything that Pauline had described. A title, *Reference #5 – Patriarchal Environment,* was added and she filed the pages in her briefcase.

She walked over to the restaurant for an early supper, then returned to the room to pack her suitcase. Tomorrow, she would be driving to Oklahoma.

# Three Hundred Miles of Prairie

Thursday, April 10, six a.m. Ellen pulled on her jeans, her favorite *Happiness is Finding Ancestors* t-shirt and quickly packed the car. On the edge of Josephine, she stopped at a gas station to get fuel, coffee, donuts, and then left for Red Cloud, Nebraska.

She drove west on a two-lane black asphalt highway. In-between the ancient oak and maple trees, she caught views of prosperous farmland and occasional creeks with tall cottonwood trees guarding the banks. Familiar billowing clouds touched a distant horizon.

∞∞∞∞

At eight o'clock, Ellen drove through the small town. Built in a typical courthouse-on-the-square plan, the retail stores advertised western antiques and collectibles; the architectural details were similar to those she'd seen in Josephine. Driving around the square, she soon found a small café that had a collection of farm trucks in front of the building. Ellen parked her car and walked inside.

"Good morning," said a waitress. "Have a seat and I'll be with you in a few minutes."

When she entered the café, everyone turned to look—she was obviously a stranger and they were curious. Ellen quickly chose a corner

133

table, scanned the menu and then surveyed the room. It reminded her of Howard Johnson restaurants from an earlier era. Slate gray Formica tables were surrounded by padded turquoise vinyl chairs with chrome legs. Above the half-paneled walls, faded sunflower wallpaper featured a collection of branding irons, cowboy hats and Coca-Cola posters. Overhead, sagging and stained ceiling tiles signified an ancient water leak. The speckled tan asbestos tile floor hadn't been scrubbed for a long time, but that didn't seem to matter to its regular customers. Their café was a familiar hang-out where ranchers could meet friends for coffee and exchange teasing comments with the waitress.

After a breakfast of pancakes, ham, scrambled eggs, orange juice and coffee, Ellen paid the cashier three dollars, and said, "The breakfast was very good. Next, I'm visiting the Willa Cather Prairie and then will continue on to Stillwater, Oklahoma. Could you give me directions?"

"Sure, go east on West Fourth Avenue to the junction of Highway 136 and Highway 281 South, turn right and drive five miles to the entrance sign, then follow the road to the parking lot. The trail has labels and photos of native grasses, wildflowers, birds and small animals. At the end of the trail you'll be on a hill overlooking the Republican River Valley. It's a wonderful tour of a native grassland area and will probably take you about an hour or so, depending on how long you visit each spot." Ellen easily found the Prairie site and parked her car. She walked the trail, stopping at each overlook to take a few scenic photos.

Ten o'clock; she reviewed her scribbled directions, and then took two-lane roads until merging with Interstate 35 South to Stillwater. The high plains landscape alternated between flat cultivated ground and low hills where cattle grazed in a vast rangeland. Fluffy clouds soared in every direction. The horizon seemed endless.

A few hours later, highway signs advertised the immigrant community of Lindsborg, Kansas. It looked interesting, she needed gas for the car and it was time to have lunch. At Exit 78, Ellen turned west, drove into town and stopped for fuel. She then turned left on Main Street and found small retail shops advertising country antiques and Swedish tourist items. She parked her car, got out, stretched, and stiffly walked into a small café.

Small copper bells tinkled as she walked through the door. The unmatched chairs and tables were painted in pastel colors, with small vases of wildflowers in the center of each table. Two o'clock, the café was empty. A waitress was clearing tables at the back of the room.

"Please have a seat. I'll be right with you." A few minutes later, the waitress came to Ellen's table.

"I'm in a bit of a hurry, and still need to drive to Stillwater today. What do you recommend for a quick lunch?"

"Oh, you've got plenty of time to eat and maybe do a little shopping. I can bring you a BLT sandwich, chips and a Coke. Would you like some home-made cherry pie for dessert?"

"Sounds perfect," she replied.

Looking at her map, Ellen calculated the distance to Stillwater. If she left Lindsborg about three o'clock, she'd arrive at the motel before seven o'clock. She had time to shop.

After lunch, Ellen walked outside, looked through a window and entered a small art gallery. The display included a small exhibit of works by Birger Sandzén, a Swedish-American artist and dean of the art department at nearby Bethany College. Exhibit labels indicated his oil paintings were considered Post-Impressionist and often compared to paintings by Cezanne. Attracted by his work, she bought a small watercolor painting that could be hand-carried on her flight home.

Time to leave. She hurried to the car, drove east until reaching Interstate 35 and turned south. Now she had to be serious about reaching Stillwater—no more serendipity stops.

∞∞∞∞

Three hours later, Ellen entered a Pizza Hut lane to order a take-out meal and then drove to the Holiday Inn. She checked in, brought everything inside and locked the car. This room had more attractive décor—the wallpaper and drapes were beige and salmon patterns, the carpet was beige plush and reproductions of western paintings hung on the walls. The furnishings were standard motel; two double beds, a small desk and side chair, a dresser with a mirror, a television set in the corner and a black telephone on the night stand.

While eating supper and watching the news, Ellen reminisced about the day. It had been twelve hours of driving and playing tourist—she had visited the Willa Cather Prairie and bought a watercolor by an important artist—both were completely unexpected events. Tomorrow, she would sleep late, unpack, call Gertrude Klein about the Saturday meeting and visit the Sheerar Museum in the afternoon.

Suddenly tired from the long day of driving, Ellen put on her pajamas, began reading *Old Jules* and fell asleep before finishing the first chapter.

# OKLAHOMA

# An Oklahoma Interview

Ellen hopped out of bed on Saturday morning and peeked through the curtains—fog. Surprised at finding pea-soup weather in Oklahoma, she dressed, walked over to the restaurant, bought a copy of the *Stillwater News Press* and found an empty table.

"Good morning," the waitress said. "Would you like to order breakfast?"

"I'll have French toast, scrambled eggs, bacon, orange juice and coffee," replied Ellen. "I'm driving to Kingmann in Adams County later today. From the map, it looks like it's about fifty miles from here, is that correct?"

"Yes, it'll take about an hour. Have a good trip."

After breakfast, another cup of coffee and catching up on the local news, Ellen returned to her room. She reviewed details about the Klein family, then placed a map, Catherine Klein's 1901 immigration details, the family photo from Helen's apartment, the *Adams County History* pages, and a small journal in her briefcase. She read *Old Jules* until eleven o'clock, had a light lunch at the restaurant and left for her afternoon appointment.

When she called Gertrude yesterday, Ellen learned her daughter would be waiting at the St. Matthew's Lutheran church in Kingmann. For the next hour, she followed asphalt roads through a landscape of ominous looking clouds, red dirt, empty pastures and scraggly trees bordering a random creek; winter wheat was starting to turn green in a few cultivated fields. Arriving in the small town, she spotted the spires of St. Matthew's and drove to their parking lot. Ellen parked her car, picked up her briefcase and walked over to the Chevrolet.

"Hi, I'm Ellen," she said, when Barbara rolled down the car window. "Thanks for offering to take me to your mother's house; I've been looking forward to this visit."

"Yes, we're excited too," Barbara replied, then unlocked the door and Ellen joined her. While driving, she politely asked questions. "My mother was very surprised to get your phone call. Now, tell me again, how did you happen to find her name?"

"I should explain . . . I've been asked to research the family of Helen Cooper. She died in San Francisco. Her mother was Marie Klein Kupper. According to their records, Marie was from Germany, immigrated to New York City, married in Nebraska and her brothers lived in Adams County, Oklahoma. At the San Francisco Public Library, I checked for a county history of Adams County, Oklahoma and found your family information. All of the descriptions matched the little bit of information I knew about Marie. So, I called your mother."

"That's amazing," replied Barbara. "My sister and I wrote that article years ago when a publisher asked for stories about families who settled here. There was always the mystery of what happened to my grandfather's sister Marie. She went to California and no one ever heard from her again.

"When we sent the story to the publisher, we didn't know if we'd ever hear from anyone in California. We're really glad that you called."

"I'm happy to meet your family too. Have you done other family history research?"

"Oh, not really," Barbara replied. "After you called, my mother found some old photographs and I've made copies for you. I also made a copy of the story my great-uncle John told about his immigration experience. When he and his brother Fred arrived in the port of *Le Havre*, Fred bought his ticket from the agent and John bought a ticket from another man who wanted to return home. John never gave anyone the details because he was afraid of being sent back to Germany. We haven't found his ship manifest."

"Yes, I've heard similar stories. Two weeks ago, I found the ship information for Marie's daughter Katherine and the grandmother, Catherine Klein. I've brought along copies for you."

"That is great!" replied Barbara. "My mother and sister Linda will be so excited. Here we are—welcome to the Klein house. There are many descendants of the original families now. This entire mile is known as Klein Row."

Parking in the dirt lane of the farmyard, they walked up steps of the back porch. Barbara opened the kitchen door and hollered "Mom, we're here." As they entered the small kitchen, an elderly white-haired woman and a middle-aged woman with brown hair turning gray at the temples, came forward to shake Ellen's hand.

"Hello, I'm Gertrude and this is my oldest daughter Linda; we're glad to meet you," she said. "Please come over to the table and sit down. Would you like a cup of tea?"

"Oh no, I don't want to bother you. I'm so glad to see you and learn more about the Klein family. Barbara and I had a nice visit on the way over here and I've brought you copies of Catherine Klein's ship records."

Ellen opened her briefcase and removed some pages. "Here, these are for you."

"Oh, my goodness. We've looked for records on Fred and his brother John and haven't had any luck," replied Linda. "Their father died in Germany and their mother brought Marie's daughter Katherine to Nebraska. But, the grandmother died a few months later and we didn't know anything else."

"Sometimes when I'm doing research, things just fall into place," said Ellen. "They arrived at Ellis Island on August 1, 1901. Apparently, the grandmother had some health problems, because they were interviewed by a Board of Special Inquiry before being allowed to enter the United States. This record shows Catherine Klein, age fifty-nine, and "senile." A panel of judges allowed them to continue traveling to Nebraska because her daughter Marie paid their tickets in advance and Marie's home in Nebraska was their destination."

"That's really interesting," said Barbara. "Mom, where are the copies we made for Ellen? She'll want to know about the rest of the family."

"Here they are," said Gertrude. "We found these photos in an old box in the bottom drawer of our walnut bureau. We're not exactly sure about the people. I can tell you what I remember from hearing stories that my father-in-law Fred told about emigrating from Germany. Fred was Marie's brother." Ellen jotted notes as Gertrude described each photo:

*Photo #1:* This is a studio photograph of Johann Reinhard Klein and his wife Sophia Katherina Kupper Klein. We don't know a year, but from looking at their worn hands and clothing style, it might be an anniversary photograph. If so, the date could be about 1891 and they would've been about forty-nine years old. We think Marie might've sent money for a studio photograph and Fred brought it along when he left Germany.

Reinhard's suit is an older style and too small for his frame. He seems to be a likeable, handsome man with a mischievous smile and a twinkle in his eyes.

His wife, Sophia Katherina, looks like she was a short, small-boned woman. She is wearing a long black veil, a two-piece black outfit with white lace trim at the neck and black lace trimming the skirt. There are old, worn shoes peeking from underneath her floor-length skirt. Katherina is holding two books, a Bible and a journal; they must have been important to her.

*Photo #2:* This is a photo of Reinhard and Katherina Klein's children. We assume it was taken in front of their house which seems to be in very poor shape; mortar is coming loose from some of the large limestone blocks, the iron-barred windows are roughly framed and don't have shutters. They're standing in front of a wooden door which opens to bare ground. There isn't any grass or flowers.

All of the children are smiling and dressed in their Sunday-best clothes. The boys are wearing suits and the girls have buttoned bodices over plaid skirts. Everyone is wearing shiny new shoes that haven't seen a lot of wear. We're not sure about some of the names and we don't know a date.

The tallest boy in the back row is John, because we have other photos of him and can match his face. We think the young man on the left is George. The two little girls in the front are Caroline and Rosina; they both died when they were sixteen, so this is the only photograph of them. We're guessing if Caroline was age eight, it could date the photograph to about 1888. The couple on the right side might be the oldest daughter Katherina Regina and her husband Fritz Ziegler; they married in 1887 and she is the only child who remained in Germany. The other children are missing from this photo; we don't know about Fred, who was twenty years old in 1888, or Lena, who would've been eleven years old. And Marie is also missing; although, she might be the photographer.

We found everything in the walnut bureau. Marie must have given this picture to her brother Fred when she left for California. We didn't find any photo of Marie.

*The Letter:* We've decided to give you this faded letter because it includes information about Marie going to California in 1935. Katie left it here when they visited in the 1940s to ask about finding her mother in California.

"Thank you for making the copies and also for this letter—it is all new and interesting information," said Ellen.

"I've also brought a photo for you. The family took it along to California and I'd like to identify the people." Gertrude had a puzzled look on her face.

"She is looking for information about Fred's Marie," said Barbara.

"Okay, I'll try to help," said Gertrude. "Linda, could you fix us some tea and lunch?" Turning to Ellen, she explained, "We still follow the old German customs. When someone visited, my mother-in-law always served hot tea and an afternoon lunch. Let me see the photo."

"This photograph was found in Helen's apartment," said Ellen. "On the reverse it is marked *Anna, Vater, Fred*. I think it's a photo of Helen, her father and her brother because her baptized name was Anna. It was taken in Omaha, Nebraska but her mother Marie isn't included in the group. I'd like to know if this man is her husband, Fred Cooper."

Gertrude looked at the photograph closely. "Yes, that's him," she said. "Their boy Fred John is younger here. When he was older, he went to the insane hospital for a while. We never knew the problem because it happened before we married. Barbara, look in the bureau drawer. We made a copy of the Fred Kupper photograph too."

"Here it is," replied Barbara. "He's younger is this photo, but it's the same man."

Ellen studied the photograph of Fred Kupper, a farmer, dressed in a worn, loose-fitting suit and wearing old scuffed-up boots. Taken in a studio at Josephine, Nebraska, there wasn't any date but Ellen remembered she'd found his 1889 *Intent to Naturalize* document at the Clayton County Courthouse. She assumed this photo was probably taken the same year.

"Wonderful! Now, I'm curious . . . did you know about Fred and Marie being divorced? According to the 1910 census, Marie lived in Josephine and Fred lived in Omaha. Last week I found their divorce papers at the Clayton County courthouse. Marie filed for divorce in 1904 because of his alcoholism."

"Why . . . I never heard anyone say anything about that. Fred and Marie were always married when they lived in Oklahoma," exclaimed Gertrude. "But, since you mention it, I do remember my father-in-law said Fred liked his beer. Marie and Fred couldn't get along with each other and couldn't get along without each other."

"I'm not familiar with that phrase," said Ellen. "What does it mean?"

"Apparently Fred and Marie were happy until he started drinking," said Gertrude. "They split up every once in a while and always got together again later."

"Since they were living here during the Dust Bowl and Great Depression, those terrible events must have affected them," said Ellen. "What happened when Marie went to California though? Their daughter Helen didn't mention anything about her father, so I don't know if he went to California."

"Fred stayed here," said Gertrude emphatically. "I remember him sitting in an old rocking chair by the stove in the front parlor of this house. When Marie went to California, Fred lived with her brother George in Nebraska for a while; then he lived here, with her brother Fred."

"That certainly explains an unanswered question! But I don't understand. Today, we'd find it odd that the husband of a separated couple would live with his wife's relatives. Maybe they did things differently in the 1930s."

"Well," Gertrude said, "when a couple married, each family considered both of them as if they were family members. There weren't any distinctions between "his family" and "her family." There weren't any nursing homes. And, the family would never have turned Fred away or asked him to become a welfare case.

"Now that you ask, I remember my father-in-law said Fred Kupper was the baptism sponsor for John, George and Lena. If Fred agreed to take care of them by being a sponsor, then it was their duty to care for him, especially if he didn't have anyone else to give him a home.

"I'm not sure what my father-in-law and his brothers thought of their sister Marie leaving for California. Everyone could have been pretty upset about it because she was leaving her husband. In the 1950s, there was a long-distance phone call but the weather was bad and the phone went dead. No one in the family ever heard from Marie again."

"This is all very interesting and new information that I didn't know. Thanks to your help, I can fill in some details now," replied Ellen.

"Lunch is ready," announced Linda. "Let's have something to eat."

Ellen gathered the photos, the 1935 letter and her notes, putting everything in her briefcase. Working together, Linda and Barbara placed utensils, plates, cups and napkins around the gingham oilcloth-covered table. They poured hot tea for everyone, then placed large platters of food in the middle of the table and sat down.

"Let's join our hands for a prayer." said Gertrude. "Come Lord Jesus, be our guest. Let this food to us be blessed."

Everyone echoed "Amen."

Barbara announced, "We just pass the food around the table and everyone takes a helping. There's plenty to eat, so don't be shy about trying everything, especially Linda's Triple Chocolate Cake."

Homemade bread, small bowls of homemade butter, mustard and mayonnaise, thick slices of American cheese, a large platter of cold cuts, bread-and-butter pickles, potato chips, and chocolate cake were offered. Gertrude said, "Please try some pears; they're the last of our best crop that I canned two years ago."

The room was quiet. Everyone seemed to be thinking about the day's events while they were eating. To break the silence, Barbara asked, "Tell us something about San Francisco. Have you lived there a long time?"

"I grew up there. My father was an Irish Catholic police officer and my mother was a homemaker. I never married, so when they died I inherited the house and have lived in the same neighborhood all of my life. It is in Noe Valley and has many old pastel-colored Victorian mansions, with gingerbread-style decoration; they're famously known as "the painted ladies." San Francisco is a large city and has a lot of hills. Most people take the trolley car or city bus instead of driving a car. It seems a bit crowded but everyone likes being near the ocean. It's been great to travel in the Midwest though; I've never seen so much land. I've enjoyed watching the sky and the clouds. It's so quiet here."

"How did you happen to get involved in family history research?" asked Linda.

"I followed my dad into police work and was a detective for many years. When the crime rates went up, the victim stories were really troubling to me, so I took early retirement. I've always been interested in genealogy, especially the German Lutheran records from my mom's side of the family."

"That explains why it is so easy to talk with you . . . on your mother's side of the family, you're German Lutheran too," said Barbara. "But, if your father was Catholic and your mother was Lutheran, weren't there some problems?"

"Not that I recall. We attended baptisms, confirmations and marriages on both sides of the family; I think these experiences have helped me to be aware of different family situations."

Glancing out the window, Ellen suddenly noticed it was raining. "I'd like to take a photo of everyone, then I'd better leave for Stillwater. I'll just have a slice of Linda's chocolate cake and be on my way."

Afterwards, Gertrude said, "Let's join hands and pray. Dear Lord, we thank you for bringing Ellen to us this day and learning so many things about our family. Please watch over her until she returns home safely to San Francisco. In the Lord's name, we pray."

Everyone echoed "Amen."

Ellen asked Gertrude, Barbara and Linda to pose for a photo in front of the old bureau. She then retrieved her briefcase, gave Gertrude a hug and said, "Thank you so much for meeting with me, it's been just wonderful. I especially want to thank you for these photos and the letter from Marie. They'll be very helpful in finding more information."

"I think we've all enjoyed your visit. It's very nice to have the ship records and we've made a new friend too," Gertrude replied.

Barbara loaned Ellen an extra umbrella, and they both ran to the car. Turning on the windshield wipers, she said, "I know the roads and can take you to St. Matthew's, then you can drive the main highway back to Stillwater. It's nearly stopped raining, so everything will be fine."

On arrival at the church, Ellen said, "I'll be in touch if I find more information. Thanks again, I really enjoyed the day." She dashed to the car, turned on the lights, and windshield wipers, then waved good-bye.

An hour later, Ellen entered the Holiday Inn parking lot in Stillwater. Picking up her briefcase and handbag, she locked the car door, unlocked the room door and placed the briefcase on the table. Removing everything, she wrote a title page, *Reference #6 – A Klein Family Interview*, stapled it to her notes, then filed the pages and the family photos.

Next, she carefully studied the 1935 letter; it included more clues. After placing the fragile pages inside an acid-free protective sleeve, Ellen added this important document to her notebook.

It had been a very good day of new discoveries and learning more about the Klein and Kupper families.

# Mercy Hospital for the Insane

When the alarm buzzed on Monday morning, Ellen peaked through the curtains and remembered she was in Oklahoma. An hour later, she walked over to the motel restaurant, bought the *Stillwater News Press*, ordered breakfast and an extra cup of coffee.

Returning to her room, she picked up her briefcase, locked the door and walked outside. Today, her destination was the Mercy Hospital for the Insane, located forty miles north of Stillwater, then another ten miles from the nearest town. Although the hospital was closed, original records could be reviewed at their administrative office.

Leaving the freeway, Ellen travelled a two-lane black asphalt highway through a landscape of flat, barren fields of red dirt until finding a sign pointing toward the hospital entrance. Driving around the perimeter of the campus, the cluster of four-story buildings had a few broken windows. Four dormitory buildings enclosed a small park, which could be glimpsed from one corner of the abandoned parking lot. She took a few photos of a dormitory building, then parked her car in front of an administration building and went inside.

"Hello, my name is Ellen O'Donnell."

"I'd like to review the files of Fred John Cooper. He was born on June 14, 1898 in Nebraska. He never married and he died in San Francisco, California on April 23, 1980. His father was Fred Cooper and his mother was Marie."

"I might be able to help you," the clerk replied. "What is the purpose of your research?"

"I'm a professional genealogist and have been hired to locate family information. Would you like to see my driver's license and other identification?"

"Yes, please complete this form, then I'll look for his file," she replied. Ellen completed the details and returned the form to the clerk.

"Thank you. The records for earlier years are filed in another building; it'll take about forty minutes to locate his file."

"Okay, is there a public coffee shop in this building?"

"Sure, just go down the hall to the right, at the first hallway turn left and you'll see the door to the lunchroom. It has vending machines where you can buy coffee and pastries."

Ellen followed the directions to the lunchroom and bought coffee. She checked her watch, found a table where she could wait and picked up a weekly newspaper from a magazine rack. Forty minutes later she returned to the main reception desk.

"Hi, were you able to find a file about Fred John Cooper?" she asked.

"Yes, I have it. Making copies is not allowed, but you may sit at the table and read the few records we have. Taking notes in pencil is okay."

After a quick survey of the contents, Ellen began manually abstracting details. The records grimly expressed how staff decisions affected the life of Fred John Cooper.

*03 June 1929 Cover Page*: Fred John Cooper, Fairfax, Osage County. Correspondents: Fred Cooper, father, Ralston, Route 3, Osage. Fred John is assigned to a guardian in Fairfax.

*County Court, Osage County, Oklahoma. Physician's Certificate, Sanity Case of Fred J. Cooper:* Born June 14, 1898. Residence: Fairfax, Osage County, Oklahoma. Father: Fred Cooper. Mother: Mary Klein. The Jail reported symptoms; he hears voices at irregular intervals. Present Location: In jail at Pawhuska for previous two weeks.

*04 June 1929 Hospital Diagnosis Report by three physicians*: Admitted: June 4, 1929. Residence: Fairfax, Osage County. Nativity: Nebraska. Education: Eighth Grade, Nebraska. Religion: None. Occupation: Farming. Social Status: Single. Race: Mixed. Age: 31, Young, white adult, good nutrition. Diagnosis: Dementia Praecox (schizophrenia).

*19 June 1929 Summary of Mental Examination*: The patient has had trouble with his neighbors for several years because Negro tenants were allowed to occupy adjoining property and they were stealing gas from him. His orientation is undisturbed. He denies hearing voices. His attitude in the clinic today is that of someone attempting to hide his true mental state and the questions are answered in a negativistic manner. Because of patient having trouble with neighbors, the fact that he was confined in jail, having hallucinations of hearing and his demeanor since being in this institution, we make a diagnosis of Dementia praecox.

*04 October 1929:* Patient was brought before the clinic and we find he has the same ideas as written above and as he answers questions more readily than before, we find other delusions and hallucinations. He thinks a gang committed him when he tried to join a lodge. He thinks this is a frame-up. The same diagnosis is continued.

*1931, date unknown:* His sister, Helen A. Cooper, signed the Visitor Register. Her address: 1870 Sacramento Street, San Francisco, California.

*12 April 1932: Physician's Report*: We find his mental condition much the same as the last time he was brought before the Clinic on 4 October 1929. Today, we find the man quiet, looking quite well physically and he answers questions readily.

He says his trouble began in 1925. It was started by Hale and his gang when they wanted to get hold of his farm. He states he was not directly approached by any members of the gang to sell the farm, but they replaced the Negroes with bootleggers.

He thinks the Hale gang controls all lodges in that community and he joined the Modern Woodman to keep from being run out of the community. He thinks the Lodge is the cause of his commitment.

The patient is well oriented, his memory is good and he can describe in detail, the people and property in the community in which he lived. He is usually quite sarcastic and easily angered. Today, he is more pleasant during examination than on previous occasions or when contacted on the ward.

The entire staff agrees the previous diagnosis of Dementia praecox is correct. It is self-evident, without any further observation, that this man is dangerous to be at large. We know it would be extremely dangerous for a man of this type not to be held under the closest supervision at all times. Continued residence in this facility is recommended.

*11 July 1932: County Court, Osage County, Oklahoma*: Order of the Court for Transportation of Fred J. Cooper from the asylum to Pawhuska, Oklahoma. This case is scheduled for a guardianship hearing in this court on 13 July 1932 therefore it is necessary for the said Fred J. Cooper to be present.

Ellen reviewed her notes a second time. From a 1986 point-of-view, the physician and staff presented contradictory evidence. After nearly three years of confinement, Fred John Cooper behaved appropriately, yet they wouldn't release him because they assumed he was dangerous. Continued residence was recommended.

On returning the file to the receptionist, she asked, "Fred John Cooper lived at the asylum about three years. Do you know the typical treatment at that time?"

"There weren't any written records kept for the particular treatment of each person. In the 1930s, they usually encouraged patients to sit quietly in their rooms or in a common area. The staff discouraged all talking or interaction with other people. They believed the most effective treatment was to avoid all excitement and give the patients a cold bath, twice a day."

"Interesting, apparently they didn't have any type of therapy," said Ellen. "Do you have any suggestions for researching asylum treatment practices during the 1930s?"

"We don't have anything here, but a library might have more information. There were legal changes affecting asylum patients during the 1930s."

"Thanks," said Ellen, then gathered her notes and returned to the car. Before leaving the Mercy Hospital parking lot, she added two items to her research list: Check for a 1932 guardianship hearing of Fred Cooper. Research Oklahoma statutes for asylum treatment in the 1930s.

Ellen left the asylum, planning to return to Stillwater. However, on the way there, she recalled the clerk had given her a strong hint about legal statutes. In thinking about this conversation, she remembered picking up a library brochure—and immediately stopped at a nearby parking lot to rummage through her handbag. If she could find a Dairy Queen and order a quick lunch, then she could locate the library.

At three o'clock, Ellen parked at the Anderson Public Library. From other research projects, she knew that finding legal details at a public library was a long shot, but maybe she'd get lucky.

Taking her briefcase with her, she locked the car and walked inside to the reference desk.

∞∞∞∞

"Hello, my name is Ellen O'Donnell. Could I talk with the Director for a few minutes?"

"Sure, go to the office door down this hallway, just knock and introduce yourself," the clerk replied.

"Hi, my name is Ellen O'Donnell. I did research at the Mercy Hospital for the Insane this morning.

"Now, I'm trying to learn if there were Oklahoma Statutes about the treatment of asylum patients.

"A staff member hinted that I could find legal information at a library."

"I might be able to help you," the Director said.

"Normally, a public library doesn't have any legal books, but a local attorney's office recently donated their collection.

"Would you like to look at the *Index of Statutes*?"

"Talk about serendipity, that's great. Yes, I'll try looking for the Mercy Hospital for the Insane and hope it has been cross-indexed to a specific statute."

For the next two hours, Ellen searched for information. Eventually, she found a 1931 law that was pertinent to Fred John's hospitalization:

*Oklahoma House Bill No. 64, Chapter 26, Article 3:* That whenever the superintendent of the Hospital for the Insane at any institution supported in whole or in part from public funds shall be of the opinion that it is best for society, that any male patient under the age of 65 years and any female patient under the age of 47 years, and which patients are about to be discharged from said institution, should be sexually sterilized. [22 April 1931]

A slip of paper also marked this page—see *Behind the Door of Delusion* by Marle Woodson. Ellen placed the volumes on the shelving cart and returned to the Director's office.

"Thank you so much for helping me. I found the reference I needed.

"Does your library also have a book by Marle Woodson?"

"Let's look in the Card Catalog," the Director replied.

Ellen followed her to the wooden cabinet, where she found the call number, then walked over to the shelf and located the book.

"I'd like to take notes if I find anything useful. What time does the library close?"

"There is a quiet corner over there," the Director replied.

"We're open until eight o'clock; I hope that gives you enough time."

"I'll start speed-reading," replied Ellen.

She settled into an upholstered chair and began reading the faded pages of an old, mildew speckled book.

The introduction to *Behind the Door of Delusion* established that Marle Woodson, a patient and former newspaper reporter, used his professional training to observe and describe the daily routine of an Oklahoma insane asylum. A few of the details were interesting:

*The Great Depression*: During this era, the number of institutionalized individuals increased in states that were affected by drought and unemployment. Considered unfit by society, the feeble-minded, epileptic or alcoholic, as well as anyone suffering from depression or dementia were placed in the asylum. During this financial crisis, hospitalized patients received shelter, food and medical care.

*1931 Legal Changes:* Due to overcrowding and the rising cost of providing room and board for a large numbers of patients, many of them were offered early release if they voluntarily agreed to sterilization *(Oklahoma House Bill No. 64)*.

*Woodson reported patient reactions*: They were frightened, excited and angry because decisions were made at the sole discretion and personal opinion of the superintendent, with court expenses paid by the state. By contrast, a patient had to personally finance the cost of appealing a decision and be given permission to write a letter, make a phone call or send a telegram to hire an attorney. Superintendents routinely denied all patient requests. Essentially, patients had no choice; they could agree to sterilization or remain at the asylum for the remainder of their life.

Although *Oklahoma House Bill No. 64* presented completely unexpected news, this ruling was potentially relevant. Admitted to the asylum in June 1929, Fred John Cooper was released in July 1932. The April 1931 law was in effect on the date of his release.

This information might or might not apply to the Cooper Estate assignment. However, the sterilization bill identified a possible family secret about Fred John Cooper.

# Osage County Courthouse

Ellen woke up, reached for the remote and turned on the television. The anchor man was reminding everyone that IRS returns were due today, April 15. She donned a gray business suit to demonstrate the seriousness of her visit to the Osage County Courthouse.

A few minutes later, she walked over to the motel lobby and bought the *Stillwater News Press*, then went inside the restaurant to order breakfast. After her usual two extra cups of coffee, Ellen returned to her room and checked the reference to *IV a) i)*. Today, she needed to review guardianship records, locate deed records and identify how the Bureau of Indian Affairs was involved. She picked up her briefcase and walked outside to the car. Leaving the Stillwater motel, she entered Cimarron Turnpike East and turned north on Highway 99.

For the next ninety minutes, Ellen followed the two lane highway and surveyed the landscape. Vast areas of sparse rangeland were interspersed with scraggly trees and a few head of cattle, randomly scattered like rust-colored accents in an Impressionist painting. As she drove closer to Pawhuska she spied coal-black oil pump jacks dotting the hillsides. Like other areas of the Midwest, an endless sky of tall billowing clouds dominated the slightly rolling landscape. Tourist billboards advertised "Welcome to the Osage Hills."

On reaching the junction of Highway 99 and Main Street, Ellen drove west into the town of Pawhuska. Two miles later, she entered a dilapidated and decaying downtown area. The six-block area didn't have any cars parked alongside the road. The sidewalks were empty. Abandoned buildings with broken windows conspicuously lined the streets. A five-story Triangle Building, reminiscent of the Flat Iron building in New York City, prominently echoed the town's former glory as a wealthy and flourishing county seat.

The desolation was startling. Unsettled by the surroundings, Ellen left the downtown area and its derelict storefront buildings. She wanted to find to a personal connection, to interact, to have a conversation with someone, to offset the crushing silence.

Looking north, a three-story domed building prominently occupied a hilltop. Two blocks later, she parked in the empty courthouse lot, locked the car and climbed two flights of stairs to the double-door entrance of the courthouse. Inside, a directory indicated District Court offices were located on the third floor and the Register of Deeds occupied a second floor office. Ellen carried her briefcase up the worn marble steps to the third floor.

∞∞∞∞∞

"Hello, I'm Ellen O'Donnell. I would like to see the guardianship records for Fred John Cooper. He was born on June 14, 1898. I've travelled from San Francisco to look at his documents. They might've been filed in the District Court. Could you help me?" she said.

"I'm sorry," the clerk replied. "Our guardianship records are closed for privacy reasons."

164

"I'm trying to identify the circumstances of Fred John's hospitalization. I can show you my genealogy certification documents and a copy of his death certificate if necessary. Mr. Cooper died in 1980; he wasn't ever married and didn't have any children, so there shouldn't be any conflict because there aren't any surviving descendants. Could you check the Guardianship Docket to see if his affairs were handled by this court?"

"Normally we aren't allowed to give anyone access to the records, but since you've travelled such a long distance, I suppose I could check the Docket book." The clerk walked into a vault, returned with a large, heavy volume and looked in the index for Fred John Cooper.

"Here it is—there are nine pages, with fifty single lines per page. Each entry summarizes a particular transaction and date of occurrence. More details are identified in the referenced document. Please wait here. I'll look at the microfilm to see if these records are still available."

Ellen held her breath; she hoped to read the individual documents.

About five minutes later, the clerk returned. "Yes, we have the records, but I'm not allowed to let you read anything because guardianships are mixed in with the probate records of other individuals. For privacy reasons, we can't let you read any part of the film because it also includes information about other people."

Trying to be diplomatic and patient, Ellen said, "Okay, could you tell me the first and last dates recorded on his Docket book pages—knowing dates would at least give me a timeframe. Also, is there a supervisor whom I could speak with about permission to view documents? I'm willing to pay for a staff member to make copies of his records."

"You've travelled so far, I suppose it won't hurt to give you the dates," the clerk replied. She looked at the Docket pages again and said,

"His records began on August 13, 1929 and closed on August 30, 1932. I can't tell you anything else unless I have approval from the Judge. Here's a form to complete. His office is down the hallway, on your right."

"Thank you. I appreciate your help." Ellen sat at a nearby table, filled in data on the release form and walked to the Judge's office.

∞∞∞∞

"Good morning, my name is Ellen O'Donnell. I'm a professional genealogist and would like to review the guardianship documents concerning Fred John Cooper. I've completed this form requesting permission to see his records."

"We don't allow anyone to read those records, they're private," answered the Judge.

"Mr. Cooper died in 1980. He never married and didn't have any children, so there shouldn't be any conflict because there aren't any surviving descendants. I'm willing to pay for a staff member to make copies of the docket pages and microfilm records. If a staff member does the copying, then I won't be reading any other records."

"No, we don't allow any copies. I don't consider genealogy research to be a valid reason for viewing any records," replied the Judge. He was adamant and unyielding.

Politely and pointedly, Ellen said, "Thank you for your time, I'm *very sorry* to bother you." She picked up her briefcase and walked out of the office, greatly disappointed. Apparently guardianship requests were routinely denied by the Osage County judge. She hadn't ever encountered resistance from other officials and wondered why there was such opposition.

# Searching Deed Records

After leaving the Judge's office, Ellen sat on a bench in the hallway to think about his refusal and decide her next step. A few minutes later, she went downstairs to the Register of Deeds office.

"Hello, I'm Ellen O'Donnell. I'd like to look at deed records for Fred Kupper but I'm not sure about a date."

"Okay, I'll show you where to begin. Here is the *Grantor and Grantee Index*; the Grantor is the seller and the Grantee is the buyer. When you find an *Index* entry, you can look at the original documents to locate a specific deed page. Our deed records are stored in the vault. If you find something that needs to be printed, it's one dollar per page. We are short of staff, so just go ahead and make the copies at the machine in the corner and pay me before leaving the office."

Thirty minutes later Ellen found several transactions that were a bit confusing; she abstracted the details and then summarized how the results affected the Kupper family:

> *05 September 1914*
> Grantor: Guardian of Indian Allottee, Osage County
> Grantee: Fred Kupper and Mary Kupper
> Deed $2,400. (160 acres)

She scanned other entries for the same description and found:

> *10 September 1914*
> Grantor: Fred Kupper and Mary Kupper
> Grantee: an individual from Osage County
> First Mortgage $1,200. (160 acres)

Fred and Mary Kupper bought land in Oklahoma as husband and wife! Previously, their 1904 divorce records were found in Clayton County, Nebraska. The latest deed records introduced the question of whether Fred and Mary married in Oklahoma or if they were merely living together again. It also raised an issue about why Mary returned to Fred—to be reunited with her son, Fred John—or to have financial support—or Fred may have convinced her to start over with him in Oklahoma. Regardless of the personal reasons involved, the 1914 transactions indicated Fred and Mary Kupper bought land together. They were living in Osage County, Oklahoma.

Ellen continued looking at the *Index*, tracing the same parcel of land. Five years later, they received a second mortgage from her brother:

> *10 November 1919*
> Grantor: Fred Kupper and Mary Kupper
> Grantee: Fred Klein – Second Mortgage
> Second Mortgage $1,200. (160 acres)

Four days later, their son, Fred J. Kupper bought 160 acres for $1,000 cash and assumed their second mortgage:

> *14 November 1919*
> Grantor: Fred Kupper and Mary Kupper, his wife
> Grantee: Fred J. Kupper
> Deed $1,000, Mortgage $1,200; the second party
> assumes and agrees to pay. (160 acres)

This transaction suggested Fred and Mary gave their son $1,000 cash which they received from the second mortgage. After filing final papers, their son returned the temporary loan to them as payment for the $1,000 deed, and assumed their previous mortgage of $1,200.

Although signed in 1914 and 1919, the mortgages weren't recorded and released until 15 November 1926. Apparently, the Kupper family had enough income between 1914 and 1926 to make payments and show a clear title. By then, Fred would've been seventy-three years old; they probably felt it was time for him to retire and turn the land over to their son.

When the mortgage was released in 1926, additional land transactions were recorded. Fred John Kupper was 28 years old:

> *25 January 1927*
> Grantor: a husband and wife from Osage County.
> Grantee: Fred J. Kupper
> Deed $1,500. (40 acres)

> *10 February 1927*
> Grantor: Fred J. Kupper of Ralston, Pawnee County
> Grantee: Guardian of Indian Allottee, Osage County
> Mortgage $1,500. (160 acres)

Fred J. Cooper bought another 40 acres, apparently by receiving a mortgage for the original 160 acres from an Indian Allottee; prices had escalated to $37.50 an acre. Both of the contracts were recorded on 15 February 1927. To place everything in context—these transactions occurred in the midst of the Roaring Twenties—Fred John Kupper was speculating in land.

169

On June 28, 1929, a hearing was held in County Court at Tulsa, Oklahoma to assign mortgages previously made under a guardianship:

> *28 June 1929.* Note of Fred J. Kupper, dated 10 February 1927, due 10 February 1932, for the principle sum of $1,500; interest paid to February 10, 1928. Security: mortgage on land in Osage County, Oklahoma.

Payments were due in 1929 and 1932. The judge assigned all outstanding notes to the Superintendent of the Osage Indian Agency, for the benefit of an Indian Allottee.

The next entry, dated 2 May 1932 in the Osage County Deed Records was a surprise. While hospitalized, Fred sold the land to his mother:

> *02 May 1932*
> Grantor: Fred J. Cooper, Jr.
> Grantee: Mary Cooper
> Deed $1.00, subject to encumbrances by
> Fred J. Cooper. (200 acres)

Two weeks later, another transaction occurred.

> *16 May 1932*
> Grantor: Mary Cooper
> Grantee: an attorney from Ottowa County
> Mortgage $750; promissory notes: $375 due 16 May 1933 and $375 due 16 May 1934. (200 acres)

By 1932, two-hundred acres were valued at $3.75 an acre, only ten percent of the original price. This transaction suggests Mary was desperately trying to raise cash and used the only resource available. She mortgaged land which belonged to an Indian Allottee.

There weren't any other land transactions after May 16, 1932. The saga ended May 18, 1935 when the United States Marshall for the United States District Court for the Northern District of Oklahoma filed suit against Fred Kupper, Fred J. Cooper, Mary Cooper, and two other individuals for foreclosure of the mortgage on behalf of an Osage Indian Allottee. The property sold on the courthouse steps at Pawhuska, Osage County, Oklahoma for the sum of $1,600.

This 1935 discovery ended their trail of deed records. Ellen printed copies of each deed transaction and filed everything in her briefcase. While paying for the copies, she asked for more information.

"I've found everything that I was looking for," said Ellen. "Next, I'd like to see the Kupper land and take a few photos.

"Could you show me how to drive there?"

"Sure," said the clerk. "Let's look at the plat map to find their section and parcel number.

"From the courthouse, take Main Street and follow it south. When you reach the town of Fairfax, go about a half mile further to the crossroads. Turn left, drive one mile, and turn left again on the gravel road. Their land is on your right side."

"Thanks, this is very helpful. Is there a café where I can get a sandwich and a drink?"

"Ernie's Café is located on Main Street. They close in one hour," the clerk replied.

Ellen gathered everything together, hurried down the marble steps and returned to the car. She returned to Main Street, found the restaurant and dashed inside to order a sandwich and Pepsi to go.

Thirty minutes later, Ellen turned north on the gravel road. She didn't know much about the value of land; however this property didn't produce any crops. The site was a sparse pasture, located at a high elevation and there weren't any trees to prevent top soil from blowing away.

After taking a few photos, she remembered the land transactions viewed earlier that day—oil company leases were scattered amongst the other deed records. Perhaps, the Kupper land was expensive in 1927 because it was located near a speculative oil field.

Five o'clock, and once again she found herself in an isolated country location. According to the map, Oklahoma Highway 18 South would lead back to Stillwater before dark. An hour later, Ellen ordered a steak dinner and glass of wine at Barney Oldfield's, then recalled her encounters at the Pawhuska courthouse.

Today was mixed results. The guardianship records would forever remain a mystery and a secret. Yet, she'd found completely unexpected details about Mary Cooper's involvement in several Oklahoma land transactions.

# A Significant Discovery

Fred John Cooper believed the Hale Gang was responsible for the loss of his land. Finding their archival records was Ellen's first priority for the day; then she planned to view a historical exhibit to learn how the oil boom affected Osage County residents.

After breakfast she checked out of the Stillwater Holiday Inn, returned to her room to retrieve her belongings and drove the frontage road until reaching I-35S, leading to Oklahoma City. Leaving the interstate, she followed tourist signs to the Oklahoma Historical Society, located in the Wiley Post building at 2100 N. Lincoln Boulevard. Parking her car, Ellen took her briefcase, entered the lobby and went to the reception desk.

∞∞○○∞∞

"Hello, my name is Ellen O'Donnell. I'd like to look at archival materials about the Hale Gang. They might be connected with the Osage County, Oklahoma area."

"Okay, please sign your name and address on this visitor register and place your briefcase in the locker. You may keep a tablet and pencil with you for taking notes. To check for the Hale Gang, look in the card catalog file; it's over there."

"Thanks," said Ellen, as she signed the register.

She placed everything except a tablet, and pencil in the locker, then slipped the key into her pocket and walked over to the Card Catalog. Under the subject category, she selected the "H" drawer and found a clipping file.

"I've found information about the Hale Gang. Here is the call number; may I look at it?"

"I'll pull the file for you. You'll need to fill out this call slip first and leave your driver's license. It's our method of making sure the file folder is returned to us."

Five minutes later, the clerk brought a 2-inch file to her table. It included articles about the Hale Gang that were published in *The Oklahoman, Tulsa Tribune, Macon Telegraph, Brooklyn Eagle, Pittsburgh Post, St. Louis Post-Dispatch, Grand Rapids Press, Milwaukee Journal, New York Evening World, Colliers* and *Literary Digest.*

By one o'clock, Ellen had scanned the various commentaries, abstracted a few main points and copied several articles for future reading. She returned the folder to the front desk, retrieved her driver's license and removed her briefcase from the locker.

"Could you tell me how to find a public telephone and recommend a good restaurant where I can have a late lunch? she asked.

"The phone booth is down the hall on your right. For lunch you might like to try Sam's Café on North Lincoln Boulevard."

"Thanks," said Ellen. She walked over to the phone booth and called the Holiday Inn to confirm her reservation, then left to find Sam's Café.

∞∞∞∞

After lunch, Ellen returned to the Oklahoma Historical Society to review a display about Osage County. In the exhibit hall, she took notes:

*Historical Background:* In 1872 an agreement between the Osage Tribal Council and the United States set aside 1,700,000 acres of land, considered worthless, for the establishment of an Osage Indian Reservation.

*The Oil Fields of Osage County:* In 1890, when Congress eased restrictions in Indian Territory, an agreement gave the Foster brothers an exclusive lease of the entire Osage Nation lands. In 1906, their lease ended. A revision to federal law allowed surface mineral rights to be held by individuals; these allotments could be sold to anyone, if the seller had a certificate of competency.

Businessmen, speculators, camp followers, gamblers, bootleggers and attorneys soon created a boomtown environment. When an extended lease expired in 1916, Osage territory land was sold by auction and created a second oil boom. Swindles were widespread; murders, that no one investigated or questioned, took place among the Osage Indian head right owners.

Residents of Pawhuska, Fairfax, Ralston and surrounding towns were afraid of the constant violence. The Dalton Gang robbed trains, banks, and hid in the dense underbrush of the surrounding hills; moonshiners and bootleggers routinely conducted their operations. One display panel had an ominous warning: "Stay Away—Strangers aren't safe in Osage County."

*The Guardianship System:* With the increased discovery and development of oil and gas production, the Osage tribe was suddenly wealthy; they built new homes, bought expensive cars, fur coats, and diamond rings. As their spending habits became more extravagant, local residents labeled the Indians as lazy and incompetent.

Under a 1912 federal amendment, state courts became responsible for appointing guardians, who controlled all land transactions, collected income, distributed payments and received a fee for each transaction. Dozens of attorneys opened offices at Pawhuska to process competency papers and request legal guardianships. These actions resulted in a system of widespread corruption. By 1924, guardianships were a mainstay of the Osage county bar, the economy and a political patronage system.

The exhibit details identified an important clue about Fred John's hospitalization. When admitted to the Mercy Hospital for the Insane, Fred John Cooper was mis-identified as Mixed Race (presumably because he lived in Fairfax, an Osage Indian area) and was assigned a guardian.

At the Osage County District Court, there were nine docket pages of transactions, with fifty items per page. In other words, Fred's guardian filed reports on a steady basis and received a fee each time. The fees were his incentive to keep Fred John Cooper hospitalized.

# The Hale Gang

Thursday morning. A loud crack of thunder rattled the windows. Ellen had over-slept, but it didn't matter because there weren't any meetings scheduled. She watched the local news, then grabbed her umbrella and walked to the motel lobby. Placing a quarter in the slot, she retrieved *The Oklahoman,* found a table and ordered breakfast.

Returning to her room, Ellen placed her notes and a stack of articles on a side table, then turned on the lamp above the upholstered chair and began reading about the *Reign of Terror.*

*William K. Hale:* From Fairfax, Osage County, Oklahoma, this self-proclaimed "King of the Osage Hills," was arrested as the organizer behind plots to murder twenty-four Osage Indians.

*Federal Authorities Intervened:* Alarmed at the rising number of deaths since 1921, the Osage Tribal Council and president of the Fairfax, Oklahoma Chamber of Commerce sent a letter to federal authorities in March 1923; they in turn forwarded it to the Federal Bureau of Investigation. At first it was difficult to find anyone who would testify against Hale. People living in

Osage County, and particularly those who lived near Fairfax, wouldn't talk about anything related to the murders. Many people, both Indian and white, abandoned their farms and moved. They were afraid.

Several suspected murderers bragged to the FBI—they personally knew every prominent and wealthy man in the area, all the judges, officers, officials, the sheriff and attorney of Osage County—all could be bought. They never expected to be convicted. During their investigation, agents found that witnesses testifying before federal, state and county courts had been bribed, and the state attorney general and the county attorney refused to comply with orders from a District Judge. Osage County, Oklahoma was completely corrupt.

*Federal Prison:* A last act of violence occurred on December 6, 1926 when Luther Bishop, the FBI agent who cracked the case, was murdered at his home in Oklahoma City. Between June 1926 and November 1929, William K. Hale and two accomplices were tried in the state and federal courts. National newspaper and magazine coverage chronicled the trials, deadlocked juries, appeals and overturned verdicts. Ultimately, all received life sentences in federal prison.

The astonishing accounts of mayhem and violence explained why Fred John Cooper was afraid. He lived in an area where murders occurred regularly.

The articles implied there might be verifiable connections between the Hale Gang, the asylum records and the Cooper deed transactions. To confirm that possibility, Ellen cross-checked names and dates, then added detailed notes to her file:

According to the deed records, the Cooper land transactions occurred in September 1914, November 1919, January-February 1927, February-May 1932 and May 1935. Every name on each transaction was checked. There wasn't any direct evidence showing names on the Kupper or Cooper deed records matched names associated with the Hale Gang.

The relevant dates of hospitalization at the Mercy Hospital for the Insane were June-October 1929, April-July 1932, and August 1932. One article indicated FBI agents found evidence of William Hale's verbal influence on the appointment of guardians and that he had conspired with guardians to swindle land from a hospitalized alcoholic patient. A comparison of the *Reign of Terror* gang members and the Insane Asylum staff didn't find any written evidence of William Hale being involved with their decisions.

*Conclusion:* There wasn't any factual evidence that linked the Hale Gang to the Cooper deeds or the hospitalization of Fred John Cooper.

Ellen added a title page, *Reference #7 – Oklahoma Evidence,* then stapled it to the articles and her notes about the guardianship system.

She glanced at her watch; it was one o'clock. She didn't want to drive around looking for a restaurant, so instead walked over to the motel restaurant to have a late lunch.

Returning to her room, the last few days of hectic research caught up with her. Waking from a two-hour nap, Ellen found the best of intentions had vanished with the afternoon sun—she hadn't written the first draft of the Research Summary. Turning on the television, she watched the news, splurged on room service for a last night in Oklahoma and packed her suitcase.

Tomorrow, she was going home to San Francisco. On Monday, she planned to visit the Multiregional Family History Center in Oakland to read the latest village microfilms. With all of her research completed, she could then organize her files and identify conclusions for the first report.

# An Itinerant Family 1875-1882

For the past three days, Ellen had visited the Multiregional Family History Center to read and print baptism and confirmation details from each village microfilm. This morning, she worked in her basement office.

Yesterday, a volunteer at the Family History Center helped her find an address for *St. Johannes Kirche* in *Altenkirchen*. First, she typed a letter to *Pfarrer* Dietrich Kraus, asking him to talk with older members of the congregation to see if they knew how to locate a descendant of Katherina Regina Klein Ziegler.

Next, she sorted the records according to year of baptism and interleaved the confirmation documents into the entire stack to confirm Oklahoma family memories and verify the possibility that Fred Kupper might've been their baptism sponsor. While reading the pages, she developed a chronology.

> *January 1864:* Katherina Regina, baptized at *St. Marien Kirche, Martinshofen.* Her mother later married Johann Reinhard Klein.

*September 1866:* Maria Magdalena, baptized at *St. Burkhardt Kirche, Heideland.*

*July 1868-January 1875: St. Burkhardt Kirche, Heideland.* Friedrich Johann baptized July 1868.

Other baptisms at *St. Burkhardt Kirche* were: Johann George (July 1870), George Heinrich (August 1872), and Michael (January 1875). Friedrich Kupper, *ledig. und Bauer von Brellohe*, was a sponsor for Johann, George and Michael.

*October 1876-1877:* Friedrich Leonhard born October 1876; died November 1876. Rosina Magdalena (Lena) baptized October 1877 at *Evangelisch Stadt Kirche, Hohenberg.* One of her sponsors was Friedrich Kupper, *ledig. von Brellohe.*

*February 1880:* Rosina Carolina baptized February 1880, *St. Andreas Kirche, Weißenfels.* One of her sponsors was Friedrich Kupper, *ledig. von Brellohe.*

*April 1880:* Maria Magdalena confirmed at *St. Andreas Kirche, Weißenfels.*

*April 1882:* Friedrich Johann, confirmed at *St. Joseph Kirche, Dorflingen.*

*August 1883-1897:* Rosina Margareta, baptized August 1883, *St. Johannes Kirche, Altenkirchen*. One of her sponsors was <u>Friedrich Kupper, *ledig. von Brellohe*</u>.

The older children were confirmed at *St. Johannes Kirche, Altenkirchen* between 1884 and 1897.

This review found that Friedrich Kupper was a baptism sponsor for John, George, Michael, Lena, Rosina Carolina and Rosina Margareta. During the years of 1870-1883, he travelled from *Brellohe* to *Heideland, Hohenberg, Weißenfels* and *Altenkirchen* to witness these important events.

Friedrich Kupper was *ledig.* (single) and he was a *Bauer* (farmer). He became a baptism sponsor at age sixteen and continued as a sponsor for the Klein family until he was twenty-nine years old.

The baptism and confirmation pages also gave important evidence about the Klein family. Even though they moved often, their children were always baptized and confirmed.

Reinhard could have left his hometown of *Südbruch* in order to open a Mill. When it failed, they had to move. However, a failure didn't explain why the Klein family continuously moved from one village to the next. Between 1875 and 1882, they were a restless, itinerant family.

More questions—more mysteries: Why did Reinhard Klein wander to different villages for seven years? Baptism sponsors were usually the siblings of the parents; how was Friedrich Kupper related to them?

With this comparison work finished, Ellen added the new details to the Family Group Sheets, filed everything and went upstairs to check the mail. On doing so, she found a surprising letter from the San Francisco Police Department.

She read it twice—and picked up the phone to schedule a Friday afternoon meeting with George Smoot.

# Research Summary I
## The Cooper Estate

Presented by:

Ellen O'Donnell

May 2, 1986

*Assignment:* IV. a) i): To identify actions by the Hale Gang which resulted in the unjustified confinement of my brother Fred John Cooper in the Mercy Hospital for the Insane and discover why the Oklahoma Bureau of Indian Affairs took away his land. These events destroyed his reputation.

*Sources:* On April 14-17, 1986 I completed research at the Mercy Hospital for the Insane, the Osage County Courthouse and the Oklahoma Historical Society; see deed attachments.

*Summary:* The Hale Gang activities were widely published. Nevertheless, Helen apparently felt it was important to publicly reveal the emotional impact of these events on her family.

Fred John blamed the Hale Gang for the loss of two hundred acres; I didn't find any written evidence of their involvement. However, he was assigned a guardian—a decision which may have been verbally influenced by William Hale according to local FBI investigations. This fact would indirectly support Fred's opinion that his hospitalization was a "frame-up."

His placement in the Mercy Hospital for the Insane caused a series of triggering events. On entering the asylum, Fred John lost his income and wasn't able to meet mortgage obligations. His failure to make payments resulted in foreclosure by the United States Marshall for the United States District Court for the Northern District of Oklahoma on behalf of an Osage Indian Allottee. Although Fred John Cooper and his sister Helen believed otherwise, this action was legitimate.

Following is a chronological account of relevant details:

*February 15, 1927*    Fred J. Cooper, age 28, mortgaged 160 acres from an Osage Indian Allottee.

*February 10, 1929*    Fred J. Cooper did not meet the scheduled annual mortgage payment.

*June 4, 1929*    On the recommendation of a guardian from Fairfax, Oklahoma, Fred John Cooper was admitted to the Mercy Hospital for the Insane. His case file stated that he was having trouble with neighbors and was confined in jail because of hallucinations. Because of his past behavior and his demeanor since being jailed, his diagnosis was Dementia praecox (schizophrenia).

*June 28, 1929*    A court hearing re-assigned Allottee mortgages to the Superintendent of the Osage Indian Agency.

*August 13, 1929*    The first guardianship report was filed at Pawhuska, Osage County, OK.

| | |
|---|---|
| *October 4, 1929* | Fred Cooper was interviewed at the asylum. The staff found he had other delusions, i.e., "he thinks this is a frame-up." They continued the same diagnosis. |
| *October 29, 1929* | Black Tuesday. The stock market crashed. |
| *April 22, 1931* | *Oklahoma House Bill No. 64* passed. Residents of an insane asylum could be released if they voluntarily agreed to be sterilized. Although potentially relevant to Fred John Cooper's hospitalization, his guardianship records were not available for review. |
| *1931* | No rain, the crops died. A blizzard of red dust from the over-plowed and over-grazed land created a drought that affected everyone. |
| *April 12, 1932* | Fred Cooper was interviewed again. His mental condition was much the same, he looked well physically; he had a good memory of the people and property in his community, was quiet and pleasant. The patient said his trouble began in 1925 when the Hale gang wanted to take over his farm. Staff agreed the diagnosis of Dementia praecox was correct. They felt it was self-evident that he was dangerous to be at large and should be held under the closest supervision at all times. Continued residence was recommended. |
| *May 2, 1932* | Fred J. Cooper sold the mortgaged land to his mother, Mary Cooper. |
| *May 16, 1932* | Mary Cooper mortgaged the same property for cash. |

187

| | |
|---|---|
| *July 13, 1932* | Fred John Cooper was unexpectedly released for a hearing by the District Court at Pawhuska, Osage County, Oklahoma. The details of this hearing were not available. |
| *August 30, 1932* | Guardianship records were closed. |
| *April 14, 1934* | Black Sunday. The worst storm of the Dust Bowl. |
| *May 18, 1935* | The United States District Court for the Northern District of Oklahoma filed suit against Fred J. Kupper, Fred J. Cooper, Jr., Mary Cooper, et al, for foreclosure of the mortgage on behalf of an Osage Indian Allottee. All of them had failed to meet mortgage payments. |

*1935:* Mary Cooper and her son Fred John Cooper moved to San Francisco, California. He became a responsible and reliable employee of the Southern Pacific Railroad Company in October 1936 and retired with a pension thirty-years later, in October 1966.

*Conclusion:* Although the past continued to haunt him, Fred John Cooper's employment history demonstrates that earlier records were not valid. In Oklahoma, extensive docket entries suggest Fred John was a victim of the guardianship system. In California, his steadfast work record proved the insane asylum diagnosis of Dementia praecox (schizophrenia) was not accurate.

# The Oklahoma Analysis

Friday, May 2. Ellen glanced out the bedroom windows; a light rain was hitting the panes. Looking at the alarm clock, she rolled over and went back to sleep.

Two hours later, Ellen dressed for the day, ate breakfast and read the *San Francisco Chronicle*. Next, as preparation for her meeting with the attorney, she reviewed Research Summary I, details about Mercy Hospital for the Insane, the Guardianship System of Osage County, Oklahoma and the Hale Gang. After lunch, she drove downtown and found an empty parking spot, then took the elevator to the fourteenth floor office of Lardner, Alexander and Smoot.

∞∞∞∞

"Hello," said George. "Let's sit here by the window and watch it rain while we talk about your trip to Nebraska and Oklahoma."

"Thanks," she replied, and joined him at the small conference table.

"It turned out to be a worthwhile trip. I found some fascinating information in the Nebraska divorce records and will include those details in the family history report. For Oklahoma, I've itemized the main points in Research Summary I, included additional references and prepared an invoice," she said, and gave him the documents.

George carefully studied everything. Looking up, he said, "The details about the Mercy Hospital for the Insane, courthouse records and the guardianship system are very perceptive. And, the information you discovered about the Hale Gang murders is fascinating. What can you tell me from reading between-the-lines?"

"It's all very interesting," replied Ellen. "*Item One* suggests that Helen identified with her brother's traumatic experiences in Oklahoma and blamed others for the foreclosure of his land. The facts give a different picture. Fred John lost his land for a legitimate reason.

"In reality, several things occurred. First, there were the circumstances of time and place. The Coopers lived in a violent area of the state. For instance, I found land swindles were a somewhat routine practice and the Hale Gang murdered Indians to gain access to their oil royalties. Fred and Mary Cooper didn't have much money, so they bought land in a less expensive area. Unfortunately, lawlessness and corruption flourished in the oil field boom towns of Fairfax and Pawhuska. The trade-off for low prices was living in a high risk environment.

"To their credit, the Coopers bought their land in 1914 and paid it off by 1926. The problems began when they sold it to their son, Fred John. He refinanced the paid-off property with a new mortgage from an Osage Indian Allottee."

"Re-financing is usually not a good decision," commented George.

"This is where we have to read between-the-lines," said Ellen. "Fred John apparently had a somewhat belligerent and demanding personality; his neighbors retaliated by calling the sheriff. He was placed in jail and classified as a person of Mixed Race.

"He was then assigned to a guardian, who transferred him to the insane asylum. The guardian collected fees as long as Fred John was hospitalized. This incentive ensured that Fred John remained in the insane asylum.

"After being hospitalized, Fred John didn't have any source of income, couldn't pay the mortgage and signed the deed over to his mother. Marie re-mortgaged the land for cash instead of making payments to an Indian Allottee. Her decision is difficult to understand—perhaps she felt it was her only option to raise money for attorney fees.

"According to the records, Fred John left the asylum two months later. Undoubtedly, their intent was to have Fred released so he could begin farming again and use the income to repay the note.

"But, the Dust Bowl interfered with their plans. There wasn't any income to make any payments. Three years later, they lost the land at a foreclosure auction."

"It would've been a final devastating event for the family," said Ellen.

Studying the Summary Report again, George said, "It looks like the details concerning his guardianship records couldn't be confirmed; that is unfortunate, since the unknown information also becomes a legacy. I suppose some answers are not available fifty years later."

"Yes, it's been a little frustrating," said Ellen.

"The good news is the family made a decision. They escaped from an environment where they were trapped by circumstances beyond their control. Mary Cooper and her son Fred John went to San Francisco after the foreclosure.

"They made the best choice. For the next thirty years, Fred John was a reliable employee and proved the Oklahoma asylum diagnosis was completely wrong. He worked at the railroad, handled the daily events of life and made sure his mother received nursing home care. By all outward indications, he was fine.

"On the other hand, Helen apparently believed her brother was emotionally stuck in the past, endlessly replaying those stressful events. His traumatic experiences are likely the reason why Helen included the *Item One* clause in her will."

"An astute observation," commented George. "You've given us an excellent analysis of the Cooper family situation. I've made some notes on your comments and will place them in the file.

"What's next on your agenda?"

"I'm afraid I must give you some disappointing news. I received a letter from my old employer, the San Francisco Police Department. They're short-staffed in several positions because of attrition or maternity leave.

"When retiring, I agreed to return on a temporary basis if needed, so I should try to honor their request. The Department has asked me to begin next week and work until Labor Day."

"This is an unexpected turn of events," replied George, as he considered how to handle her request.

"Tell me," he said, "how far along is the research project?"

"The unfinished research is related to *Item Two*. I have some good leads on being able to answer Helen's question about family history, but I'll need to go to Germany to find definite answers. Last week, I sent a letter to the pastor in *Altenkirchen* and to the *Landesarchive Baden-Württemberg* asking for a referral. I'm hoping a local guide can take me to the villages where the Klein family lived."

"Sounds like a good plan," replied George.

"Will that finish the assignment?"

"Not completely. It would be helpful to spend a few days of research in New York City. I'd like to identify where Marie lived and worked from 1888 to 1892. This was probably a very formative time period in her life and it may have influenced her later decisions.

"Altogether, I estimate three days in New York City and one week in Germany to get everything wrapped up. Then, it'll take about a week to write a report. I can have a final summary completed in October."

Listening carefully, George mulled over how the delay would impact a final review and acceptance by the San Francisco Heritage Association. A few minutes later, he made a decision.

"You've made very good progress throughout this assignment and the reasons for the extended travel make sense," replied George. "Go ahead and help the Police Department. I'll approve your travel plans for visiting New York City and Germany.

He continued, "This summer I'll be in Boston because we're opening a new branch office and I need to manage all the arrangements. I'm not returning to San Francisco until September anyway, so everything for the Cooper Estate project can wait until October. I'll tell my partners and John Hawthorne about the schedule change."

"Thank you," replied Ellen. "I appreciate your understanding of the situation."

Relieved to have these details taken care of, Ellen put away her notes. They shook hands, George then escorted her to the elevator and she returned to Noe Valley.

On arriving home, Ellen placed her briefcase in the basement office and then called the travel agency. She asked the agent to make arrangements for September flights, a rental car, an international driver permit and lodging in New York City and Germany.

Next, Ellen called her boss at the San Francisco Police Department and said, "I'll be there on Monday."

Glancing at the clock, she decided it was time to quit for the week. Ellen went upstairs to have a glass of wine and celebrate. A major requirement of the Cooper bequest had been completed.

# *NEW YORK CITY*

# Castle Garden Clues

Tuesday, September 9, New York City. Ellen was sleeping soundly when the telephone rang. At first disoriented, she then remembered—her temporary assignment ended last week.

Yesterday, between the early check-in at the San Francisco International Airport and the five hour flight, it had been a very long day. On arrival, she took a tax to the Stonehurst Guest House, dropped off her luggage, and then went to Macy's for late-afternoon shopping.

Becoming side-tracked by all the choices, she didn't leave until seven o'clock. By that time, the throngs of workers emerging from the subway had slowed down a bit, but the sidewalks were jam-packed with singles, couples and families who were shopping or looking for restaurants. Threading her way through the crowds, she soon found a cozy café and ordered Pasta Primavera, Caesar Salad, a glass of Merlot and New York Cheesecake for dessert.

After dinner, she hailed a cab, went directly to her room at the Stonehurst, watched the late evening news and fell asleep.

This morning, by the time she arrived in the dining room for breakfast, the other guests had already assembled. They included a young couple from Paris, France, a recently retired couple from Canada, a university professor from Boston and a middle-aged couple from Kansas City. Ellen helped herself to coffee from the sidebar, chose a selection of gourmet breakfast items from the extensive buffet, then sat down and listened in on the conversation.

When the hostess asked Ellen to present herself, she replied, "I'm a genealogist and this is my first visit to New York City. A San Francisco family asked me to find information about their mother who emigrated from Germany to New York City in 1888. Today, I'm visiting the immigration history display at The New-York Historical Society."

"I've heard it's a very good exhibition," said the professor.

"Our interest is the Statue of Liberty, so that's our destination," the young woman added.

The group visited for a few more minutes before leaving. Ellen returned to her room to get a jacket, her handbag and a small journal and then asked the hostess to call a taxi.

∞∞∞∞

At Seventy-Seventh Street and Central Park West, she recognized an impressive Beaux-Arts façade, including Ionic columns and a massive classical pediment over the main entrance door. On entering The New-York Historical Society, she paid the admission fee, studied the brochure for directions on where to begin, then walked through the immigration history exhibit and noted comments in her journal:

*Introduction*: Located in Battery Park, near the tip of Manhattan, Castle Garden operated as an immigrant processing center from August 3, 1855 to April 18, 1890.

*The Statue of Liberty*: The immigration experience achieved legendary status as new arrivals wrote home to describe their impressions of the Statue of Liberty, the bureaucratic procedures at Castle Garden and their first glimpse of Manhattan.

*Arriving at Castle Garden:* After a long sea voyage, immigrants completed medical inspections while onboard the ship. Next, their ship sailed into the harbor, anchoring near the Battery. Passengers hurried to barges, ferries or steamer tugs which delivered them to the pier at Castle Garden; it was a massive two-story round brick structure with additional wings for the Labor Exchange and the Ward's Island Department, who detained destitute or sick emigrants. New York City policemen were standing nearby to keep order and protect immigrants from being molested, swindled or robbed.

*Admission*: On arrival, luggage went one direction while passengers were sent in another direction. Throngs of men, women and children waited in a large Hall to be interviewed by a Registry Clerk, who recorded their names, nationality, previous address and destination. If questions occurred, a male clerk known as an Interpreter, helped them.

*Emigrant Aid Societies*: Women were only allowed to leave Castle Garden if they were married, had a male escort who was a relative, or were sponsored by a missionary from one of the Emigrant Aid Societies. Located on State Street, only a short distance from Castle Garden, these social service agencies offered temporary lodging, translation and letter-writing services, assistance with railroad tickets and helped new immigrants find employment. One of the agencies was the *Lutherisch Emigrantenhaus Association*.

*Next Steps*: Female immigrants who planned to remain in New York City waited for a male escort to take them to a local destination. Other immigrants took a ferry to New Jersey and bought railroad tickets for the remainder of their journey.

Two hours later, Ellen had absorbed all of the events that Marie Klein would have encountered. She strolled across the hall to the Café and ordered a sandwich, chips and tea.

While waiting for lunch to arrive, she jotted notes in her journal: In October 1888, Marie Klein arrived at Castle Garden in New York City. Missionaries from the *Lutherisch Emigrantenhaus Association* met new arrivals. Marie wasn't employed at Castle Garden; Interpreter and Translator positions at this immigration depot were only held by men.

∞∞∞∞

Walking outside, it was a pleasant fall day and perfect weather for a Statue of Liberty tour. She caught a cab to the ticket office.

Taking the ferry across the Harbor, Ellen was awestruck by the powerful magnetism of the magnificent statue; everyone paused in reverent silence. She completed the guided tour, kept the brochure for future reference and walked around the perimeter to view the harbor.

Afterwards, she rushed to catch the last boat to Manhattan and stood at the railing among a packed crowd of other tourists. As the ferry chugged along, Ellen quietly watched a familiar skyline and thought of Marie. She would have experienced a similar skyline, being simultaneously thrilled and overwhelmed by an environment that was completely different from her home in *Mittelberg*.

∞∞∞∞∞

When the boat docked in Manhattan, Ellen walked up the hill to State Street, hailed a cab to the Stonehurst and found a lively evening reception in progress. An hour later, the couple from Kansas City, the professor from Boston and Ellen continued their animated conversation at a near-by restaurant. Over an excellent steak dinner and several glasses of wine, she learned of another research event. The professor mentioned he was giving a lecture at the quarterly meeting of the YWCA.

"What is your topic?" asked Ellen.

"My specialty happens to be New York City in the nineteenth and early twentieth century. They've asked me to talk about the German immigrants who lived in the *Kleindeutschland* tenements," he replied.

"Marvelous! Thursday is my last day in New York and I'd love to attend your lecture."

"I presumed you might be interested," he said. "I'll check with the director of the YWCA and ask if you may attend as a special guest."

"Thank you. I'm going to The New York Public Library tomorrow to look for the city directory address of my young lady. She could have lived in those tenements."

Everyone returned to the Stonehurst and said "good-night." Ellen retrieved her journal and added a note about the YWCA lecture meeting. Serendipity had struck again.

# The New York Public Library

Wednesday morning. Ellen had tossed and turned all night, dreaming about unanswered questions. On waking, she resolved to set her mind at ease by creating a timeline for the years when Marie Klein lived in New York City:

| | |
|---|---|
| *October 1888* | Marie arrived; she emigrated from *Antwerp* on the *SS Vaterland.* |
| *Unknown* | The Adams County, Oklahoma History article said Marie worked as a Translator but it didn't give any dates or the name of her employer. |
| *July 1889* | Her brother, George, arrived; he met with Marie and received money for a railroad ticket to Nebraska. |
| *1891* | Her brothers, Fred and John, arrived and met with Marie. She gave them money for railroad tickets to Nebraska. |
| *1892* | Her sister Lena arrived; she continued on to Nebraska. Marie married in Nebraska in June 1892. |

Using these details, Ellen listed her goals for the day: Look for census and 1888-1892 city directories. Search the archives catalog to locate information about the *Lutherisch Emigrantenhaus Association.*

She then dressed, placed the notes in her briefcase and left it in the foyer. Entering the dining room, she chose several items from the buffet and hurriedly ate breakfast while the other guests were leaving for their excursions. She then asked the hostess to call a taxi.

∞∞∞

Twenty minutes later, Ellen walked up the steps of The New York Public Library. Located at Fifth Avenue and Forty-Second Street, the two famous Lion sculptures "Patience" and "Fortitude" stood guard on either side of the main entrance to the attractive Beaux-Arts building.

Walking through the portico into the lobby, she followed the signs and entered the Public Catalog Room. Other genealogists had told her the Library resources were incredible—*The Stacks* included ninety miles of books and archival documents in eight levels of underground storage.

Ellen signed the register, stored her belongings in the Check Room and then searched the Card Catalog for census records and New York City Directories.

She would've liked to review the 1890 federal census, but it was destroyed by fire in 1921. An 1890 Veterans Census was a substitute, but this record wasn't relevant. A New York Police Census of hospitals, orphanages and prisons didn't fit her criteria either. On the other hand, an *1892 New York State Census* was available on microfilm. Ellen copied details to submit a call slip at the Microforms Division, Room 100.

She then searched for a City Directory reference. An *1890 New York City Directory* and *1891 Trow's City Directory* were available; these citations were added to her list.

In Room 100, she turned in a call slip for the *1892 New York State Census*. On receiving it, Ellen threaded the microfilm, made focus and lighting adjustments, then took notes:

> *1892 New York State census (as of February 16, 1892):* This census only listed names by Ward; it did not include any street addresses. There weren't any entries for a Mary, Marie or Maria Klein, Kleen, Klien or Kline. There was a Mary Klein, born 1862 Germany, and three other individuals named Mary Klein, born in 1865, 1868 and 1870; all were born in the United States.

The 1892 census was a dead-end. None of the details were relevant to her criteria. However, all the citations hadn't been exhausted yet.

She returned the film to the reference desk, then located the Milstein Division in Room 121 and submitted two call slips for the *New York State City Directories*. About twenty minutes later, the books were delivered and Ellen began searching for clues about Marie Klein.

> *1890 New York City Directory (May 1889-1890):* There were 257 Klein entries, but no Mary, Marie or Maria. There were 14 Kleen entries, 10 Klien entries and 7 Kline entries, but no Mary, Marie or Maria were found under any of these surnames.

Disappointed, she reviewed the requirements; only individuals who were a Head of Household were included in the 1890 directory. That explained why a single person, renting a room or apartment, wasn't listed in the City Directory.

The next microfilm was threaded onto the machine:

> *1891 Trow's City Directory (May 1890-1891):* Under the Klein, Kleen, Klien and Kline names, there wasn't anyone named Mary, Marie or Maria.

After searching three hours, there wasn't any street address information for Mary, Marie or Maria Klein, born 1866, living in New York City. Although discouraged by this conclusion, collateral information might offer more clues.

Ellen delivered the City Directories to the reference desk in Room 121, then returned to the Public Catalog Room and checked the card files again. She found an archival reference card titled *Emigrantenhaus / Emigration Assistance* and turned in a call slip; it would take about forty minutes to locate the materials.

∞∞∞∞

Placing her research notes inside the briefcase at the Check Room, she picked up her handbag, then walked around the hallways until finding the food kiosks and dropped in some coins; a sandwich, chips and drink fell into the take-out slot. Walking outside, she spied an empty bench, sat down to have lunch, enjoyed the sunshine, and watched people strolling, skating, shuffling or rushing to a destination.

An hour later, Ellen stopped at the Check Room to store her handbag and retrieve previous notes. She then picked up the new research file and walked to a nearby table. The folder included an 1883 article of instructions titled *Emigration to America,* an Emigrant Missionary Card, and several pages describing the *Lutherisch Emigranten Mission.* Several details were relevant:

*Assistance for emigrants*: Aid was given at many of the shipping ports in Germany. Special communion services were often held on the night before emigrants left Germany; sermons offered advice, warnings and farewell messages to everyone who was departing from their homeland. Local congregations in Germany often gave their members a *Kirchenpass* to help them join a new parish; they also provided addresses of Lutheran pastors in America.

*Immigrant aid societies*: These agencies helped foreigners become settled in their new home. Most often associated with religious organizations, they provided temporary lodging, employment referrals, and directions to organizations that provided English language classes or emergency cash.

*New York City*: The *Lutheran Almanac* recommended contacting Pastor Keyl, a missionary, who could be found in the debarkation building at Castle Garden; he met every ship. New arrivals were strongly advised to visit *Das Deutsche Emigrantenhaus* to find low-cost lodging and employment.

*Emigrant Missionary Card:* A card identifying Pastor S. Keyl, *evangelisch lutherischer Emigranten Missionar* in New York, was also in the file. The card announced that German immigrants would receive every kind of advice and support, at no cost. Instructions indicated the emigrant should wear the card in their hat or on their coat. The missionary would then take the new arrival to a lodging place.

A review of other *Lutherisch Emigrantenhaus* records found more information. Under the management of Rev. Stephanus Keyl, this organization provided lodging, advice and assistance for German Lutheran immigrants:

> The *Lutherisch Emigranten Mission* sponsored a boarding house, named *Lutherisch Pilgerhaus*, at No. 8 State Street, New York City. The letterhead of the *Emigranten Mission* included a drawing of the *Lutherisch Pilgerhaus* building. Its mission was to assist German Lutheran immigrants in their spiritual and secular requirements, with all information and advice given free of charge. *Pilgerhaus* charged 25 cents per night for lodging and 25 cents per meal, although those who were destitute were not required to pay. The boarding house had five floors, with twenty-three rooms for couples or families and one room for unmarried women.

Finally! After many hours at The New York Public Library, clues about Marie's life in New York City had been discovered. She returned the file, retrieved her handbag, walked outside and hailed a cab.

∞∞∞∞∞

At the Stonehurst, Ellen dropped off her briefcase in her room, then returned to the foyer, picked up a glass of wine from the tray and joined the professor and young couple from France. The young woman was describing their visit to the Statue of Liberty and the reason for their interest; her great-great-grandfather was one of the workers who helped Auguste Bartholdi construct the statue, although they didn't know what happened to him when Lady Liberty was completed. It was a fascinating family story.

An hour later, they walked to a local restaurant, debated about what to order, then agreed on two bottles of fine Italian wine and ordering a large salad to pass around the table along with individual orders of an Italian specialty so they could each sample other selections.

While waiting for the food to arrive, the professor leaned over and said, "I'm glad to see you again so we can talk about the YWCA meeting tomorrow."

"Yes," Ellen replied, "I've been wondering how things turned out."

"I talked with the Director this afternoon and she'd be delighted to have you attend. If we catch a taxi around eleven o'clock, we'll arrive early enough to visit with the other guests. The Y has also arranged for a bus tour of *Kleindeutschland* after the luncheon. I hope you'll be able to attend."

"I'll plan on it. I'm looking forward to hearing your lecture and will be in the foyer at eleven o'clock."

"Good. How was your day at The New York Public Library?"

"Unfortunately, I wasn't able to locate a specific address for my young lady. However, I did learn about the *Emigrantenhaus Mission.* One of their missionaries, Rev. Stephanus Keyl, met German Lutheran emigrants at Castle Garden and helped them find employment or make further travel plans. It seems logical my young lady would've had contact with this organization."

The young woman from Paris listened to Ellen's reply. "That sounds like an interesting and relevant piece of information," she said. "Was it a surprise?"

"Yes," replied Ellen, "but, you never know what turns up until you start digging—sometimes you hit a goldmine and sometimes you find only one part of the puzzle."

Before leaving the restaurant, everyone exchanged business cards and all encouraged each other to get in touch if travelling to San Francisco, Boston or Paris. The new friends returned to the Stonehurst together, said "good-night" and each returned to their room.

# A *Kleindeutschland* Tour

On Thursday morning, Ellen dressed and walked over to the dining room to have breakfast. Since the professor from Boston hadn't arrived yet, she sat next to the guests from Kansas City and Canada. They were exchanging opinions about the sites they visited yesterday. The Kansas City couple had seen John Lennon's Strawberry Fields Memorial in Central Park and walked through the park to the Museum of Modern Art, while the Canadian couple had explored Greenwich Village, Little Italy and China Town.

The conversation turned to looking at brochures and deciding which theatre production to attend that evening. Ellen listened a few minutes and said, "I've been eaves-dropping on your conversation—I don't have any plans for the evening—could I tag along?"

"No problem," replied the woman from Canada. "We're going to ask the hostess how to order tickets and you can talk to her also." Before long everyone had finished their breakfast, chosen a theatre performance and bought their tickets.

Ellen returned to her room and re-organized her briefcase so everything was in the proper file. At eleven o'clock, she placed a small journal in her handbag and met the professor in the lobby.

213

At the YWCA, he introduced her to the Director, who in turn presented both of them to other members of the Board, donors and special guests. After some polite chit-chat, everyone looked for their assigned seats and sat down for the elegantly catered lunch.

While dessert was being served, the Director introduced Dr. Thomas Cunningham. He illustrated his lecture with photographs by Jacob Riis and paintings by The Ash Can School, a group of artists that painted scenes of the tenement neighborhoods. Ellen quietly jotted notes:

*History*: *Württemberg* immigrants lived in Ward Seventeen.

*Architecture*: The *Kleindeutschland* district included rows of four-to-six-story brick tenements where nearly every building resembled its neighbor. The rented space included basement level workshops, street-level retail shops with merchandise being sold underneath a sidewalk awning, and upper level apartments. Schools, churches and synagogues were built by prominent German-American architects.

*Immigrants:* By 1890, the area had nearly 40,000 residents. Most immigrants were educated or skilled craftsmen. The *Weisse Garten* area included beer gardens, libraries, shooting clubs, German theatres, schools, churches and synagogues.

*Social Services:* In 1888, the YWHA (Young Women's Hebrew Association) offered classes to newly arrived immigrants and taught them about American customs. Non-Jews were also welcome. The YWHA was the forerunner of the YWCA.

With this link to the YWCA, the professor concluded his lecture. He also asked everyone to join a private bus tour of the tenement district.

Ellen walked to the front of the room, found the YWCA Director and thanked her for being able to attend their quarterly program, then went outside to board the bus. A few minutes later, the driver chauffeured the group through Orchard Street and Hester Street while Professor Cunningham talked about the typical crowded living conditions. Ellen began reading the handout while he identified various features of the tenement district:

*Boundaries:* During the 1890s, the *Kleindeutschland* boundaries were Broadway on the west, the East River, Fourteenth Street on the north, and Grand Street on the south. This area was later known as the Lower East Side.

*Crowded Tenement Conditions:*
• The dirt streets were muddy when it rained or snowed.
• Owners were not required to meet any regulations.
• No privacy or security. The entrance was never locked.
• A front parlor had the only window for fresh air.
• Interior rooms were dark or used kerosene lamps.
• A kitchen coal stove was the only source of heat.
• The two room units were known as cold water flats.
• There wasn't any running water or hot water.
• Most people washed their clothes outside, using a faucet.
• There weren't any indoor toilets.
• Laundry hanging over the balcony was a common site.
• Garbage accumulated near the front door.

*Other landmarks of Kleindeutschland were:*
YMHA Educational Alliance Settlement House
*Freie Bibliothek und Lesehalle*
*Deutsche Dispensary*
*Schützen-Gesellschaft Hall*

At each location, Professor Cunningham described the architecture, date of construction, its architect and patron. As the bus returned to the YWCA headquarters building, Professor Cunningham closed the tour by recommending the film *Hester Street* and handing out copies of the ward maps for the *Kleindeutschland* area. The maps identified districts where emigrants from various German provinces usually lived.

When the tour ended, Ellen walked over to Professor Cunningham and said, "Thank you so much for introducing me to the *Kleindeutschland* district. I suspect my young lady may have lived in the Ward Seventeen area. This map will be very useful."

"I'm glad it worked out," he replied. "I'm sorry we won't be able to meet for supper this evening. If you ever come to Boston, give me a call."

"I'll certainly do so," replied Ellen. They shook hands and each took a taxi; Professor Cunnningham went to the airport and she returned to Stonehurst.

Arriving in her room, Ellen gathered her notes about the Castle Garden exhibit, research at The New York Public Library as well as the *Kleindeutschland* information. She added a title page, *Reference #8 – New York City*, stapled it to the other pages and then filed everything.

Before leaving for the evening theatre performance and dinner, Ellen listed her itinerary for tomorrow. She planned to check-out early in the morning and buy a thank-you gift for Professor Cunningham while visiting the Museum of Modern Art. After lunch, she would return to the Stonehurst to pick up her luggage, then take a taxi to the airport and check-in at Lufthansa for her flight to Frankfurt, Germany.

# GERMANY

# St. Johannes Kirche at Altenkirchen

S unday, September 14. Germany. Ellen woke at first light, glanced out the windows at a dense thicket of trees and remembered arriving at *Hotel Schloss Dorflingen*.

Yesterday, when the Lufthansa flight reached Frankfurt, she'd exchanged dollars for *Deutsche Marks*, bought a map, picked up a Volvo from the rental agency and drove two hours. When registering at *Hotel Schloss Dorflingen*, she found there wasn't any elevator, carried her luggage, briefcase and handbag up two flights of stairs and placed everything inside the room. Returning downstairs, she ordered lunch at their Golden Ox restaurant and then spent Saturday afternoon recuperating from jet lag by taking naps and walking around the village.

A few minutes later, Ellen's recollections were interrupted by a wake-up call. She couldn't stay in bed any longer; she had to get dressed for the day, have breakfast and drive to *Altenkirchen*. Yesterday, she'd called *Pfarrer* Dietrich Kraus and confirmed her appointment to meet him at the church. Visiting *Altenkirchen* was important because the Klein family worshipped at *St. Johannes Kirche* from 1882 until 1901.

Leaving *Dorflingen*, Ellen drove across the river bridge, then followed a narrow one-lane road. It led to the village of cobblestone streets that followed a natural terrain of steep hills. Crowded together in every available space, the houses varied from one-story cottages with thatched roofs to two-story houses built in the half-timbered *Fachwerk* style. Pots of red geraniums were blooming on the window sills. Shuttered windows were decorated with white lacy curtains. *Altenkirchen* was an enchanting picture-postcard village.

Turning on *Zellerstrasse*, she parked in a tiny space, opposite the church. While walking uphill to take photos of the steeple, the bells began ringing. From behind her, two young children were laughing and racing each other down the cobblestone street. About mid-way down the hill, they scampered up the sidewalk, opened a door and went inside a two-story *Fachwerk* building. Their young parents calmly followed them down the steep hill; dressed in somber Sunday-best clothes, the mother carried a baby wrapped in a pastel blanket.

After taking a few more photos, she walked downhill; an arrow pointed north to the *Evang. Kirche St. Johannes Friedhof.* The asphalt lane climbed another steep hill. An old barn and thatched-roof houses were on the left side; a vine-covered hill was on her right side.

At the top of the hill, an arched stone entrance with several wide flagstone steps announced the main entrance of *St. Johannes Kirche*. Ellen walked under the arch and entered the cobblestone churchyard to meet *Pfarrer* Dietrich Kraus.

*"guten Morgen,"* said Ellen, shaking hands with the smiling black-robed pastor. "I'm sorry I don't know much German but I want to thank you for meeting me and being able to attend church services today."

"It is okay," replied *Pfarrer* Kraus. "I know a little English. Today is special because we're having a baptism. If you like, you may go inside the sanctuary and look at the flowers. After the service, we can look at the 1888 baptism records and meet *Frau* Schäfer. She has information about the Klein family."

*"Danke.* May I take photographs of the church interior?"

"Yes, it is okay. I'll be here, welcoming our parish members."

The bells continued ringing, calling everyone to worship. Young and old, everyone walked up the steep pathway to the church courtyard and greeted their pastor.

Ellen entered the vestibule, then walked into the main sanctuary. Established in the thirteenth century, the stone altar held an open Bible, fresh flowers and candles. Above the altar hung a gilded figure of Christ on the Cross; sunlight streamed through a single stained-glass window behind the statue. Delicate fresco paintings of religious scenes covered the surrounding walls. Katherine Marie Klein knelt before this altar when she was confirmed in 1901.

Parishioners entered the sanctuary to find their pews; dressed in black, everyone quietly said *hallo* to each other and also greeted each child. With a flourish of organ music, the service began; it included familiar hymns as well as the familiar cadence of the Lord's Prayer. During the last musical chorus, somber-faced ushers stood beside each row to allow an orderly exit from the service.

Walking outside, Ellen photographed the façade, tombstones and the flagstone wall which surrounded the church and cemetery, then walked to the eastern edge of the ancient stone wall and photographed the distant mountains.

∞∞∞∞

Near the church entrance, *Pfarrer* Kraus was talking with an older woman. He saw Ellen and they came over to greet her.

"I'd like you to meet *Frau* Schäfer," he said. "She doesn't know much English but her husband does. They'd like to invite you to their home to talk about the Klein family." Ellen shook hands with her and in turn, *Frau* Schäfer warmly greeted Ellen with a hug.

"*Ja, ja, mein Mann kann bringen Sie unsere haus,*" she said. "*Was day kommst du?*" *Pfarrer Kraus* translated. "My husband can bring you to our house. What day do you want to come?"

"Oh my, that's very nice," replied Ellen. "I'm at *Hotel Schloss Dorflingen*. I'm driving to Frankfurt on Wednesday afternoon, but I can come in the morning. Is Wednesday morning okay with you?" She looked at *Pfarrer* Kraus; he translated for *Frau* Schäfer.

"*Ja, ja, ist okay,*" she replied. "*Mein Mann können Sie auf ten o'clock.*" Ellen looked at *Pfarrer* Kraus. He asked Ellen if a ten o'clock pick up time was alright, then relayed her answer to *Frau* Schäfer.

"*Ich muss gehen. Mein namen ist Theda und mein Mann ist Heinrich. Wir vill sehen Sie am Wednesday morning,*" she said. *Pfarrer* Kraus translated. "I must go now. My name is Theda and my husband is Heinrich. We'll see you on Wednesday morning."

"*Danke,*" replied Ellen and gave *Frau* Schäfer a hug.

Ellen then turned to *Pfarrer* Kraus and asked, "I'm sorry to take so much of your time. May I look at the 1888 baptism records?"

"*Ja*, it is okay. The originals are kept at our main office because the books are very fragile. I have a copy for you." They went inside the church, entered a small side room and sat down at a table to look at the 1888 document. *Pfarrer* Kraus translated the record:

> Mother: Maria Magdalena Klein.
> Father: blank.
>
> Child's Name: Maria Katherina Klein, illegitimate, born 23 May 1888, baptized 17 June 1888, *Mittelberg*.
>
> Sponsors: Friedrich Ziegler, and his wife Katherina Regina (Klein) from *Waldberg*, and Johann Klein, *Bauer* in *Mittelberg*.

Carefully studying the copy, Ellen said "This is very interesting. Her family said the child was named Katherine Marie—this document shows Maria Katherina. She must've been named first after her mother Maria, and secondly after her grandmother, who was known as Katherina."

"Can you tell me when and where she was baptized?" asked Ellen.

"Maria Katherina was baptized twenty-five days afterwards, on June 17, 1888," replied *Pfarrer* Kraus. "It would've been unusual for a baptism to occur three weeks later. Perhaps the father's family caused a delay. The Klein family probably wanted to have the child baptized as soon as possible; most often it occurred within one week.

"The baby was baptized at home, in *Mittelberg*. Apparently, the family chose a home baptism instead of a church baptism where everyone witnessed the event."

"Fascinating," said Ellen. "It looks to me like the name of the father wasn't identified. Was this a common practice?"

"This happened about a hundred years ago, so it's hard to know the circumstances," *Pfarrer* Kraus said. "I've been told—in poor families, the midwife tried to have the young woman declare the father's name, so the child wouldn't be a welfare burden to the community. But, if the father came from an important family, his name was never recorded and the mother was often banished; she had to leave her baby. Regardless of the circumstances, the child was baptized but they often had difficulty in finding suitable marriage partners or employment when they became older; the sin of illegitimacy followed them."

"Amazing. The situation you described is likely what happened to Maria Magdalena Klein—she left *Mittelberg* after her daughter was born. Thank you so much for locating these details." said Ellen.

*Pfarrer* Kraus gave her the baptism copy and they walked outside. It was a beautiful fall day. The courtyard was empty. Everyone had left.

"You've been most helpful," said Ellen. "I know it's nearly lunchtime but you mentioned yesterday that I might be able to visit *St. Joseph Kirche* at *Dorflingen*. I'm staying at *Hotel Schloss Dorflingen*. Is the church located near the *Schloss*?"

"Yes, I'm also the *Pfarrer* for their congregation. We can meet at *St. Joseph Kirche* in *Dorflingen*."

"Great . . . I'll see you there."

∞∞∞∞∞∞

Ellen re-traced her route to *Dorflingen* and parked in the small lot next to *St. Joseph Kirche*. First, she took a few photos of the local scene. The village was surrounded by a forest; it included wide cobblestone streets and large two-story half-timbered *Fachwerk* style houses.

*St. Joseph Kirche* was constructed of white stucco with a red shingled roof. It had an impressive bell tower on the southern façade and a steep exterior staircase on the eastern façade, which faced the parking lot.

They entered a side door. This structure was smaller in size and simpler in decoration than *St. Johannes* at *Altenkirchen*; it didn't have any painted fresco scenes or stained glass. The heavily inset oval windows gave evidence of two-foot thick walls, suggesting the building may have been used as a fortress at one time.

In a small niche at the front of the sanctuary, the stone altar was covered with a lace-edged cloth where a large Bible, two candles and a flower arrangement were displayed. Immediately behind the altar, a gilded statue of Christ on the Cross, dominated the small space. On the right side of the altar, steps led to a canopied lectern decorated with paintings of religious symbols. Prominently displayed below the lectern, a stone baptism font covered by a lace cloth had its tall carved baptismal hood placed on the floor nearby; it was too heavy to lift.

Above the altar, an ornate pipe organ dominated the second level. A balcony continued around the perimeter of the sanctuary with painted scenes of the saints, all of them looking down on the pews below. Overall, the church seemed to be a retreat from worldly cares and concerns.

The *Pfarrer* stood quietly to the side while Ellen concentrated on photographing the interior. When finished, she said, "Thank you for allowing me to take photos. Instead of emphasizing decorative elements, this sanctuary seems to have an air of humility about it."

"Yes," replied *Pfarrer* Kraus. "It is a comforting space for the community. This smaller congregation couldn't afford frescoes and stained glass. The church was built in the sixteenth century when the parishioners of *Dorflingen* wanted a separate place of worship instead of crossing the river and attending services at *Altenkirchen*."

"I'm glad you've shared the history of this congregation. I wanted to visit this church because Fredrich Klein was confirmed here in April 1882. May I look at his record?" Ellen asked. "I'd like to identify his father's occupation at that particular date, since the family seemed to move around quite a bit."

"Yes, I assumed you would like to see it. I have a copy from the official *kirchenbuch* and have translated it for you."

> *Confirmation 16 April 1882:* Friedrich Johann Klein, born 25 July 1868, *Südbruch*. Parents: Johann Reinhard Klein, *Tagelöhner, Altenkirchen,* and Sophia Katherina (Kupper).

"This page indicates Reinhard was a *Tagelöhner,* that is, a day laborer," said *Pfarrer* Kraus. "The Klein family was living in *Altenkirchen.*"

"The two villages are not very far apart. Did you find this family in the *Heimatbuch*?" asked Ellen.

"No. I asked our local historian to look in the village book and he couldn't find Reinhard Klein as a resident. It probably means he didn't own property. He might have lived in *Altenkirchen* but attended church at *Dorflingen.*"

"I'm a bit disappointed but apparently there isn't any other evidence available in *Dorflingen*," said Ellen. "Thank you so much for helping me. I'd like to give you a donation for your congregation." She handed him forty *Deutsche Marks.*

"*Danke,* I'll place the money in our Mission Fund. I like history too, so I'm glad help you. If you think of other questions, please let me know."

"Yes, I'll stay in touch," she replied, and they left the church.

Ellen moved her car to the nearby *Hotel Schloss Dorflingen* parking lot, then walked into the Golden Ox, chose a table by the window and looked at the menu. When the waitress arrived, she said, "I'd like to order *Salate*, choosing *Wurstsalat, Rotkohlsalat* and *Pikanter Moehrensalat*; she also requested a basket of *Brot* and *Stille Wasser*. She enjoyed the variety of salads, the delicious bread and was glad to have a glass of water.

∞∞∞∞

Returning to her room, Ellen reviewed the brochure that she'd picked up yesterday and consulted the map. The *Schloss* at *Kirchberg an der Jagst* was presenting a late afternoon Chamber Music concert in the Great Hall. This event would give her a chance to hear a musical performance in an ancient building and return to *Dorflingen* before dark. It was a once-in-a-lifetime opportunity.

An hour later, Ellen drove through forests, then past large open fields on the Autobahn, and exited toward the medieval city of *Kirchberg an der Jagst*. Cautiously, she maneuvered through the narrow cobblestone streets, found a parking space and then entered the nearest retail store to buy a concert ticket.

Next, she followed others who were walking uphill and through the massive stone gates. The crowd followed signs pointing toward the side entrance of a castle and up three flights of marble stairs to the Great Hall. Ellen chose a seat toward the back of the room.

Looking around, it appeared to be a former ballroom; elaborate Baroque scenes enclosed by gilded frames decorated the ceiling and portraits of elegantly-dressed men and women lined the walls. While waiting for the performance to begin, she watched the crowd. The audience included college students and retired folks; all were dressed conservatively in long-sleeved blouses or shirts, skirts or slacks, sturdy wool or tweed blazer jackets and well-made walking shoes. About one hundred people from the village or near-by localities chatted with their friends and neighbors while waiting for the recital to begin.

When the concert master walked on stage, everyone clapped and waited patiently for an introduction of the young musicians and their program. They played a violin, cello, viola and the piano, featuring a selection of music from the seventeenth century by Haydn, Mozart, Beethoven and Shubert. Afterwards, the crowd gave their approval by applauding enthusiastically. The musicians played one or two more selections; then everyone began quietly leaving the room.

Ellen followed the crowd down the long hall, three flights of marble stairs, went outside to a courtyard in front of the castle, and walked downhill through the massive town gate, to re-locate the Volvo. She then drove through the cobblestone streets until reaching an exit to the Autobahn and returned to *Hotel Schloss Dorflingen*.

By six o'clock, she was ready to order dinner at the Golden Ox restaurant. "I'd like to begin with a small glass of *Schwarzriesling* wine, and order *Karamelisierte Creme von Kastanien-Suppe mit Speck Croutons*," she said. "I'll have a main course of *Wiener Kalbsschnitzel mit Preiselbeeren und Petersilienkartoffeln*. For dessert, I'd like *Nougat-Crème brûlée und hausgemachtes Eis mit Orangen-Kompott und Kaffee*. Everything was excellent; the chestnut soup was tasty, the veal with cranberries and potatoes was scrumptious and the dessert was delicious.

The dinner capped a great day of research and the concert at an ancient castle was an unexpected bonus. Returning to her room, Ellen checked her schedule. During the next two days, she would be seeing villages where the Klein and Kupper families lived.

# Visiting Klein Hometowns:
## *Südbruch* and *Heideland*

By Monday morning Ellen had become accustomed to the time lag and woke up as usual. She glanced around her room; it was similar to American motel rooms. Although the bathroom was tiny, the room included a single bed with a reading light on the wall above, a night-stand and telephone, a bureau for clothing, a television, an upholstered chair and small table for a glass of wine. The only noticeable variation was the bed linens. In Germany, they used a Duvet for the bed covering instead of blankets and a bedspread.

At eight-thirty, Ellen went downstairs to the lobby to wait for her tour guide. Before long, Ingrid Bauer walked through the lobby door. An attractive young woman with auburn hair and sparkling brown eyes, she was wearing dressy slacks, a lightweight sweater and paisley scarf. Ingrid smiled cordially and introduced herself.

"I'm glad to meet you," said Ellen. "Let's go to the restaurant for breakfast and we can talk about an itinerary for the day."

Ellen chose a table near the window overlooking the garden. The tablecloth and napkins were snow-white linen. Fresh flowers filled a small vase.

Both ordered coffee, Ellen ordered orange juice, Ingrid ordered apple juice. At the breakfast buffet, they surveyed the choices—a basket held a variety of hard rolls and fruit pastries, bowls held grapefruit slices or sliced cooked applies, platters held an assortment of cold cuts and several types of sliced cheese, or they could choose sausages, bacon or boiled eggs, and hot cereal or cold cereal. Ellen and Ingrid filled their plates and returned to their table overlooking the garden.

"This breakfast looks delicious," said Ingrid. "Thank you for asking me to help you. Please tell me about your research project."

"I'm a little astonished by all these choices," replied Ellen. As she buttered a roll and began eating, she described the Klein family project.

"I'm so glad to find a researcher who speaks English and can help me with the remaining pieces of this project. I've found quite a bit of information in the microfilmed *Kirchenbuch* records but some things are still puzzling.

"The Klein family had eleven children and lived in five locations between 1875 and 1882. Their daughter Marie left her baby in Germany. Katie was raised by her grandparents.

"I came to *Württemberg* to see where they lived, where they attended church during those years, and to understand the reasons why they moved so often. In *Martinshofen*, I'd also like to look at Kupper family records since Marie married Friedrich Kupper and the maiden name of Marie's mother was also Kupper."

Listening carefully, Ingrid replied, "I have your letter with a list of the villages you'd like to see and have contacted a local guide in each settlement. I'm assuming you would like to see the villages in chronological order?"

"Yes, that would be best. By touring each village according to the years they lived in the area, I'll be able to place everything into context according to Reinhard's occupation and the size of each community."

"Okay, my itinerary will work. This morning, we'll visit the community of *Südbruch* and *St. Burkhardt Kirche* in *Heideland*. In the afternoon, we can go to the village of *Ehrenfeld* and *St. Marien Kirche* at *Martinshofen*.

"Sounds great to me. I have my research notes and camera in my bag. We can take the Volvo to the various locations. Do you have a map?"

"*Ja, ja*, I have marked everything on a map. I'd like to drive my BMW though; I'm more familiar with driving a smaller car and we'll be going on some switch-back one lane roads through mountainous areas."

"Oh, I didn't realize," said Ellen. "Okay, I'll pay you for the petrol." After breakfast, they began the tour in Ingrid's navy BMW convertible.

∞∞∞∞∞

As she drove away from *Hotel Schloss Dorflingen*, Ingrid began telling Ellen about the rural area. "Here we are in the midst of a forest," she said. "Later we'll see more open, flat land that is suitable for farming. *Südbruch* is more of a settlement than a village. Their *hausbarn* architecture is very interesting."

As Ellen watched the countryside, she raised a question. "I'm curious. My room is at the *Hotel Schloss Dorflingen*. What does the term *Schloss* represent?"

"*Schloss* means castle," said Ingrid. "Most often a *Schloss* is named after the family who originally built it as protection over their surrounding territory. We have many small castles in this area; the most famous is *Schloss Waldberg*. It is near *Mittelberg*." Recognizing the name

*Mittelberg*, Ellen opened her handbag and quietly added a note to her research journal.

She then checked her reference page and mentioned to Ingrid, "This place is important because Johann Reinhard Klein was born here. When he married Sophia Katherina Kupper in 1866, they lived in *Südbruch* until 1875. During that time period, they had seven children."

Ingrid zipped along confidently on the one-lane road. It followed a jagged route, twisting and turning through large fields, then continued through dense forest before breaking into another area of large open fields as they reached *Südbruch*.

"This village has large *hausbarns*, but no street names or *haus* numbers," said Ingrid. "We'll be meeting a representative at the village crossroad."

A few minutes later, Ingrid saw their local guide and parked the car. Bringing along her notepad and camera, Ellen and Ingrid walked across the road to meet him.

∞∞∞∞

"*Hallo*," said Johann, as they all shook hands. "Did you want to see where Reinhard Klein lived from 1866 to 1875?"

"Yes, that's my primary interest," replied Ellen. "Did you find his house?"

"Unfortunately, no. I've talked to many people in the community and no one remembered them. Would you like to walk around and look at some of the buildings? *Südbruch* was established by only a few families. They built the large *Fachwerk hausbarns*."

"Okay, I can at least take photographs of the typical architecture," Ellen replied. As they walked down the solitary road, she observed the four-story houses were nearly as large as their attached barn. And, many of them were in poor shape.

"The area appears to be deserted," she commented. Ingrid agreed and asked Johann for an explanation.

"The original owners had many children to help them with the farm work. As time has gone by, most of the homes have been kept as family property but many of the children have moved into larger towns to find work; consequently, some of the houses were abandoned. You can tell by the size of the barns and the large surrounding fields that *Südbruch* was a prosperous farming community at one time. Unfortunately, things have changed now."

"This settlement seems to be all barns and houses; there aren't any retail shops or public buildings," Ellen said. "Where did the children go to school?"

"Everyone in *Südbruch* went to school at *Heideland*. The children walked there each day and attended school through the eighth grade. The school is about four kilometres from here."

"I have another question," said Ellen. "The Klein family lived here for about nine years and then moved to several other villages. Reinhard held *Bürgerrecht* here but not anywhere else. Did he lose these citizenship rights by moving away from his hometown?"

"*Ja*, that's true. If a person with citizenship rights left the village, he also lost his right to live there again. He wouldn't be allowed citizenship rights in any other village because he could only hold *Bürgerrecht* in his hometown. When moving to a new community, Reinhard had to demonstrate good character in the previous town, pay village fees, and have employment."

"Hmmm, that's very interesting" replied Ellen. "The records indicate the Klein family moved about every two years after leaving his hometown of *Südbruch*. Why would this happen?"

"There was probably some difficulty with his reputation. Reinhard might've had arguments with neighbors or he may have been an alcoholic whose behavior others found intolerable. It's hard to tell unless there is a public record. If the family moved often, there was a problem."

"We call it "living in a wagon," said Johann. "After a period of time, the community might have learned of previous problems or else Reinhard demonstrated that he wasn't a reliable person. As a consequence, the family had to move again. They were living in a wagon."

"That is such an unusual phrase," said Ellen. "Thank you for explaining the village rules."

"You've been very helpful but we need to leave for our next village," said Ingrid. They all shook hands. Ingrid snapped a photo of Ellen and Johann, and they left *Südbruch.*

∞∞∞∞

The road to *Heideland* led past dormant grain fields and continued through low mountains and dense stands of trees. Seven kilometres later, Ingrid parked the car on a cobblestone street lined with pastel-colored stucco houses outlined in half-timbered *Fachwerk* beams. They walked uphill to *St. Burkhardt Kirche.* It was large, imposing, and situated on a towering hill; the church dominated the countryside.

"*Hallo,*" said Ingrid, as she greeted her friend. "This is Ellen. She is interested in seeing the church and would like to take photographs."

"I'm glad to meet you," replied Sophia. "*Ja,* photographs are fine. Our church was established in the late ninth century by Irish catholic monks.

It is known as the oldest congregation in the region and is the "mother church" for the communities of *Südbruch*, *Ehrenfeld* and *Martinshofen*."

Wide, flagstone steps led up to an entrance that was dwarfed by a massive thirteenth century white stucco bell tower. Surrounding the bell tower and church, an eight-foot high wall of massive stones protected the church and its granary from invasions by territorial enemies.

Across the courtyard from the church, a three-story pink stucco building identified the location where Johann Reinhard Klein and his children attended school. Ellen took photos of the imposing tower, the church façade, the surrounding wall of ancient boulders and the school. Then, she walked over to the bell tower to meet Sophia and Ingrid.

"The sanctuary has been remodeled," said Sophia. "But, you might like to see the original altar; it is enclosed by a thirteenth century Romanesque arch." Ellen took a few photos of the altar but was disappointed to find the sanctuary had been renovated. Visually, it wasn't the same space where the Klein family worshipped.

Turning to Sophia, she said "Reinhard Klein was born in *Südbruch* and was a member of this congregation from 1866 until 1875. I'd like to learn about his occupation while he was a member at *St. Burkhardt*. May I look at the *Familienbuch* records?"

"*Ja*, I have a copy of their family register and can translate for you."

> Johann George Klein, *Bürgher* and *Köbler*, born 19 February 1807, *Heideland*, died 16 April 1872, *Südbruch*. Married 23 September 1840 *Heideland*, Catherina Barbara. Arndt, born 19 September 1804, *Südbruch*, died 21 July 1889, *Mittelberg*.
>
> Children: 1) George Michael Klein, illegitimate, born 21 March 1831, died 01 April 1831, *Südbruch*. 2) Johann Reinhard Klein, born 9 April 1842, *Südbruch*, confirmed 20 April 1856, *Heideland*.

"This record indicates Johann Reinhard Klein was an only child, since his older brother died in 1831. Also, his father, Johann George Klein, was a *Bürger* and *Köbler,*" said Ellen.

"*Ja,* replied Sophia. "A *Bürger* was a citizen of the community. He was also a *Köbler,* which translates to an occupation of small farmer, while a *Bauer* would have owned a larger farm. I also found a marriage record for Johann Reinhard Klein and his wife."

> Johann <u>Reinhard</u> Klein, *Bürger* and *Köbler,* married
> Sophia <u>Katherina</u> Kupper, from *Ehrenfeld,*
> 30 January 1866, *St. Burkhardt Kirche, Heideland.*

"Great!" said Ellen. "Johann Reinhard Klein, was also a citizen and small farmer. But this raises a question about what happened when he left his home village of *Südbruch.* Yesterday, in *Dorflingen,* the records indicated Reinhard's occupation had changed to a *Tagelöhner.* I wonder why his status changed?"

"I'm sorry, I don't know. Maybe someone from another village will be able to help you. It's about noon—would you like lunch?"

"Oh no, we had a huge breakfast. Before leaving though, I would like to thank you for helping me and give a donation to the church." Ellen handed her twenty *Deutsche Marks.*

"Of course, we wouldn't mind having a little dish of fruit and maybe some bread, cheese and a cup of tea," said Ingrid. "That could tide us over for a while."

"Okay," replied Sophia. "Let's go to my house. I live one block downhill from the church."

After a pleasant lunch at Sophia's home, Ingrid took a photo of Ellen and Sophia, then with a final "good-bye" they left *Heideland.*

# Touring Kupper Hometowns:
## *Ehrenfeld* and *Martinshofen*

Ingrid checked her map, "We should be at *Ehrenfeld* in about ten minutes." She followed a one-lane winding road which led through hills and forests on either side until they reached a small valley with the distant view of a village.

*Ehrenfeld* was established on the bend of a small river. It included about a dozen well-kept three-story *Fachwerk* style homes, a few large *hausbarns* and a five-story *Muehl*, built in the *Fachwerk* style. Sheep grazed in a small pasture near the river. They stopped on a hillside above the village; Ellen took photos of the *Muehl*, the river, and the *Fachwerk* homes—it was a charming story-book scene.

∞∞∞∞

Ingrid parked the car and they crossed the road to meet Hermann.

"*Hallo,*" said Ingrid, as she waved to an older man. Ingrid spoke to him and then translated her greeting. "I'm Ingrid and this is Ellen. Thank you for meeting with us about the Kupper family."

Hermann shook hands with them and then pointed toward the steep hill behind them.

239

Ingrid explained his remarks, "We should walk to the clearing on the right side." She directed Ellen to an abandoned plot of land.

When they arrived, Hermann gave more details and Ingrid translated, "The Kupper family lived in the *Old Shepherd's Haus,* below the forest. There was a flood in 1880 and the house washed away, but this is the location."

Ellen checked her notes. This was the first evidence of a dwelling related to the Reinhard Klein family. This was the site where his wife, Sophia Katherina Kupper Klein, was born and raised. Her father, Johann Georg Kupper, was a *Bürger,* (citizen), and *Bauer* (farmer).

Since Sophia Katherina Kupper, became pregnant before marriage, this is also where Katherina Regina Klein was born in December 1863.

The *Adams County Oklahoma* article referred to Reinhard Klein selling his farm and using the cash to buy a Mill. As a young man, he may have worked at the *Ehrenfeld Muehl* and met his future father-in-law there. The *Muehl* was located downhill and across the bridge, only a short distance from the Kupper house site.

Ingrid and Hermann visited while Ellen took photographs. She didn't want to keep the others waiting, but she had a question.

"This is very helpful," she said. "Do you know where Sophia Katherina Kupper went to school and where her family went to church?" Ingrid translated for Hermann and then translated his answer for Ellen.

"That bridge crossing the river wasn't built until 1900," Hermann replied, as he pointed downhill toward the bridge.

"Before that time, children who lived in the village went to school in *Heideland* and children who lived outside the village went to school in *Martinshofen.*"

Indicating a path behind the house site, he said, "Sophia Katherina Kupper would have followed that path over the low mountain and through the forest, walking four kilometres to reach the school. It is across the courtyard from *St. Marien Kirche* at *Martinshofen*."

Ingrid looked at her watch; they needed to leave for the next village. Turning to Hermann, she explained their itinerary and thanked him for showing them the Kupper location.

They shook hands with Hermann and Ingrid took a photo of them. Ellen glanced at the *Old Shepherd's Haus* site for a final time; then they returned to the BMW.

∞∞∞∞∞

The route to *Martinshofen* followed a curving one-lane road for six kilometres. From *Ehrenfeld*, it first led through a forest but they soon drove past a large area of grain fields.

Ellen explained to Ingrid, "The next village is important because *St. Marien Kirche* is the home congregation for the Kupper family. This is where Sophia Katherina Kupper was baptized, her parents were buried and her son Michael was buried.

"At this location, I'm most interested in tracing other Kupper family relationships."

On arriving, Ingrid parked the car in a small space near the church and they walked up another steep hill to *St. Marien Kirche*. At the entrance, they were met by Dirk.

∞∞∞∞∞

"*Hallo,*" said Ingrid. "This is my friend Ellen. Thank you for helping us today."

"I'll be happy to show you around," he replied.

Ellen was glad he spoke English and asked, "May I take photos?"

241

"Of course, it is okay," he answered. "*St. Marien Kirche* at *Martinshofen* was established in the thirteenth century as a daughter congregation of *St. Burkhardt* in *Heideland*. The exterior is the original façade, although the interior has been modernized."

Surveying the scene, Ellen took photos of the impressive buildings. The immense and imposing limestone bell tower was located on the right side of the sanctuary; its third story was built in the *Fachwerk* style, with alternating crème-colored stucco and dark wooden beams.

An exterior view of the sanctuary included tall stained-glass windows that were deeply inset into two-foot thick walls; the third story of the sanctuary also featured the *Fachwerk* style. A steep red-tiled roof complemented the entire architectural scheme.

Directly across the cobblestone courtyard from *St. Marien Kirche*, Ellen took photos of a two-story peach colored stucco building. This was the site where Sophia Katherina Kupper attended school.

∞∞∞∞

Ellen turned to Dirk and said, "The family I am researching lived in *Ehrenfeld*. Sophia Katherina Kupper was baptized here at *St. Marien Kirche*; however, I'm most interested in trying to identify her relationship to Friedrich Kupper. Can we trace Sophia's father, Johann George Kupper, and the other Kupper families in the *Familienbuch* records?"

"*Ja*, I can help you," he replied. "I have a copy of the church records in *Martinshofen* and the *Pfarrer* at *Altenkirchen* has been kind enough to give me a copy of their *Familienbuch* records.

Using these documents, I have traced backwards to the parents of Johann George Kupper. Let's go inside the church to look at the old records. I will translate them."

Here is the first document I found:

Johann Andreas Kupper and Maria Elizabetha Dorothea Mayer, married 22 May 1787 *St. Johannes Kirche, Altenkirchen*. [They had six children.]

This record identifies Johann Andreas Kupper's youngest son:

Johann George Kupper, born 17 May 1803 *Altenkirchen*, married 16 June 1835 *St. Marien Kirche, Martinshofen*. Sophia Barbara Ott from *Ehrenfeld*. [They were the parents of Sophia Katherina Kupper.]

Next, is a marriage of Sophia Katherina Kupper:

Johann Reinhard Klein and Sophia Katherina Kupper, married 30 January 1866 *St. Burkhardt Kirche, Heideland*. [Their daughter was Maria Magdalena Klein.]

The fourth page identifies Johann Andreas Kupper's oldest son:

Johann George Friedrich Kupper, born 09 April 1792, *Altenkirchen*, married 21 January 1821 *St. Burkhardt Kirche, Heideland*, to Anna Rummler from *Ehrenfeld*. [They had one child, Johann Friedrich Kupper.]

Next, I found a marriage record of Johann Friedrich Kupper:

Johann Friedrich Kupper, born 25 February 1827 *Ehrenfeld*, married 15 June 1851 *St. Marien Kirche, Martinshofen*, to Johanna Tiedemann from *Braunfels*.

[Their son was Friedrich Kupper, born 07 September 1853, *Braunfels; ledig.* and *Bauer, Brellohe*. The *Familienregister* entry for his name didn't show a marriage or death in Germany. Friedrich Kupper must have immigrated to America.]

"Thank you for locating this information!"

"When charting these details," said Ellen, "the children of Johann George Kupper and his older brother Johann George Friedrich Kupper, were Sophia Katherina Kupper and Johann Friedrich Kupper. They were first cousins.

"The children of the first cousins were second cousins. In other words, when Marie Klein married Friedrich Kupper in America, she married her second cousin."

"*Ja, ja*" said Dirk. "In Germany, it is not allowed. The records show Maria Klein and Friedrich Kupper had the same great-grandfather: Johann Andreas Kupper.

"They grew up in different villages. If anyone checked the records, the *Familienregisters* from *St. Johannes Kirche* and *St. Marien Kirche* would've shown their true relationship."

Pleased by learning these new details, Ellen exclaimed, "Thank you so much—this is the verification I've been looking for since February!"

"May I have a copy of these pages?"

"*Ja*, it's already done," he said. "These are for you."

Ingrid looked at her watch; it was four-thirty. "We need to leave now so I can take Ellen to *Dorflingen*. Thank you very much for locating these records and being able to take photographs of the church and schoolhouse."

"You're most welcome," replied Dirk. "I hope you have a safe journey."

Ellen retrieved forty *Deutsche Marks* from her handbag and handed it to him. "Please give this donation to *St. Marien Kirche*," she said.

Ingrid then took a photo of Ellen and Dirk. Everyone shook hands and said "good-bye."

While Ingrid drove to the *Schloss*, Ellen reviewed the day.

"I'm so pleased about everything we've discovered. I didn't realize these communities would be so closely linked with each other.

"Nearly everyone remained in the same place for many years and seldom left their hometown.

"And, they were all connected by having similar occupations, by attending the same schools and churches and by knowing the same families over several generations."

"I agree. It has been a good research day," answered Ingrid. "What time should I pick you up tomorrow?"

"Let's follow the same routine as this morning, it worked out pretty well," said Ellen. "If you could be at the restaurant about eight-thirty, we can have breakfast again and plan the day. Is that alright with you?"

"*Ja*, it is okay," replied Ingrid. "Here we are."

∞∞∞∞

Ellen walked into Golden Ox. When the waitress came to her table, she said, "I'll have a glass of *Trollinger* wine while I look at the menu."

When reviewing the choices, Ellen began with *Fried weichen Ziegenkäse im Blätterteig, Kürbis-Chutney und Salat aus geräuchertem Rote Bete* and ordered a main course of *Filetsteak mit hausgemachter Kräuterbutter, Zucchini und Knoblauch Kartoffein.* The goat-cheese pastry and smoked beet salad were tasty, the steak was excellent and the vegetables were delicious. She topped off the meal with a dish of vanilla ice cream topped with cherry sauce.

A few minutes later, Ellen walked up two flights of stairs to her room. Today, she'd discovered significant details that would answer *Item Two* of the Helen Cooper bequest.

Tomorrow Ingrid would take her to the villages where the Reinhard Klein family lived after they left his hometown.

# Seeking New Opportunities

At eight-thirty the next morning, Ingrid greeted Ellen, "*guten Morgen,* did you sleep well?"

"Yes, I was really tired, although now I'm ready for another day of research. Let's go to the restaurant and have some breakfast." They ordered coffee and juice, chose buffet selections from a variety of pastries, cold cuts, cheese, and fruit, then returned to their table.

"What did you think of the villages we visited yesterday?" Ingrid asked.

"I enjoyed seeing everything and took several photos, so I'm happy. What's the driving sequence for today?"

"We'll start with *St. Jacob Kirche* at *Arnsberg.* It is the first village where Reinhard moved after leaving his hometown of *Südbruch.* That will give you a chance to see the difference between the two locations."

"Good. What's the itinerary for the rest of the day?"

"Next, we'll follow the family to *Hohenberg* and stop in *Dinkelsbühl* for lunch. Then we'll drive to *Weißenfels* and later return to *Dorflingen.* Except for *Dinkelsbühl,* which is a tourist destination, we'll be following a sequence of where the Klein family lived."

"Great. On Sunday, I visited *Dorflingen* and *Altenkirchen*, so your itinerary completes the chronology. Tomorrow I'll be visiting neighbors who knew the Klein family when they lived in *Mittelberg*. I have my research notes and camera in my handbag. Let's go."

As she left the *Hotel Schloss Dorflingen,* Ingrid began describing their route. "This morning, we'll drive on well-traveled roads until we reach the village of *Unterharnsbach*. Then, we'll follow a narrow road along the river, drive through a forested area and climb higher until we reach *Arnsberg*. We'll be there in about thirty minutes."

Located on steep hills, the streets of *Arnsberg* were lined with old trees and large three-story pastel stucco homes with red-tiled roofs; shuttered windows featured lace curtains and red geraniums. Ingrid drove three blocks, found the small church, parked the BMW and they walked across the lot to meet their guide.

∞∞∞∞

"*Hallo*," said Meta. "Welcome to *Arnsberg* and *St. Jacob Kirche*."

"*Danke*," replied Ingrid. "Ellen is interested in the history of the church and would like to take some photographs if it is okay."

"*Ja, ja*, it is fine, please come inside."

On entering the white stucco building, the small size of the space was noticeable; it was only 20' wide and 40' feet long. The thick walls included deeply inset windows. At most, four people could sit in each of the twelve pews.

Religious symbols decorated each wall of the barrel-vaulted altar niche and sanctuary. A white lace cloth covered the stone altar that held an open Bible, a small vase of flowers and communion vessels. Immediately behind the altar, morning sunlight flooded a single stained-glass window; it highlighted a gilded statue of Christ on the Cross.

Ellen turned to Meta. "There is a Latin charter hanging on the wall. Do you know when this church was established? And, I've never seen these symbols before. Do they have a special meaning?"

"*Ja, ja*. They're known as "Apostles Crosses" and were placed on the walls of the church when it was consecrated in the fourteenth century. This was originally a Catholic congregation and later converted to Protestantism. The statue of Christ and stained glass window were added in the eighteenth century, however we don't know any other history."

"It is okay. I'm happy to see where the Klein family worshipped. On the microfilm records, Reinhard Klein was a *Köbler* in *Arnsberg*, but I didn't find any record that he owned a Mill. The film stated the Klein family lived here for only six months and then moved to *Hohenberg*. Are there any records of where he lived?"

"*Nein*, I'm sorry. I've talked with several Klein families who live here. They've looked at their family history and couldn't find anything. I also asked the village historian about civil records. He couldn't find anything either."

Ingrid asked, "If Reinhard was a tenant or renter, would there have been any official records?"

"I don't think so. The *Heimatbuch* only identifies those who owned property. Maybe he leased the Mill from a relative, but didn't stay in *Arnsberg* very long. Perhaps that is why a church membership is the only record."

"Okay, we tried," replied Ellen. We need to go to the next village although I'd like to take photographs of the exterior before we leave."

Walking outside, Ellen surveyed the building. A red-tiled roof contrasted with the white stucco exterior of the walls. The west façade was constructed of large limestone blocks, with contrasting gray stones emphasizing the corner *quoins* and an arched entrance doorway. On the east side of the church, a large bell tower displayed the Protestant symbol of a rooster.

Even though she hadn't learned any new details, Ellen was very pleased about visiting the small church. She gave Meta a twenty *Deutsche Marks* donation for *St. Jacob Kirche*. Afterwards, Ingrid snapped a photo of Meta and Ellen before they returned to the BMW.

∞∞∞∞

As she drove, Ingrid explained, "Now we're going to *Hohenberg*; it is a large city in comparison to the other villages. We'll be driving on narrow mountain roads until we reach open fields outside the town walls."

Forty-five minutes later, Ingrid zipped around a curve and Ellen spied her first glimpse of the impressive castle. Expertly driving uphill on the crooked cobblestone roads, Ingrid found a space to park.

After photographing the flags and armorial cartouches of *Hohenberg*, they walked underneath its impressive stone gate. Directly in front of them was a turreted castle; it was surrounded by an empty moat which had been converted into a sunken garden.

Ellen and Ingrid kept walking and looking up, until they noticed a tall Baroque steeple in one corner of the town wall. They followed a cobblestone street toward the tower and read a sign attached to the building.

The pale blue stucco façade of the *Evangelisch Stadt Kirche* was difficult to photograph. An elaborate cartouche above the sixteen-foot bronze doors could only be seen from an oblique angle because the church entrance was squeezed between other buildings located on the same narrow street.

Entering the church through a side door, Ellen was disappointed. The interior had been remodeled in the Art Deco style and didn't have any resemblance to the sanctuary where Rosina Magdalena Klein was baptized in 1877. She didn't take any interior photos.

Noticing her frustration, Ingrid proposed looking for the *Pfarrer's* house. Asking a local resident for directions, they quickly found his four-story *Fachwerk* home. Ingrid banged the brass door knocker loudly.

∞∞∞∞∞

When an older woman answered the door, Ingrid said "I'm sorry to trouble you. My friend Ellen has travelled from America to find records about the Klein family. They lived here from 1876 to 1880. Could you help us?"

*Frau* Weber replied and Ingrid translated, "Yes, please come in. What is the name of the family? Do you know of baptism or confirmation dates?"

Ellen looked at her notes. "I'm looking for the Reinhard Klein family. They had a son, Friedrich Leonhard Klein, born in October 1876 and died November 1876. They also had a daughter, Rosina Magdalena, born 29 September 1877 and baptized 04 October 1877."

*Frau* Weber looked a little confused. Ellen showed her notes to Ingrid; she translated the request to Frau Weber.

"*Ja, ja, Ich kann sehen,*" she replied, and abruptly disappeared into another room.

Twenty minutes later, *Frau* Weber returned with copies.

> Friedrich Leonhard Klein, born 20 October 1876, died 01 November 1876. Parents: Johann Reinhard Klein, *Köbler* and *Fuhrmann*, Sophia Katherina (Kupper).

> Rosina Magdalena Klein, born 29 September 1877, baptized 04 October 1877. Parents: Johann Reinhard Klein, *Köbler* and *Fuhrmann*, from here, and Sophia Katherina (Kupper).

Ingrid translated. "Both documents give essentially the same information. Reinhard Klein was a *Köbler* and *Fuhrmann* at *Hohenberg* from October 1876 through October 1877. A *Köbler* is a small farmer and the word *Fuhrmann* translates to coachman or driver."

"*Danke*," said Ellen. Reaching into her handbag, she retrieved twenty *Deutsche Marks* and handed them to *Frau* Weber. She looked at Ingrid and said, "Please tell *Frau* Weber this is a donation for the church. I really appreciate this information."

Ingrid relayed Ellen's message and explained they had to leave. Everyone shook hands. Ingrid took a photo of Ellen and *Frau* Weber in front of the impressive arched doorway. Then, they retraced their steps through the massive stone gate, returning to the BMW.

As they walked, Ellen excitedly talked about the newly discovered details. "This is an interesting piece of information—a coachman in a larger city such as *Hohenberg* means Reinhard could have received better wages to support his growing family."

*"Ja,"* commented Ingrid. "Even though the first move from his hometown of *Südbruch* to *Arnsberg* apparently wasn't successful, he must have had some connections in *Hohenberg* who helped him find steady work as a coachman; perhaps he worked for local merchants or other important people. It raises some interesting possibilities."

∞∞∞∞

Forty-five minutes later, Ingrid squeezed her navy BMW into a small space in the *Altstadt* area of *Dinkelsbühl*, jumped out to pay the meter and looked for a café.

On every street, the architecture and street scenes were fascinating. Pastel three and four-story houses were outlined by *Fachwerk* beams and the sidewalks were filled with colorful hand-lettered signs that announced menus, various services or specialty goods for sale.

Ingrid found a tiny café tucked away on a side street. As they hurriedly sat down at one of the few empty tables, Ellen snapped a photo of the café scene; it brought memories of her home in San Francisco.

"Let's order something that is quick and easy," said Ellen. Ingrid looked at the menu and ordered for both of them—*Gemüsesuppe, Brot mit Käse, Wasser* and *Zucker Cookies*.

Checking her watch, Ingrid said. "We don't have much time but we could stroll through one or two streets to find a souvenir."

"I'd like that . . . how far is the next village?"

"About an hour."

"Okay, I'll watch the time."

"Let's walk this way."

Before long, they found a tiny, cramped retail shop that sold postcards. Continuing for another block, Ellen spied an art gallery and ducked inside; it didn't take long to choose a small pen and ink drawing of *Dinkelsbühl*.

Afterwards, they followed the crooked streets and returned to the BMW, then left for the next village.

# Living in a Wagon

Ingrid retraced her route, taking the Autobahn until exiting toward *Weißenfels*. The narrow road led up another steep hill of cobblestone streets lined with pastel-colored stucco houses. She parked at *St. Andreas Kirche*.

An older gentleman walked across the asphalt parking lot to meet them. "*Hallo*," he called, "I'm Ernst. I'll be your guide for *St. Andreas*, welcome."

Ellen and Ingrid shook hands with him. Ingrid asked "Do you speak English?"

"*Ja, ja,*" most of the time I can translate and give a reply," he said.

"Great," said Ellen. "I'm looking for information about the Klein family, but perhaps we could see the church first. May I take photos?"

"*Ja*, it is okay. Our church is being renovated. It was established in the eighteenth century; the congregation includes people from the village and farmers who live near-by. Our school is across the courtyard."

Ingrid visited with Ernst while Ellen snapped photos of the exterior. An elegant three-story building, *St. Andreas Kirche* was constructed of white stucco walls with *quoins* in contrasting gray stone on each corner and a dark gray mansard roof. The western and eastern façades featured a prominent cartouche above each entrance door; the doors were balanced by tall narrow windows. The bell and clock tower, with its steep slate gray roof, dominated the southern façade. An ancient stone *Mark-Grafer* wall enclosed and protected the church from a surrounding countryside of large fields.

On the north side, a crème stucco two-story schoolhouse was directly across from the balcony doorway. Since Maria, Friedrich, Johann, George and Michael Klein attended this school, Ellen took more photos.

She then walked over to where Ingrid and Ernst were chatting. "This is a very impressive church, I'm glad it's being preserved."

"*Ja*, we're grateful that our government believes in saving the old structures and mandates a tax to maintain our historical buildings."

"I'm hoping to locate records about the Reinhard Klein family," said Ellen. "Their tenth child, a daughter named Rosina Carolina Klein, was baptized at *St. Andreas Kirche* in February 1880, and their second-oldest daughter, Maria, was confirmed here in April 1880.

"I'll go to the parsonage now and bring you copies from the church records. We can meet inside the sanctuary to look at everything."

While Ernst retrieved the documents, Ingrid and Ellen entered the sanctuary. The altar was located inside an impressive bell tower niche. Above the altar, the pipes of an elaborate Baroque organ soared upwards on the second and third levels. Opposite the tower niche, three sides of the sanctuary were surrounded by a two-story balcony. The interior space confirmed her first reaction on arriving in the parking lot; *St. Andreas Kirche* served a large congregation.

A few minutes later, Ernst returned and translated the pages:

> Rosina Carolina Klein, born 04 February 1880, baptized 09 February 1880. Father: Johann Reinhard Klein, *Oberknecht*.

> Maria Magdalena Klein, confirmed April 1880. Father: Johann Reinhard Klein, *Dienstknecht*.

"Thank you," said Ellen. "Could you tell me the meaning of *Oberknecht* and *Dienstknecht*?"

"*Ja, ja*. An *Oberknecht* is a head servant, while a *Dienstknecht* is a manual laborer or servant."

"Interesting. Before moving to *Weißenfels*, the family lived at *Hohenberg* from 1876 to 1880. Reinhard's occupation in *Hohenberg* was *Köbler* and *Fuhrmann*. According to these records, he began employment in *Weißenfels* as an *Oberknecht* in February 1880. However, by April of the same year, his occupation had declined to a *Dienstknecht*. When Reinhard moved to *Mittelberg* two years later, his occupation was a *Tagelöhner*. Can you suggest an explanation?"

"It's hard to know what might have happened one hundred years ago," explained Ernst, politely. "A new resident had to meet several qualifications."

"I'm trying to understand local customs," said Ellen. "Our guide in *Südbruch* said if a person with citizenship rights left his hometown village, then he lost his right to live there again, and he wouldn't be allowed citizenship rights in any other village either. Was that true in *Weißenfels*?"

"*Ja, ja*, it is correct. Did you say the family had ten children?"

"Yes, although a twin and one other son died shortly after birth, and their oldest daughter, Katherina Regina, likely worked for another family because she was past confirmation age. Five school-age children, a toddler and an infant lived here with their parents."

"That might be one of the problems; the village didn't accept large families because they didn't want to provide welfare support for new residents."

"Village rules were very strict," he continued. "Reinhard could remain in *Weißenfels* if he was Lutheran, paid the village admission fees and had full-time employment within three days of arrival. Most importantly, he had to be considered of good character, be reliable and have a good reputation.

"Occasionally, when a new resident arrived, their past history caught up with them. If a problem occurred, the village would investigate and the new resident could lose their employment status or be asked to leave the village. This might have been the case when Reinhard began work as an *Oberknecht* and later became a *Dienstknecht*."

Listening to their conversation, Ingrid observed, "Although Reinhard was doing well in *Hohenberg*, his family was getting larger. He might've been seeking a better opportunity by moving to *Weißenfels*. Perhaps an event occurred after he arrived. If there weren't any relatives or patrons to protect his standing, his employment status could have declined."

"If good character, reliability and reputation were the primary criteria" said Ellen, "then, something must have happened. He may have had a drinking problem, argued with his neighbors or simply wasn't a dependable worker. These documents suggest his employment status fell while they lived in *Weißenfels* and declined further when they moved to *Mittelberg* in 1882."

"We call this "living in a wagon," said Ernst. "If the father wasn't accepted by the community, the family had to move from one place to another. Their housing situation only improved if they moved in with a relative or if they lived in a house owned by another family member. It seems strange today, but those were the village rules at that time."

Ingrid looked at her watch; four-thirty. "I'm sorry, we need to leave. Thank you for helping us," she told Ernst.

Ellen chimed in, "I had no idea there were so many restrictions. Your explanations have helped me understand the Klein family. Please accept this donation of twenty *Deutsche Marks* for the church. Thank you for meeting with us."

"I'm glad the information was useful," he said. "You may keep these copies." They shook hands and went outside to take a photo of Ernst and Ellen, then returned to the BMW.

∞∞∞∞

Ingrid followed a one-lane zig-zag road leading to *Dorflingen*. Twenty minutes later, she stopped to fill the car with petrol and then drove to the *Schloss.* On arrival, they went inside for a cup of coffee.

"I've been considering the Klein circumstances," said Ellen. "From everything I've learned, it seems that Reinhard and Katherina left a long-term and familiar family environment. They had a series of experiences—some were good for the family and some were not so good.

"They moved from a farming community to a mountain village but didn't stay long; something unexpected must've happened. Next, they lived in a larger city, where Reinhard found steady employment for four years. Then, they moved to a village where he didn't have any relatives or patrons who might help him.

"The employment didn't work out. In fact, his occupational status declined shortly after arrival and continued falling. By 1882, they were living in *Mittelberg;* it was located near *Altenkirchen,* where his wife's grandparents lived. Their housing situation stabilized; however in terms of wages, he never recovered. Reinhard Klein was a *Tagelöhner* for the next twenty years."

"*Ja, ja,*" replied Ingrid. "You've identified everything very well."

"As the German saying goes, *Alles Gute,*" replied Ellen. "I've found nearly all the answers I was seeking. Thursday morning I'll fly to New York, then home to San Francisco."

"Thank you for contacting me about this research assignment. I've enjoyed it very much," replied Ingrid. Ellen paid her invoice, then walked with Ingrid to her navy BMW convertible and took a photo. They gave each other a hug and promised to stay in touch. Then Ingrid left and Ellen returned to the Golden Ox.

She found a favorite table by the window, ordered a glass of *Schwarzriesling* wine and studied the menu, choosing *Schweinemadaillons "Provencale" mit Schafskäse überbacken, Böhnchen, Tomatensalpicon, und Salate der Saison,* and *Apfel Strüdel* for dessert. The pork and baked beans were scrumptious, the salad was delicious and the apple cobbler hit the spot.

Tomorrow, she would meet Heinrich and Theda Schäfer.

# A *Mittelberg* Interview

Wednesday. Ellen woke early; yesterday's conversation was on her mind. Instead of trying to remember every nuance of the discussion, she summarized the comments about living in a wagon and added a title page, *Reference #9 - Village Rules*. She then filed the notes and documents from *Altenkirchen, Dorflingen, Heideland, Martinshofen, Hohenberg* and *Weißenfels* in her briefcase.

After completing these tasks, Ellen dressed for the day, then carried her luggage and briefcase down two flights of stairs and placed them in the car trunk. When paying the bill, she explained the Volvo would be in their parking lot until early afternoon; then she waited in the Lobby.

∞∞∞∞

Promptly at ten o'clock, *Herr* Schäfer walked through the door. "*Hallo*, I'm Heinrich Schäfer," he said. "You talked to my wife Theda on Sunday. I'll bring you to our house in *Unterberg*."

"*Danke*," replied Ellen. "It's usually hard to find someone who has stories from the turn of the century, so I really appreciate the opportunity to talk with you and Theda. Can you translate our conversation?"

"*Ja, ja,*" Heinrich replied. "I had to know both languages for my job. Let's leave now . . . we can talk while driving." From *Dorflingen*, he crossed the river, drove through *Altenkirchen* and continued toward *Unterberg*.

Ellen asked, "It feels like the altitude is getting a little higher. Am I imagining this?"

"*Nein*, you aren't dreaming." he replied. "*Unterberg* and *Mittelberg* are a collection of houses on the side of a mountain. You'll see when we get there."

A few minutes later, Heinrich stopped at a road sign: *Unterberg – Mittelberg*. Ellen took a photo; then Heinrich continued on the unpaved one-lane road until they reached the Schäfer house. Theda was standing in the doorway, waiting for their arrival.

∞∞∞∞

"*Hallo*," she said. Heinrich translated her greeting, "I'm glad to see you. Please come in."

When Ellen entered the vestibule of their contemporary-style home, Theda ushered her into the dining room, which opened into an adjoining solar room. Astonished, Ellen looked at Heinrich and asked, "May I go into the sunroom and look at the view?"

"*Ja, ja*, it is okay." Heinrich followed Ellen into the glass roofed room while Theda disappeared into the small galley kitchen.

The sunroom overlooked the peaceful scene of cattle grazing beside a few trees and a small creek. In the distance, there was a large stone castle at the top of a mountain. Anticipating her question, Heinrich said, "That's *Schloss Waldberg*. It was built in the thirteenth century but it became a private hunting lodge in the nineteenth century."

Overhearing his comment, Theda said something in German and Heinrich translated, "Later we'll go to the Klein house site. It's on the road that leads to the *Schloss*. Everything is ready to eat. Please have breakfast with us."

Ellen and Heinrich sat at a dining room table decorated with a rust-colored tablecloth, dark brown linen napkins, a centerpiece of colorful Mums, delicate china plates and silverware. Theda brought the food—a tray of pastries and banana bread, a platter of cold cuts and several types of sliced cheese, another tray of home-made wheat and rye bread, a bowl of fresh orange slices, another bowl of fresh grapefruit wedges—and then she poured coffee.

"Oh, my goodness," said Ellen. "I didn't expect a huge breakfast. I assumed we'd just have coffee and talk about the Klein family."

"It is okay, Theda likes to cook," said Heinrich, as he smiled, picked up one of the trays and began passing it around the table. While eating, they chatted about the history of *Unterberg* in comparison to the neighboring communities of *Mittelberg* and *Altenkirchen*. When Theda poured a second cup of coffee, they began discussing the Klein family.

"I've been thinking about this meeting. Perhaps first, you could tell me how you knew the Klein family?" said Ellen. Heinrich translated for Theda and then repeated her reply to Ellen.

"My father purchased their house about 1902, after *Frau* Klein died in America. It's a large house—I found a photograph to show you."

"I didn't expect to find a photo!" exclaimed Ellen.

Theda smiled and handed her the picture. Heinrich translated as Theda described the house and Ellen took notes:

*The Klein Home:* They lived in a large frame house. The sheep and a milch cow were kept underneath the house, in the limestone half-basement that was built into the hillside. The first level included a kitchen with a fireplace, space for a large table, and one or two bedrooms. The unheated second floor either had three rooms or was a large open space used as a bedroom. There's not much land near the house. They likely carried water uphill from the creek for their garden. I don't know if they had a horse and wagon.

"I remembered something else," continued Theda. "My mother said whenever anyone was sick, they would see *Frau* Klein. She was known as a healer and made home remedies from plants in the forest or meadow. Everyone walked to her house in the forest to ask for help."

"That's very interesting. And, looking at a photo of their home is also great. According to the records, Reinhard was a *Tagelöhner*. What does this term mean?"

"A *Tagelöhner* was a day laborer who did odd jobs for local people," said Heinrich. "He probably cut wood for the *Graf* because the *Schloss* had many rooms with fireplaces and they also needed wood for cooking in the kitchen. He might've helped flush deer and other game from the woods when their English guests came to the lodge for the fall hunting season. He could've been their carriage driver when the family needed to be taken to another location or to a special event."

"I've read about old castles in England, but I don't know much about Germany. Did the *Graf* have servants who worked for their family?"

*"Ja, ja.* They would've had one or more *Dienstmädchen,* which are female servants who helped with cleaning, laundry, cooking and taking care of the children. The *Dienstknecht* were male servants that harvested crops and did other farm work. Some families also had a private tutor. The servants had quarters in the ground level of the *Schloss."*

While Ellen and Heinrich talked, Theda looked at the photo again. Heinrich translated her question, "How many children were in the Klein family?"

"They moved to *Mittelberg* sometime in 1882 and continued living there until 1901," replied Ellen. "In 1885, there were ten people in this house: Reinhard and Katherina Klein, his mother, Catherina Barbara Arndt Klein, their oldest daughter Katherina Regina and her baby, as well as Maria, George, Lena, Carolina and Rosina. Since Friedrich and Johann were past confirmation age, they likely worked for relatives or neighbors and didn't live there."

"Do you know where the children went to school?" asked Ellen.

"All of the children in *Unterberg* and *Mittelberg* went to the school in *Altenkirchen.* It is located next to *St. Johannes Kirche.* They walked down the mountain every morning and walked home on the same one-lane road again in the afternoon; it's about three kilometres distance."

"Isn't that a coincidence. I didn't realize it was a school, but took photos of that building when I visited the church on Sunday." Looking again at the Klein house photo, Ellen said, "From my big-city perspective, they must have been very isolated; there weren't any immediate neighbors and the nearest village wasn't very close to them either."

*"Ja, ja,* it seems so today, but it wasn't unusual at that time," replied Heinrich. "Theda wants to take you to their house now."

Everyone buckled their seat belts and Theda carefully backed the car out of their short driveway. She followed the narrow one-lane road up the side of the mountain. Reaching a switch-back U-turn in the road, Theda parked in the grass and pointed to a pile of timbers and stones.

Heinrich said, "That was the Klein house."

Ellen, Heinrich and Theda walked over to the site. A jumble of limestone blocks and wooden beams littered the ground. Remnants of a half-cellar foundation could be imagined but the upper level of the house was completely demolished. In front of the house, a few wildflowers were growing in a meadow and a steep hill led down to a creek. Immediately behind the house, tall fir trees dominated the mountainside.

The isolated forest scene was very different from the places where Marie lived in America. New York City was an urban environment, crowded with people. Nebraska and Oklahoma held vast fields of grain with endless horizons of clouds and sky. By contrast, the *Mittelberg* home was enclosed by a dense forest with occasional sunlight filtering through the canopy of tall trees. Ellen took photos of the abandoned home site, the nearby meadow and surrounding forest.

Afterwards, she asked Heinrich, "Where does that steep narrow road behind the house lead—it goes uphill to someplace."

"It is the only road to the *Graf's* hunting lodge. The castle is about one-half kilometre from here, on top of the mountain. Did you get all the photographs you wanted?"

Ellen snapped pictures of the castle road and its relationship to the Klein house. "Yes, I'm very pleased. Even though the house is gone, it's fascinating to see where Marie lived during her teenage years and where her daughter Katie was born and raised by grandparents. Thank you."

"We're glad to help you," said Heinrich. "Would you like to have another cup of coffee?"

"Thank you, but no," said Ellen as she looked at her watch. "I should be on my way and I don't want to get caught in late afternoon traffic while driving in an unknown city."

"It is okay," said Heinrich, and translated her comments to Theda.

Ellen memorized a view of the abandoned home and then everyone returned to the car. Heinrich turned it around carefully in the narrow road and drove down the mountain, through *Altenkirchen* and across the bridge to *Dorflingen*. On arrival, Ellen pointed to her Volvo and said, "Please drop me off by the car, I've already checked out of the *Schloss*."

Heinrich parked next to her car. Ellen asked if she could take a photo of him and Theda, then Heinrich snapped a photo of Ellen and Theda.

"This has been a great visit," said Ellen. "I really appreciate everything you've done."

Heinrich smiled and looked at his wife Theda, "I think we've enjoyed it as much as you did."

With a final round of hugs, everyone left. Heinrich turned south to return home and Ellen drove north a few blocks. She parked in front of a *Blumenladen* shop and went inside to order an exotic houseplant for delivery to Theda Schäfer. She then retraced her route to the Autobahn.

∞∞∞∞∞

Two hours later, Ellen arrived in Frankfurt, returned the Volvo to the rental agency and pushed a luggage cart through the halls of the huge international airport until finding the Marriott Hotel.

In her tenth floor room, she immediately sat at the desk and began writing, trying to remember everything from her visit with Heinrich and Theda Schäfer, then added a title, *Reference #10 – The Klein Family Home.*

Tonight she hoped to find a nice restaurant in the airport mall to celebrate the end of a successful trip. Tomorrow morning, there was an early flight from Frankfurt to London, then a second flight from London to New York City. By mid-afternoon, she would arrive in New York City, take a taxi to the Stonehurst, attend their evening reception and tag along with other guests to a local restaurant.

A flight home to San Francisco was scheduled for Friday morning. Next week, a final report for the Cooper Estate would be completed.

# SAN FRANCISCO

# Research Summary II
# The Cooper Estate

Presented by:

Ellen O'Donnell

October 6, 1986

*Assignment*: IV. a) ii): To identify the family history of Helen Cooper's parents and determine why Mary Cooper insisted her children, Helen and Fred John, should never marry.

*Sources*: In February, I compiled the 1900 and 1910 census records of Fred and Marie Kupper and their children, using resources at the San Francisco Public Library. Subsequently, I located immigration records for Marie Klein (1888), Fred Kupper (1889), Catherine Klein and Katherine Klein (1901) at the National Archives. To document an accurate family history, I found birth, marriage and death records for the families of Marie Klein and Friedrich Kupper at the Oakland Multiregional Family History Center. In April, other relevant details about their family were discovered during courthouse research as well as interviews with local historians and family members in Nebraska and Oklahoma. Information about Marie Klein's 1888-1892 experiences in New York City was found at The New York Public Library, The New-York Historical Society and during a tour of the *Kleindeutschland* tenement district in September. Afterwards, I reviewed church documents and interviewed local residents in Germany to compile an account of circumstances affecting the Klein family from 1866 to 1901. Ten *Reference Reports*, Family Group Sheets, photos of the family and where they lived, are enclosed.

*Summary*: Mary Cooper's instructions to her children were based on factual evidence and three other reasons: events she experienced during her teenage years in Germany, her immersion into American culture in New York City and a repetition of negative circumstances during her marriage, divorce and reunion with her husband.

## I. An Itinerant Family Life in Germany:

An extensive review of family history versus village expectations identified that Marie's father—Johann Reinhard Klein—was apparently a likeable fellow who consistently talked his way into new ventures but didn't have a good reputation. This behavior affected his ability to earn sufficient income to support his growing family.

In the hometown villages of Germany, being reliable and having a good character were the most important criteria for continuous tenure. A new resident had to be a Lutheran, pay village admission fees, have full-time employment, and a small family. New residents could be expelled because of continuous disagreements with their neighbors, or else, they were sometimes banished because they didn't meet the village rules.

At the time of his marriage in 1866, Johann Reinhard Klein was a *Bürger* (citizen) and *Köbler* (small farmer). In 1875, he left the hometown village and lost residency rights. Subsequently, his status changed from a *Köbler* (small farmer) and *Fuhrmann* (coachman-driver) to *Oberknecht* (head servant), then fell to *Dienstknecht* (servant) and *Tagelöhner* (day laborer) by the age of forty. His status declined each time they moved. Although disagreements or alcoholism may have been a factor, no public records of a problem were found.

## II. New York City

After emigrating from Germany, Marie supported herself and became independent. On arrival at Castle Garden, the *Emigrantenhaus-Mission* most likely hired her for a Translator position. While living in the *Kleindeutschland* area, she may have attended the YWHA (Young Women's Hebrew Association); they offered classes that introduced immigrant women to American customs and provided information about their legal rights.

## III. Repetitive Family Patterns

Marie's father may have been an amiable "quiet alcoholic" whose behaviors were tolerated by his wife and children. Her husband was a known alcoholic. Marie repeated childhood patterns; she endured his behavior for twelve years.

In her youth, the Klein family moved about every two years. During her marriage, Fred Kupper was a tenant farmer, moving every year from 1892 to 1903. After the divorce, Marie moved often; she lived with a different employer every year.

*IV. Factual Evidence*

A search of the *Martinshofen Kirchenbuch* found Maria Klein and Friedrich Kupper were second cousins. This was the family secret and skeleton-in-the-closet which Mary Cooper would not discuss and her reason for insisting that Helen and Fred should never marry. In Germany, the church prohibited marriage to the fourth degree of consanguinity. Maria Klein and Friedrich Kupper had the same great-grandfather, Johann Andreas Kupper. Their children, Helen and Fred, were the offspring of an incestuous relationship.

Although unverified, her son Fred John could have agreed to sterilization in exchange for his release from the Mercy Hospital for the Insane. Mary Cooper may have considered sterilization a drawback to marital happiness and insisted that he remain single.

*Conclusion:* Mary Cooper wanted to protect her children by requiring them to remain single. Helen and Fred John agreed to her request. They never married.

# The Cooper Family Analysis

At one o'clock, Ellen placed an invoice, Research Summary II and the 1935 letter in a file folder, then added the folder to her briefcase. She then retrieved Marie's journal, the family photos and documents received from George Smoot, adding them to the briefcase. Next, she picked up her research notebook which held the ten *Reference Reports*, updated Family Group Sheets, additional family and site photos, along with the documents she had accumulated during the Cooper Estate assignment. Placing everything in the car, she drove downtown and parked near their office. She carried her notebook and briefcase into the offices of Lardner, Alexander and Smoot.

∞∞∞∞

"Hello Ellen, how are you?" George asked. "Let's sit over here for a nice view of The City. I've been looking forward to learning about your New York City and German research."

"I'm fine, thank you. I'm returning the Cooper Estate items that I received earlier and have added photos from Oklahoma and Germany. I've also brought Family Group Sheets and several reports that give background details.

"The main points are itemized in my Research Summary," she said. "I've included factual information but thought it would be better to talk about other circumstances and the new information that I discovered."

George studied the Summary. "The details about the village rules in Germany and how they affected family living conditions are remarkable. Apparently, it was a very structured society."

"Yes, that seems to be the case. When Reinhard Klein left his hometown of *Südbruch*, he lost citizenship rights. Village representatives said if someone didn't have a good reputation, he would've lived in the new village until the past caught up with him, then he had to move again. They described the family circumstances as "living in a wagon." Reinhard's search for permanent residency didn't end until 1882, when they moved to *Mittelberg*."

"Fascinating," commented George. "How did this affect his daughter Marie?"

"She apparently reacted to adversity by developing a strong personality and becoming independent. In Germany, she learned English before immigrating. In New York City, she earned good wages and learned about women's rights. In Nebraska, she filed for divorce due to domestic abuse. Then, after ten years of working as a housekeeper, she bowed to family pressure and reunited with her alcoholic husband. Fred and Mary lived in Oklahoma until the 1935 foreclosure proceedings. She then reasserted her independence and moved to California."

"Were you able to learn why Mary Cooper insisted that her children should never be married?"

"Yes. It involved quite a bit of digging but everything was discovered in the *Martinshofen* records. Church documents verified that Maria Klein and Friedrich Kupper were second cousins. Their children, Helen and

Fred, were the offspring of an incestuous marriage. That was the reason their mother insisted Helen and Fred must remain single."

"Interesting. You mentioned finding some new information. Was it a complete surprise?" asked George.

"Very much so!" replied Ellen. "This family had a habit of keeping secrets. For instance, no one ever mentioned the likelihood that Marie's father was a quiet alcoholic with a poor reputation; yet, his declining employment status implied there was a problem. We've already talked about the second cousins secret; however, the children apparently never knew about their parents' tumultuous divorce, so that's another secret. Anna changed her name to Helen; this kept her identity hidden from the Nebraska relatives. Whenever they filed an official document, Helen and Fred John told "little white lies," giving a different age or year of birth in each record. Then, there is the possibility that Fred John may have agreed to sterilization; another secret.

"The greatest surprise—which no one in the family ever discussed—was the identity of Katie's father. I asked the pastor at *Altenkirchen* about this question and he looked at their baptism records. The *Pater* column is blank; no one is named as Katherine's father. The pastor said this wasn't unusual if the paternal family held an important position in the community. And, her baptism occurred at home; this was considered rare because it was not witnessed by the community. He couldn't tell me anything else. The records were silent."

"I've brought you a letter dated June 2, 1935," said Ellen, as she handed it to George.

*Dear Katie,*

*We have lost everything. I am writing to let you know my plans. Anna said I must get away from all the headaches in Oklahoma and live with her in San Francisco. She has always been very independent, like I was many years ago. Since she never married, we will live with her. Anna will help Fred John find a good job. She is sending ticket money. We are leaving on the train next week.*

*My brothers do not understand how difficult it has been to live with Fred. I left him once—everyone in the family was upset until I returned. My brothers said I should do whatever Fred wanted, but when things were bad, they blamed me instead of him. This Indian lawsuit is the last straw. I am leaving. Fred will live with my brother George in Nebraska.*

*Now I must explain things that happened many years ago. The Graf had a hunting lodge in the forest about a half mile from our house. My father cut wood for him and did other small jobs. When I was twenty years old, I became their nanny and lived in the servant quarters. They also had an English tutor for the older children. After a year of being a good helper and nanny, I asked to learn English—an older son said he would teach me.*

*At first we met only two times a week, but before long we were meeting secretly, more often. My prince was three years older, very handsome and told me stories of places where he traveled. He was my true love. It became a hopeless situation— he was high-born and my parents were very poor—we would never be allowed to marry. When it became known that I was having a child, his parents insisted we must both leave. He went to England. They paid my ticket to America. Everyone agreed you would be raised by my parents in Mittelberg. All of us had to swear to the pastor at St. Johannes Kirche that we would never mention your father's name—even today I cannot give his name because his relatives are still alive. They live in Württemberg.*

*When you were four months old, I had to leave, and cried nearly all the way from Antwerp to New York City. My friends on the ship convinced me to find a good job and send for you later. I didn't realize how many years would pass and how much I would miss in watching you grow up.*

*Now, because of my age and poor health, I may not see you again. I take comfort in knowing you have a very good husband who will take care of you and five children to give you a happy life. I have decided to always remember you by changing my name to Mary Catherine—like your baptism name of Maria Katherina. I'm not sure when I will be able to write again. Everything is in turmoil.*

*With love always — your Mother*

*P.S. Our pastor asked the Ladies Aid to make a Signature Quilt. We embroidered our names in the center of each block and then made a border from scraps of old clothing. The middle square was embroidered with the title of Oklahoma 1935. When the quilt was done, we had an auction to raise money for the poor. Anna sent me one hundred dollars to make sure that I would be the highest bidder. I am taking this quilt to California. It will help me to remember my home and friends in Oklahoma.*

Stunned by the unexpected disclosures, George exclaimed, "What a surprise! It's astounding to know that Katie's father was a prince from *Württemberg*. This letter gives important details about the Kupper and Klein family dynamics and it explains why the Nebraska, Oklahoma and California families were estranged. It's all very relevant to their story."

"I thought it was amazing too," said Ellen. "When I visited the site of their abandoned home in *Mittelberg*, I photographed the narrow road that leads to the *Schloss.* Last week, I traced the *Graf's* genealogy in the *Wappenbuch* heraldry series at the San Francisco Public Library and learned they had a son who was three years older than Marie.

"In thinking about everything," she continued, "I'm not sure whether this letter should remain tucked away with the private legal papers about the Cooper Estate or whether it should become part of the public record and given to the San Francisco Heritage Association. From a provenance point-of-view, the Klein family didn't think it necessary to keep the letter because both Mary and her daughter Katie are deceased. They gave it to me. Now I am giving the letter to your firm because it is relevant to the Cooper family."

"Thank you," replied George, as he recovered from his initial reaction and resumed a professional tone. "I appreciate your ideas about how to handle the letter. I'll discuss this situation with my partners and ask John Hawthorne for an opinion. It'll probably depend on whether the letter is considered relevant to Helen's bequest or if it has historical value for the Association. You've definitely found significant information.

"Now we have to talk about the next step," he said. "A check will be sent to you next week. I'll also place these pages with your first report and schedule a meeting with my partners so they can review everything. We'll talk with John Hawthorne about the 1935 letter and decide how to handle the final distribution of Helen Cooper's estate."

"Thanks for asking me to work on this assignment," said Ellen. "Even though the project was a little tedious, I've enjoyed finding the answers. I'm glad the San Francisco Heritage Association was named as a beneficiary."

"Yes, everything has turned out very well," George replied. "The reports look pretty good to me. If any questions occur when I talk to everyone else, I'll give you a call." They shook hands, he escorted Ellen to the elevator and she thanked him once again.

∞∞∞∞

Ellen returned to her small Victorian home in the hills of Noe Valley, parked in the basement garage and checked the answering machine. Glancing around, the office was a mess. Books and papers were stacked everywhere. She closed the door and went upstairs.

Pleased with the results of the day, Ellen called a few friends and asked them to meet her at the La Roca restaurant for an impromptu celebration that evening. They all knew she was working on a research assignment that involved travelling and wanted to hear about her latest adventures. Ellen described the endless horizons of the Midwestern landscape, the interesting people she'd met in New York City and the fascinating *Fachwerk* architecture in the medieval villages of Germany. "It was a great assignment," she declared.

The next morning Ellen checked her calendar. No deadlines. She could resume her retirement routine of working in the garden, looking for antiques, visiting art galleries and completing needlework projects. *Alles Gute!*

# The Gift

The magnificent lobby was abuzz with a crowd of members, donors, patrons, and guests. The chandeliers were stunning, the Art Deco murals were dramatic, a pianist entertained everyone by playing jazz music. The men wore black-tie; their wives dressed in formal gowns and displayed their opulent jewelry. It was a festive occasion—the Annual Gala Dinner of the San Francisco Heritage Association, Saturday evening, November 15, 1986.

Ellen joined the crowd at the *hors d'oeuvres* buffet and accepted a glass of champagne from one of the servers. Before long, a staff member quietly asked the audience to take their seats at the large round tables. Ellen spied George Smoot, who had invited her to the celebration.

"Hello," said Ellen. "Thanks for asking me to the Annual Gala."

"You're quite welcome," George replied. He introduced Ellen to his wife, the other partners and their wives. Everyone found their assigned seat. The waiters began serving the gourmet dinner and more wine. Afterwards, while the tables were cleared and dessert was being served, the Director of the San Francisco Heritage Association walked to the podium.

"Ladies and Gentlemen," announced John Hawthorne, "I appreciate the wonderful turn-out and want to thank all of you for coming this evening. Before we hear our main speaker, I'd like to ask Michael Lardner, president of the Association, to make a special announcement."

"Good evening and welcome," said Michael. "Tonight, I am happy to announce the San Francisco Heritage Association has received an anonymous gift of two million dollars." Everyone gasped in astonishment.

"The Board has decided this grand Art Deco building has served us well for many years, but it needs some up-dating. We're going to remove the old asbestos insulation from the interior rooms and bring everything up-to-date by installing new equipment.

"As you know, for many years we've provided typewriters so patrons may transcribe archival documents for their research notes. One of our board members is an executive at Intel and has told us major changes will be happening in the next ten years. To prepare for the future, we're also remodeling the Sutter Gallery by installing cubicles where each space will have its own electrical outlet, a word processor and a dot-matrix printer. We're very excited about receiving this gift and all the benefits it will bring to our Heritage Association."

Suddenly, the crowd was standing and applauding enthusiastically.

"And now," he continued, "I'd like to ask the Director to introduce our speaker for the evening."

In the short break between the introduction and the beginning of the lecture, George Smoot leaned over and whispered to Ellen, "The Association wouldn't have received this donation without your help. They're very pleased about everything."

She just smiled and said, "Thank you."

# *EPILOGUE*

## Fact vs. Fiction

Silent Legacy is a fictional account based on the life of my great-grandmother. When I asked about our family history, her descendants always said "no one ever heard from Marie after she disappeared to California." For me, it was a mystery waiting to be solved.

Fiction often evolves from a scrap of fact and such is the case with this story. Marie, her daughter Helen and son Fred John died in San Francisco. The trail of clues began with Helen's death in 1986 and eventually led to an 1853 document in *Württemberg*.

The surnames of Marie, Fred, their children and ancestors, as well as locations in Nebraska and Germany, all dates and genealogical records have been altered for privacy reasons. Like many German-Americans, names changed as immigrants assimilated into American society—born Maria, she became Marie after immigrating and Mary in later years. Likewise Friedrich was known as Fred or Fritz. Maria's mother, sister and daughter were known as Katherina; to avoid confusion, her mother is identified as Sophia Katherina, her sister as Katherina Regina and her daughter as Katherine or Katie.

In Nebraska, all records are accurate, although the location has been fictionalized. In Oklahoma, the FBI investigated the guardianship system of Osage County and the 1921-1929 activities of the Hale Gang and its *Reign of Terror*. Fred John lived in an insane asylum for three years; however, the name and location of this institution has been changed. The sterilization bill, known as *Oklahoma House Bill No. 64*, became law on April 22, 1931; it was repealed by *Oklahoma Senate Bill No. 15* on April 29, 1983. The Oklahoma deed records are accurate and foreclosure occurred; Marie and Fred John left for California in 1935.

Archival records indicate Rev. Stephanus Keyl managed the *Lutherisch Emigrantenhaus Mission* from 1869 to 1905. Marie's employment as a Translator and her tenement lodging in New York are based on family tradition, likely encounters and typical customs of the era. Concerning kinship, the second-cousin relationship of Fred and Marie is accurate. The letter identifying Katie's father is fiction, although it is based on a few relevant facts.

This has been an interesting journey of discovery with more twists and turns than I ever expected to find. Originally, I hoped to locate a picture of Marie. I have photos of her children, her parents and her siblings—a photograph of Marie has never been found.

# ACKNOWLEDGEMENTS

R esearch for this book began nearly thirty years ago, was often set aside due to other obligations, but later continued on random evenings and weekends as I looked for details in a multitude of public records. First and foremost I would like to express my appreciation to the librarians at the Dallas Public Library Genealogy Department and the courthouse clerks of Nebraska and Oklahoma. Willing to answer any question, no matter how trivial, these public servants were instrumental in helping to find the elusive and relevant details of this story.

During a time span of several years, I also completed microfilm research at various Family History Center locations. I would like to acknowledge and extend sincere appreciation for their continuous support of genealogical research. The FHC microfilm records were an invaluable research tool and their volunteers were consistently helpful in every location I visited.

To learn about events that Marie, her mother, and her daughter experienced, I visited the Red Star Line Museum in Antwerp, the Statue of Liberty and Ellis Island, where a tour guide comment about social service agencies located on nearby State Street led me on another quest for details. Years later, more questions surfaced. A helpful email from Barry Moreno, Ellis Island Immigration Museum, explained the distinction between a Translator and an Interpreter occupation. His book, *Castle Garden and Battery Park,* Arcadia Publishing, 2007, is a highly recommended reference.

While writing the first draft of *Silent Legacy*, it soon became evident there were more facts to check and descriptions to be verified. Pamela Storm, at SFgenealogy, was a delight to work with; she recommended Noe Valley as Ellen O'Donnell's neighborhood and also provided historic preservation references that added interesting details to the story. Thomas Carey, Librarian for the San Francisco History Center at the San Francisco Public Library, explained the 1986 day-to-day procedures of the San Francisco Public Library; his assistance was very helpful.

Finding answers to research questions also brought opportunities to meet new friends and other family members in Germany. For their gracious hospitality, delightful conversations and willingness to share information, I sincerely thank Charlotte Braun, Susan Fielder, Kathrine Green, Carol Harper, Werner Loechner, Hilde Stein, and Pauline Whitnah.

After the initial writing phase was completed, the next stage involved reviews by genealogists and general readers who made helpful suggestions for improvement. A special thank you goes to Kristin Dorn Burnett, Sheila Carskadon, Bill Crumpler, Connie Dake, Cheryl Meints, Don Meints, Lewis Miller, Nancy Miller and Pamela Storm.

On a flight from Germany in 2010, I sketched a rough outline for this novel. My thanks to everyone who subsequently offered encouragement and assistance. The years of research and myriad of circumstances mingled together to become a *Silent Legacy* saga.

CPSIA information can be obtained at www.ICGtesting.com
Printed in the USA
LVOW01s1808270115

424574LV00008B/289/P